DRAGONS' WRATH

Benny strained to hear what they were saying.

'I should close it up,' the newcomer was saying. 'They've sent in a cryvok.'

The heavy doors swung shut, leaving Benny and Nicholas alone in the room. Ahead of them they could see the Gamalian Dragon illuminated by its spotlight. A shining beacon in the gloom.

'Er.' Benny hesitated. 'What exactly is a cryvok, do you suppose?'

'I'm afraid we may be about to find out.'

The noise was getting louder, echoing round the room so that it was impossible to tell quite where it was coming from. The sounds resolved themselves, as the volume rose, from growls to barks. The scratching became the sound of sharp claws slapping into the flagstones of the floor as the creature ran at full pelt towards them. It launched itself towards Benny and Nicholas as they stood frozen in the gloom. As it leapt, it passed through the light of one of the flambeaux. A glimpse of death in the darkness.

THE NEW ADVENTURES

DRAGONS' WRATH

Justin Richards

NA

First published in Great Britain in 1997 by
Virgin Publishing Ltd
332 Ladbroke Grove
London W10 5AH

Copyright © Justin Richards 1997

The right of Justin Richards to be identified as the Author of
this Work has been asserted by him in accordance with the
Copyright, Designs and Patents Act 1988.

Bernice Summerfield originally created by Paul Cornell

Cover illustration by Fred Gambino

ISBN 0 426 20508 1

Typeset by Galleon Typesetting, Ipswich
Printed and bound in Great Britain by
Mackays of Chatham PLC

*All characters in this publication are fictitious and any resemblance
to real persons, living or dead, is purely coincidental.*

This book is sold subject to the condition that it shall
not, by way of trade or otherwise, be lent, resold, hired
out or otherwise circulated without the publisher's prior
written consent in any form of binding or cover other
than that in which it is published and without a similar
condition including this condition being imposed on the
subsequent purchaser.

*For Alison and Julian, as ever, with love.
Thanks for the Time and Space.*

Extract from Nicholas Clyde's doctoral thesis:

Ambitions of Empire, the rise and rise of Hugo Gamaliel
It is impossible today to think of Gamaliel without thinking of the Dragon. Like a latter-day St George, he is remembered for this rather than his actual accomplishments. The fact that one can apply to see the Gamalian Dragon on display in the Castle of Ice and Fire on Tharn only bolsters this association (though few would be brave enough to apply to its current owner for a viewing and fewer still would be granted it).

We have already examined Gamaliel's accomplishments. We have tried to distinguish between the myth of the all-conquering hero and champion of the people and the somewhat less successful campaigns that he actually prosecuted. In fact, when separating the legend from historical reality, only the Gamalian Dragon and the Battle of Bocaro seem to live up to the legend.

It is not the purpose of this paper to examine the Knights of Jeneve. But no study of Hugo Gamaliel would be complete without a mention of the Order. In fact, it is a simple matter to recount what is known about the Knights, since there is so little. The bulk of extant information comes from studying the legends surrounding Bocaro and Gamaliel's capture of the Dragon of Jeneve – usually referred to, of course, as the Gamalian Dragon. What information we do have seems to be in complete accord with the myths and legends, and we can assume therefore that there is at least some truth in these.

The loss of most of the documentation of Gamaliel's reign during the wars in which his successors rapidly lost all the territory he had gained has robbed us of validated source materials. But the surviving secondary sources of the day seem for once to be accurate. While Brahmyn's holovid and the romances of Anton Phelps paint an overzealous picture of Gamaliel, the same cannot be said of the Knights of Jeneve. And we know from the local newscasts of the time that Gamaliel's victory at Bocaro was as brilliant and unexpected as the subsequent mythology suggests. The so-called 'Gamalian Gambit' is referred to within days of the battle.

The rest of this paper will demonstrate how Gamaliel's expansionist ambitions were accomplished with renewed vigour following his victory at Bocaro. We have seen that the Gamalian Dragon was a symbol that galvanized his armies and brought terror to his enemies, evoking the memory of his tremendous victory against the Knights of Jeneve. But first, let us recap briefly on what actually happened.

The legend tells how the Knights of Jeneve (sometimes spelt *Geneve*) were founded to protect a great secret. With typical vagueness, it does not relate what this secret was, and so we must doubt that in fact there ever was one. The Knights of Jeneve guarded a beautiful jewelled statuette in the form of a rearing Dragon breathing fire. It was their emblem and their standard. The stories tell how the Knights fought in its shadow, and the Dragon watched over everything they did and kept the Knights 'to the ways of justice and chivalry' (Phelps, *op cit*).

But apparently, the Knights 'fell into evil and knew not the proper ways'. Quite what Phelps means by this arcane expression is far from obvious. Brahmyn is even less helpful. The opening narrative of *Dreams of Empire* says only in effect that the Knights were evil and Gamaliel was 'chosen' to end their power. It is implied within the main drama that they somehow fell from grace and neglected their duties. But what these duties are is unclear. The holovid makes great play of their Dragon emblem somehow seeing the Order fall into disrepute and calling to Gamaliel to rescue it from their clutches. The famous opening voice-over continues in the melodramatic way that sets the tone for the rest of the piece:

> *Gamaliel, ruler of all known space, heard the Dragon's wrath. He answered the call and exposed the Knights of Jeneve for what they were. And he hunted them through space, guided by the call of the Dragon.*

This does rather ignore the fact that, until he defeated the Knights at Bocaro, Gamaliel had very little territory or support from outside his own system. He was certainly not 'ruler of all known space'.

But for whatever reasons, Gamaliel engaged the far larger forces of the Knights of Jeneve at the communications station world of Bocaro (sometime *Bosarno*). By means of the Gamalian Gambit he completely defeated and routed the superior forces of the Knights, and captured their Dragon emblem. He then adopted the Dragon as his own motif and standard, using it as a rallying call to the increasing number of worlds and peoples dissatisfied with Earth's remote and, as they saw it, unfair rule.

According to legend, the Dragon kept watch over Gamaliel's works. Certainly, it was after Bocaro that Gamaliel's crusade really began.

Extract from Examiner's Comments on Clyde's Paper

. . . This curious lack of balance is most apparent in the short description of the Battle of Bocaro, the Knights of Jeneve, and the Gamalian Dragon. Given the detail with which you go through the data for the subsequent period (even if you do, as I have noted already, tend to agree with current interpretations rather than challenge or expand them), this seems rather unbalanced. I expected more, frankly.

The work is good as it stands, but to excel you would need to expand on this section in particular, and relate your arguments to the present day. You make much play of how the Gamalian Dragon became a rallying point for the unease and dissatisfaction with Earth's continued rule, for example. But you do not comment on the similarities of the current situation or how the political landscape has changed post-Gamaliel. Could any of the power brokers in the area today assume ascendency over the others, for example? Of course, the answer to this is not difficult. But if Gamaliel had never lived, if there was no legacy to pass on, how would the answer be different?

Unless and until you learn to consider these sorts of things, and address questions such as the continued potency of the Gamalian Dragon as a popular symbol, you will not make a truly great historian.

DEATH IN THE NIGHT

'A copy, of course. But I pride myself that it is now worth more than the original.' Newark Rappare was surprised his voice was so steady. 'May I?' He reached out for the fragile vase, intending to lift it delicately from Mastrov's grasp and replace it on its plinth.

Mastrov let go of the vase just as Rappare's fingers grazed its deliberately crazed surface, and he had to scrabble to grab it as it fell. His breath was ragged and chipped and he stumbled towards the plinth. With trembling hands he positioned the vase somewhat off centre.

Mastrov watched from the shadows, face concealed in the near-darkness. 'You know why I'm here.'

'Of course. But I wish you wouldn't just let yourself in. If I hadn't realized who you were, I could have killed you.'

Mastrov smiled through the gloom. 'I doubt that.'

Rappare was indignant, still embarrassed and annoyed. And scared. 'There's a lot of valuable art in here, you know.'

'Craft, maybe.'

'How did you get in, anyway? I was assured the studio systems were intruder-proof.'

'Tricks of the trade. And talking of trade . . .' Mastrov's voice faded.

A small metal case gleamed in the darkness as it slid across the tiled floor towards Rappare. He grabbed at it, lifting it up to eye level as he sat down. It fitted snugly into the palm of his hand. Mastrov waited while he checked the contents.

'Yes, yes. Well, that seems to be in order.' Rappare smiled, and stuffed the plastic card back into the padded case. 'I'll just get your, er, merchandise.' He took the case with him into the next room. A few moments later he returned, carrying another, larger case. He passed it to Mastrov.

'Light.'

Rappare switched on the nearest spotlight. 'Sorry.' Rappare glanced nervously towards the shuttered windows, hoping that the light was not seeping out and betraying his presence into the night outside. He watched Mastrov open the case. Inside, the two items were held firmly and safely in place, resting neatly in the cavities Rappare had cut from the extruded foam packing. 'You'll see that I have labelled the pieces, just so you don't get them confused.'

Mastrov snapped the case shut. The sound was a gunshot echoing off the bare walls of the studio. 'Good. Splendid.'

'You don't want to check it more carefully?'

'I don't think so. I know your reputation. And anyway, if there's a problem I can always call back.'

Rappare gulped, and his voice wavered as he said quickly, 'No, no problem. I assure you.'

Mastrov nodded slowly, then smiled and made for the door, but stopped and turned before reaching it. 'There was one other thing. Your contract stipulated that you should keep the mould.'

'Ah, of course.' Rappare slapped his sweaty forehead with the palm of his hand, as if remembering. 'I have it right here.' He reached behind the plinth where the Ming vase stood askance and lifted out a white cylinder. He held it more carefully than he had cradled the vase, and pulled it apart into two halves so that Mastrov could see the hollow shape inside. 'The only way to get the definition and line accurate enough for a job like this is to use a plasticrete compound. The lasers cut through the composite, but it re-forms when the laser has passed through. Only the form in the centre remains free and can be removed by cutting open the surrounding material –

what we call the mould, and of course it could be used as such. It's very fragile.'

Mastrov took the two halves of the mould from Rappare, lifting them with care from his slightly trembling hands.

Rappare actually jumped. Not so much at the sound, but in sheer disbelief and horror. The noise was deafening, an explosion ricocheting round the walls and glancing off the paintings and artefacts. He barely noticed Mastrov leave, hardly registered the click of the door closing. He stood, mouth open, hands sweating and clenching, as he stared at the white starburst of powder and fragments spread across the dark floor.

It took Rappare several minutes and several stiff drinks to recover from the shock. But after a while he decided that things could be worse. He had never expected to see the mould again anyway, although the destruction of any art was against his instinct and inclination. But the job was completed, collected and paid for. In full. He had expected some push-back, some last-minute refusal to pay the full price. He had no illusions about who Mastrov was, or about who was really paying for the work. Yes, all in all it had gone rather well. And he still had one more move of his own to make. He placed the call.

The videomail system cut in on the second tone and Rappare cursed.

'The party you were calling,' the glossy female voice of the system announced, 'is not available. Please leave a message.'

Rappare hesitated, then left a short message. A pity, it had all been going so well.

Too well, perhaps. It was time to leave, Rappare decided. Time to cash in and move on. He looked round the dimly lit room, and raised his glass to the *Mona Lisa*. Then he swung her aside, and peered into the retina-scanner mounted in the frame of the safe set into the wall behind.

* * *

The door clicked open and a figure emerged from the gloom within. For a moment he was silhouetted against the opening, caught in mid-turn as he pulled the door shut. Tableau. Targeting information – distance, size, estimated body weight – were fed across the bottom of the image.

The man was slight of build, bulked out by the heavy cloak pulled tight around his neck. A wide-brimmed hat was pulled down low over the eyes, which glistened faintly as they caught the gleam of a distant street light. His warm breath appeared in rhythmic misty clouds in the cold night air. The cloak swirled as the figure turned, opening slightly to reveal that the man was carrying a battered Gladstone bag. His boots clipped on the paved pathway as he started furtively away from the door. The sound became more rhythmic, more confident, as he went.

A shadow detached itself from the blackness nearby, and set off silently after Newark Rappare. The heat signature registered strongly on the retinal display; details blurred into red and orange as Rappare moved. The shadowy figure stayed well behind, watching and following. For the moment. They were still in the residential areas, and the slightest sound might attract attention, might be noted and remembered afterwards. Artificially enhanced hearing registered every footstep as a richly textured burst of aural input.

Rappare was moving more quickly now, his exact speed and energy output flitting across the display surgically implanted between eyes and brain. They were out of the residences and into Kalba Square. A hideous sculpted assortment of scaffolding and plastic slabs loomed over Rappare's hurrying figure.

Rappare reached the far side of the square and started clumsily up the steps towards the alleyway. The strategy program had marked the area in green on the map the neural implants projected into the cerebral cortex. The pursuer's pace quickened as they entered the killing ground.

Rappare was just starting along the alleyway, a short cut, when he heard the faintest of sounds from behind. He paused, and turned. Somewhere on the edge of conscious vision a shadow deepened, seemed to shy away from his gaze. Rappare watched for a moment longer, then continued along the alley, the night air cold and clammy against his face. He was nearly at the back entrance to Cordelia's – if there was someone behind him he could duck inside for a quick drink, and let them pass. He turned again, rapidly, hoping to catch a glimpse of his potential follower. Again, nothing but a deepening of blackness.

But it was enough. Rappare ran.

His cloak was blown out behind him as he raced down the alleyway. The bag was a weight which slowed his progress just as the blood pumping in his head was a distraction and the echo of his boots on the pavement was the footsteps of his pursuer. He could see the door to Cordelia's ahead, and this gave him more energy. A ragged holograph of a female dancer flickered in and out of focus as she twisted and turned above the doorway. Then, with an electric buzz, she flicked out of existence, and the lights inside the door also went out. A high-pitched sigh of panic forced its way through Rappare's lips as it occurred to him that it was well past closing time.

But even as he watched, even as he realized that the footsteps behind were neither echoes nor imagination, the door opened. He lunged forward, the weight of the cloak pulling at him.

A figure emerged from the opening, suddenly, as if pushed through. And the door slammed shut behind it. Rappare heard the security systems engage in the same instant as he cannoned into the figure now standing in the alleyway outside Cordelia's. They both collapsed in a tangle of limbs and cloak. The bag skidded across the pavement.

Rappare pulled himself to his feet, ignoring the woman's curses and insults. There was no pretence now. He could see a figure running up the alleyway towards him, could see the assassin's smile in the night. He looked towards the bag, lying the other side of the woman, back down the alley towards the approaching killer. Rappare hesitated just long enough to solve the equation which opposed the contents of the bag against his life. Then, with a renewed strength born of panic, he raced away down the alley.

Bernice Summerfield watched the strange man as he fled into the darkness. She glanced down the alley in the other direction, but whatever the man had seen or been running from was gone now. If it had ever existed. It was bad enough, she reflected as she pulled herself to her feet, being thrown out of the bar simply because it was closed. But being knocked down by a terrified clown in fancy dress running from his own shadow was enough to drive you back to drink. She shook her head and started down the alleyway in the opposite direction to that taken by the man, towards her apartment.

She had taken just three steps when her foot connected with something in the darkness. Whatever it was skidded slightly on the ground. Benny reached down and fumbled for it. It seemed to be a bag. A heavy bag. She lifted the battered black shape into the half-light, and pulled at the catch. Perhaps inside there would be some clue to the address of the owner.

But there was only one thing inside. She tilted the bag to try to let more light in, then pulled out the thing inside, staring at it in disbelief. The bag dropped to the floor.

Somewhere, a door slammed. The sound brought Benny back to reality, and she looked round quickly and guiltily. Not that she needed to feel guilty. Whoever the strange man was, he would be certain to report it missing. And even the vaguest description would establish the owner's credentials.

Benny stuffed the strange item back into the bag, and set off for home.

Rappare was gasping by the time he reached the building. He allowed himself a moment's rest outside the main door, bent over, hands on knees as he struggled to draw the cold air into his lungs. He staggered towards the glass doors. The department's symbol, a stylized mask of a human face, was etched across them. One side of the face was happy, the mouth curled into a smile. The other half was sad, a teardrop falling from the eye and trailing down the cheek. The doors remained closed, even when Rappare leant his forehead against them and peered through the glass.

The inside of the building was in darkness. But this was just what Rappare needed. If he could find the right office, he could wait for the man he wanted to see to arrive in the morning. He looked round, but there was no sight or sound of pursuit. He doubted his pursuer had given up, but it seemed that he had thrown the assassin off his trail for the moment.

The card-reader glowed as he swiped the plastic through it. There was a pause, and Rappare pushed tentatively on the door. Come on! What was the delay? A tiny light flashed red on the top of the badge-reader, and Rappare swiped the card again. The same result. He held the card up to check he was holding it the right way up, though he knew the reader should be able to detect the on-board chip whichever way.

It was the wrong card.

A movement. Rappare saw something, a flash of motion blurred in reflection on the glass doors. He scrabbled for his university identification, pushing the transaction card back into his pocket. This time the reader flashed green, and with a quiet click, the doors swung open for him. Rappare jumped inside, willing the doors to close again quickly. He crossed the atrium at a clumsy run, looking back over his shoulder expecting to see a figure detach from the shadows and race for the doors as they swung shut. But there was nothing.

He turned and walked slowly backward away from the doors, watching carefully for any movement. His artist's eye subconsciously noted the lighting outside, the way the shadows were cast and images on the glass reflected. And with a sudden certain stab of fear, Rappare realized his mistake. He had not caught a glimpse of movement reflected in the glass doors. The angles were all wrong. There was nothing outside.

What he had seen was the movement of someone *inside* the building. In the atrium. He braced himself ready to run back towards the main doors, hoping they would open to let him out. And a hand clamped down on his shoulder.

'I think you and I have some business to conclude,' a voice said quietly.

It was the smell that struck her first. It was a too-fresh odour, artificially overscented, which reminded her of air-freshener, wet floors and hospital.

Benny had woken late, sworn at her chronometer and at Joseph, her small spherical porter, then leapt for the ultrasound shower. Pausing just long enough to accept a mug of coffee from Joseph to deaden the fogginess inside her head, she grabbed the pile of books by the door, waved to her cat Wolsey and let herself out of her apartment. She always left the books ready for the next day before she went out in the evening. It took her a few minutes between the end of the day and the start of the evening, but they were minutes she could better spare then than in the blind panic of the morning rush. Most mornings this had the effect of keeping her almost on time for her first seminar. It did not seem to matter what time the day started, Benny was late before she got going. And after cycling for all she was worth across the campus to make up the time, she would arrive out of breath.

But today was different. Perhaps she had misread the clock, or perhaps she was in more of a panic than normal, but whatever the reason she found herself taking her usual short cut through Prospero Plaza over ten minutes early for her seminar discussing techniques in the recovery of Etruscan organic remains. As she passed the front of the Theatrology building, she glanced out of habit over at the imposing glass frontage, the sun shining through the top of the high atrium.

The first day Benny had cycled across the square, she had been struck by the uncharacteristic splendour of the building. It was completely out of keeping with its dull brown surroundings. A glass cathedral of theatrical proportions plonked down in the middle of the mud-hut architecture of St Oscar's. Benny had been too overawed to be surprised, and despite being late had found herself standing on the threshold of the building, bicycle leaning against her thigh. The doors had swung ponderously open, and she had stepped into the high atrium, looking up into the glass pyramid ceiling. Behind her the glass doors swung silently closed, completing the two distinct halves of the happy-sad face engraved on them.

It had hardly been a surprise, rather a realization, when Benny saw the small brass plaque set into the wall. In clean, clear lettering it said: 'Department of Theatrology: Shakespeare Building. Sponsored and Opened by Irving Braxiatel, Head of Department.' She had laughed out loud, a sudden stifled snort of mirth. Then she looked round quickly, smiling in embarrassment at the looks of surprise she had drawn from the students and staff milling round at the start of the day. As she left, she wondered distractedly what had attracted everyone's attention – her snort of laughter, or the fact that she was the only person in the building wheeling a bicycle.

Benny had first met Irving Braxiatel some years earlier. Apart from masterminding a convoluted plan to overthrow a ruthless dictator, Braxiatel had been an obsessive collector. She gathered from people who had known him better and for longer than she that he had always been an obsessive collector. He collected everything. And his knowledge seemed to span just about every conceivable subject, though theatre was a particular love of his. Literature and history were not far behind, Benny supposed because he had read an awful lot and lived through so much of history between his reading.

Benny had no idea how old Braxiatel really was, and since he undoubtedly had access to time-travel technology, she doubted if he knew himself. But she had heard stories that Braxiatel had helped organize the Armageddon Convention in Venice in the seventeenth century, and she was quite prepared to believe it.

The last time Benny had seen Braxiatel was at her wedding, standing characteristically by the champagne. She smiled to herself as she remembered their verbal sparring. He had been calm and quiet, happy to concede a point if it was well made. And she had been desperate to make the points, appreciating and respecting the fact that his concessions were not lightly given. Braxiatel had many qualities, but suffering fools gladly, or even at all, was not one of them.

Benny had waited a few days, then asked at the Theatrology information desk if she could leave a message for Braxiatel. The woman at the desk had smiled sadly. 'Mr Braxiatel is away at the moment. In fact, he is not with us very often.'

Benny nodded. 'Just pops in every decade or so to see how you're coping without him, and sort out the mess, I expect.' The woman gave her a sideways look. 'I've heard of similar arrangements,' Benny assured her. Then she smiled and left. There was probably plenty of time to leave a message.

Every time Benny passed the building she was reminded of that first visit – every time she looked over at the sheer glass frontage, and smiled ambivalently back at the happy-sadness of the engraved mask. Recently the impressive frontage had been enhanced, if that was the right word, by Menlove Stokes, Artist and Sculptor in Residence. He had constructed an arrangement of tubes and pipes up the side and across the roof of an adjacent block. The garish clashing colours reflected off the glass building, and a single strand of piping stretched across the walkway dividing the two, joining to a supporting strut of the Theatrology Building. Benny had asked Stokes about this single tubular incursion, and he had stared at her as if she were mad. 'Umbilical,' he barked at her, and strode off in a huff. She asked no more.

But today the smell made more of an impression than the building or the sculpture opposite. It caught at the back of her throat as soon as she turned into the plaza. She looked across at the building, and the bicycle coasted to a slow stop. The doors of the building were open. The atrium inside was deserted. In front of the building, an area of the square was roped off, yellow-and-black-striped tape strung between low posts forming an uneven rectangle in front of the doors. Several porters hovered at intervals over the tape, almost lost against the building behind. A couple of university security guards were standing by the tape, laughing and joking together. Their humour seemed artificially exaggerated, and it took Benny a moment to work out what seemed so forced about it. They were nervous, she realized with a shock. It was gallows humour.

And standing in the doorway, looking out across the square, his expression suggesting that he was not seeing it, stood the tall, thin figure of Irving Braxiatel.

Benny dismounted and wheeled the cycle across the plaza. She was very close before Braxiatel even seemed to notice her. If he was surprised to see her he did not show it. She studied his angular features for a flicker of emotion, and found none. 'Trouble?' she asked brightly.

'What makes you think that?' His voice was quiet, with only the faintest hint of sarcasm.

'Oh you know, the usual. Cordoned-off area, porters out in force, security guards swapping war stories.' Benny smiled. 'The fact that you're here.'

Braxiatel frowned. 'Trouble's your middle name,' Benny told him. But she was beginning to worry. Had she made some mistake? This was not the way she had envisaged the conversation going. It was hardly the merry banter and sarcastic kidding back and forth she was used to from Braxiatel.

He rubbed his chin thoughtfully for a moment. Then he leant forward over the tape barrier and looked at Benny, his gaze careful, steady and intense. At last he straightened up and smiled politely. 'Have we met?' he asked.

Benny opened her mouth to reply. Then closed it again as it struck her that he was serious. In fact, now she thought about it, he had a point. 'Yes,' Benny told him, 'we have met. But perhaps not yet.'

'Ah.' Braxiatel took this in his stride. 'Then this is probably going to be one of those awkward conversations where we don't know what to say or what tense not to say it in.' He turned and walked slowly along parallel to the fluttering tape. One of the porters moved rapidly out of the way. Benny walked beside him, the chain of the bicycle clicking over the ratchets. 'Are we friends?' Braxiatel asked suddenly. 'I do apologize,' he added before Benny could reply, 'but it's best to be sure of these things. Especially in the current circumstances.'

'Absolutely,' said Benny. 'I mean, you're right. And yes, we are.' Braxiatel nodded slowly. 'You came to my wedding,' Benny told him.

'Will I? Oh good.'

They stopped walking and looked at each other. Benny felt it was her turn to say something, but she was not quite sure where to go from here. Then she realized what Braxiatel had just said. 'What circumstances?' He raised an eyebrow. 'Well,' Benny reasoned, 'if we're going to be friends.'

He laughed. Not out loud, just a sudden curl of the mouth. Then it was gone. 'A man died here. Last night.'

'Anyone we know?'

'Well, somebody knew him. They're checking the access records from the badge-reader and running a DNA match against the university records, in case he was a student or on the staff.' Braxiatel reached down and carefully tore the tape. The two ends fluttered to the floor beside him, and he ushered Benny through the gap. 'Come with me,' he said. 'You can leave your bicycle there. It'll be quite safe, I'm sure.'

At first Benny thought the body had been left lying where it had been found in the atrium. It even cast a shadow. Then, as she watched, the holograph misphased for an instant, guttering like an oily flame. 'Natural causes?'

'So it would seem. So, I don't think so.'

Benny smiled. Braxiatel hadn't changed. Or rather, he wouldn't change. 'Murder then.'

'Made to look like massive heart failure.' Braxiatel shook his head, angry rather than upset. 'As if someone would dress up like a second-rate music-hall villain, then traipse over to Theatrology in order to drop dead in the foyer. Too melodramatic for real life, and too imaginative for a student prank.'

'What,' Benny chided, 'and in our department?' When Braxiatel did not respond, she looked again at the holographic figure. It was a man, overweight and middle-aged. Rather improbably, he was wearing a long heavy cloak. A virtual wide-brimmed hat lay nearby. 'He looks so peaceful.'

'There are two sides to everything, even death,' Braxiatel said quietly. 'The peaceful all-embracing silence of the aftermath, and the gut-tearing agony of incision as the laserknife rips through the stomach, cauterizing as it goes so the scars seem like old trophies of survival rather than the trappings of murder.'

Benny grimaced. 'What a long sentence.'

'A long sentence will certainly be in order when I find the culprit.'

'You think you will?'

'Oh, I'll move Burnham Wood to Dunsinane to that purpose, if you'll allow me to complement your earlier allusion.' Braxiatel turned and gestured for Benny to precede him back to the doors. 'Do you like our engraving?' he asked as they returned to the plaza.

Benny paused, and looked at the grinning crying mask on the doors. 'It's all Greek to me,' she said.

Braxiatel laughed. Out loud this time. 'Till we meet again,' he said, shaking her hand. 'And I'm sure we shall.'

Benny nodded, waited for the security guard to untie the knot he had just made in the black-and-yellow tape, and stepped through the cordon. She wondered, as she picked up her bicycle, why the figure lying sprawled in the atrium had seemed vaguely familiar. Then she glanced at her watch, realized she was every bit as late as usual, and started pedalling.

MEETING PEOPLE

'Ah, Summerfield.'

Benny gritted her teeth so hard she was afraid that Professor Follett would see her jaw clench from behind. She resolved the expression into an approximation of a smile and turned to face him. Her seminar had just ended, and she had hoped to make a rapid escape back to her rooms to recover before the rigours of her lecture that afternoon. Lunch or a 'cosy chat' with Follett was not high on her list of must-dos for today. Or any day. But Professor Divson Follett was after all the head of the Archaeology Department, so Benny clenched a smile and waited for him. Just so long as he wasn't going to ask her to lead the annual field trip for latecomers to the first year. Or the graveyard shift, as the staff called it.

Follett wheezed and slushed along the corridor, winking politely at the students who fled before him clutching handkerchiefs to their olfactory organs. The chlorine-laced steam rose from him in a pungent green cloud as he approached Benny. 'Glad I caught you,' he said in his husky voice, and tapped her on the arm in a friendly manner.

Benny resisted the urge to wipe the stain from her sleeve. She kept her smile fixed in position and tried desperately not to inhale. She failed. 'Professor, how nice,' she coughed.

'You got my note?' Follett set off down the corridor and Benny walked slowly beside him.

'I did, yes. But it really wasn't me, you know. Probably

one of the students. I'm sure the staff all appreciate how much you enjoy your mollusc-enriched diet.'

Follett waved a scaly hand. 'Not that note, Summerfield. Not that note. My other note.'

'Er . . .'

'About the meeting today at, well, in a few minutes' time. We can walk over together.'

'No.'

Follett stopped in his slimy tracks.

Benny gulped, and drew breath through the farthest corner of her mouth. 'I mean, no I didn't get the note. What meeting?'

They had reached the lifts, and Benny let Follett press the call button. 'Over at History,' he explained. 'With old Winston – dreadful old woman but means well. Got some off-worlder with a proposal.'

The lift arrived, and Benny squeezed into a corner away from Follett. She watched in horror as the doors slid to and closed them into the confined space together.

'And money,' Follett hissed. 'There's an offer of some money. And you know how desperate the department is for that.' He nodded emphatically. 'So mind your manners, I know what you're like.'

Emilia Winston was indeed an old woman. She had run the History Department of St Oscar's with a rod of tempered duralinium for longer than anyone would admit to remembering. Benny had never met her before, but she seemed pleasant enough as she ushered them into the conference room. Two men were already seated at the large, oval, glass-topped table. They both rose politely as Benny, Follett and Winston entered, and Benny saw there was a huge difference in their heights.

'I thought we'd all be more comfortable in a larger room,' Winston said pointedly as she gestured for Follett to sit in a chair set well apart from the others.

Benny chose one of the chairs closer to Follett. But not too close. Then she looked round at the others. One of them she recognized from the staff meeting earlier in the week. He was short and fat and his name was Mappin Gilder. Benny sighed: there was indeed some money involved. Gilder was the Archaeology Department's new 'facilitator'. He was responsible for saving as much money from the paltry department finances as he could, and looking for new sources of funding and sponsorship. Given that what little money industry had left to invest was likely to be channelled into more specific and 'applied' scientific research than archaeology, Gilder would be cutting budgets rather than enlarging them.

If Gilder was aware of Benny's disdain, he did not show it. He smiled insipidly, wiped a sweaty hand through his lank hair, and then examined his perfect fingernails.

'I think we're just waiting for Doctor Kamadrich, now,' Winston said as she took her seat well away from Follett. 'She'll explain what this is about.' She settled herself at the table and pulled out a palmtop reader. In a moment she was busily reading through her mail.

'We haven't been introduced,' said a quiet voice close to Benny. The tall man had moved round the table and was sitting down beside her. He was well built, his hair short and dark and his eyes a startling grey-blue. He reached out his hand. 'Nicholas Clyde.'

'Professor Summerfield,' Benny said. 'But my friends call me Benny.'

Clyde nodded. 'You're with Archaeology, I assume.'

'And why do you assume that?'

'Because you came in with Follett, and because I'm with History.' He smiled. 'I gather you're pretty new here too.'

Benny studied Clyde's features. He had a nice smile, for sure, and he seemed intelligent enough. 'I've been here a little while. And yourself?'

'Just a couple of weeks. I finished my doctorate at Kai-Tec last month, and got an attachment here as a specialist lecturer.'

Benny nodded. 'And what are you a specialist in?'

Nicholas Clyde, it turned out, was a specialist in the life, times and campaigns of Hugo Gamaliel. Benny feigned an appreciation of this famous historical figure of whom she had never heard, and Nicholas talked quietly and knowledgeably about his interest. Benny listened carefully, filing away the information for future reference. Nicholas was someone she might well spend some time with.

Gamaliel, it seemed, had been a local dictator who conquered and ruled a large area some centuries previously. His origins were something of a mystery, most of the records of the time having been lost in the subsequent wars. 'He is also, of course,' Nicholas continued, 'famous for exposing the existence of the Knights of Jeneve and defeating them in battle. There are lots of legends about his exploits and heroism, but that at least seems to have some historical basis.'

'Have you researched any of the legends in detail?' Benny asked. She was wondering who on earth the Knights of Jeneve might have been. A few open questions might draw the answer out of Nicholas without her having to ask outright. And she had nothing better to do at the moment. Winston was doing her mail, and Gilder and Follett were both sitting stewing in their own juices – almost literally in Follett's case.

'I've done some research, yes. But the extant sources are pretty vague and ambiguous. At least, the ones at my disposal anyway.'

Benny frowned. Had she missed something? 'Sorry,' she said, 'I thought you were doing research for a doctorate at Kai-Tec.'

Nicholas nodded. 'That's right.'

'So, well, surely you haven't just been relying on extant sources, as you put it.' Nicholas looked blank, so Benny went on: 'I mean, haven't you been to the sites of the battles, poked about on his home planet? Tracked down oral traditions and dug up incriminating relics?'

Nicholas laughed. 'You're joking! On a history doctorate's

budget.' He caught sight of Benny's expression. 'No, you're not joking, are you. Well, I'm sorry to disappoint you, but history is mainly digging around only metaphorically in books and archives, rather than literally at battlefields and ancient sites.'

Benny shook her head in disbelief. 'But how can you call it research if you've never been to anywhere that this Gamaliel guy lived or fought? What original information can you get from existing sources?'

'You get knowledge, and you interpret it. You might find a new slant on existing evidence, or develop a new theory that explains anomalies in the existing information. That's what history is about. It's about explaining the past, not raking it up. You're confusing the two things. You do the digging, and we interpret, and reinterpret, what you find. We refine and codify the knowledge.' Benny just stared at him. 'Knowledge above all,' he said, so quietly that she almost missed it.

Benny wanted to say that she thought he was missing the point entirely, and that raking over the past was the only way of truly discovering anything interesting and new about it. She wanted to say that if that was history then she'd stick with archaeology until it crumbled to dust around her. But while she was still fumbling round in her mind to frame the words, the door opened, and a woman walked in.

The woman was about Benny's age, younger if anything. But she immediately exuded a self-confidence and a presence that made Benny feel like a new student in freshers' week. She was tall and slim, and carried a briefcase. Her long, straight, blonde hair, perfect make-up and deep blue eyes contrasted with the grubby overalls she wore. She moved quickly across the room, her eyes darting to and fro as she took in her surroundings. Her gaze lingered for a fraction of a second on Benny, then moved on. She looked at Nicholas for slightly longer, and Benny felt him tense slightly. The woman's searching stare had unsettled him in the same way as it had unnerved her. Or nearly.

'Doctor Kamadrich,' Winston said, 'how kind of you to join us.'

The woman, Kamadrich, switched on a sudden smile, and sat down next to Winston at the table. 'Well now,' she said in a cut-silk voice, 'my name is Truby Kamadrich. And when we've finished the introductions, I have a proposition to put to you.'

The proposition was straightforward. Kamadrich had financing for an archaeology expedition to a planet on the edge of the sector, and she was looking for some cheap but plausible help. At least, that was how Benny read it. She wanted professional assistance at a reasonable rate. St Oscar's was nearby and the fact that most of the sponsorship was directed into the sciences and research into technology with an indirect or not so indirect military application was hardly a secret.

'So,' Benny asked when Kamadrich finished her brief explanation, 'what's there?'

'I'm sorry?'

Benny leant forward, hands clasped together on the cold glass of the table top. 'You've told us you want to excavate on this planet Stanturus Three. But you haven't told us why you need expert help from us. This isn't just a shot in the dark, is it? You expect to find something there.' Benny sat back, happy with the sudden tension round the table. 'So, what is it?'

'Good,' Kamadrich said after a pause. 'Very good. I can see you will be a great asset to us, Professor Summerfield. You're right of course.' She looked round the table, pausing for a moment as if about to reveal a dark secret. 'We believe that there was once an ancient civilization on Stanturus Three. We fully expect to find evidence to support this theory.' She looked directly at Benny, her eyes steely points of reflective blue. 'Happy?'

Benny nodded. 'Hardly an original excuse, but it gets me every time.'

'So what?'

There was a startled silence for a second. Kamadrich

was still looking at Benny; Gilder had been jotting some figures and making calculations based on the sponsorship Kamadrich had mentioned; Winston was doing her mail again; Follett was grinning at Kamadrich's compliments to his professor. And Benny was feeling pleased with herself. So Nicholas Clyde's question took them all by surprise.

'Sorry,' he apologized. 'That's the difference perhaps between an archaeologist and a historian. Benny wants to know what, and I'd like to know why. What does it matter if there's an ancient civilization there or not? As Benny points out, they are ten a shilling out there, so what's special about this one?'

'Why should there be anything special?' Gilder looked up from his scribbles. 'Doctor Kamadrich is willing to pay, isn't that enough?'

'I think that's my point, actually. What exactly is so special about this planet that someone is willing to pay to investigate it?'

'Why do you ask?' Kamadrich's voice seemed calm and reasonable, but there was an edge to it that was not lost on Benny.

Nicholas smiled. 'I'm asking because I think we both know the answer. Because it's information that you haven't proffered, but which I think is important in deciding whether or not to accept your kind offer.'

Gilder almost choked. 'Whether or not?' he spluttered. 'You heard how much money's involved.'

Winston smiled, and Follett stirred in his vapours. Nicholas shook his head slowly. 'Again, that's exactly my point. So much money on the off chance we might find something? I don't think so, I really don't think so. Not given the current economic climate, not given the standing of Doctor Kamadrich in the archaeological world, and not given the strategic position of Stanturus.'

Suddenly everyone was talking at once. Everyone, Benny noticed when she'd given up trying to be heard above them, except Nicholas and Kamadrich. They were sitting silent and still, staring at each other. After a moment, Kamadrich reached down and lifted her briefcase on to the table. She opened it and took out a small, black box. She made a brief gesture with the flat of her hand, and a holographic projection shimmered into existence above the table. The noise stopped.

The image showed a star map, and as Benny and the others watched, the picture seemed to expand and flood out into the room. Points of stellar light reflected off the glass of the table as they sped outwards, until the central image was of a single planetary system.

'The Stanturus system,' Kamadrich said quietly. 'We are interested only in Stanturus Three.'

Benny had never heard of Stanturus before, but within a few minutes she was as aware as anyone of its importance. In fact, it was simple. The Stanturus system was on the edge of the sector of space where Dellah was situated. And it was on the edge closest to the next civilized sector. In effect it was the gateway to and from the whole of local space.

Stanturus Three was special as it was the only naturally inhabitable planet of the system. There were four planets in total, and two of them were now terraformed and had small communities living on them. But the third planet of the system was a wilderness of jungle and desert inhabited by a predictable complement of birds, mammals, reptiles and fish.

The lights dimmed again as Kamadrich gestured to her puter and it spat out another image. It was the face of a middle-aged man. He was clean-shaven with short, black hair and sideburns. His bushy eyebrows made his brown eyes seem more deeply set than they probably were, and the wrinkles beginning to show on his forehead and around his mouth made him look older than he probably was.

Nicholas snorted, though whether in mirth or surprise Benny could not tell. 'Romolo Nusek,' he said quietly. 'I should have guessed.'

'Nice guy to work for?' Benny asked casually. But she

reckoned from Nicholas's thinly disguised look of contempt that she already knew the answer.

The DNA from the corpse had eventually been matched with a personnel record in the university's database. Braxiatel had stood over the nervous operator as she coaxed the antiquated AI search engine in its task of going through each of the staff and student files in turn and extracting, then comparing, the genetic information.

He tutted and snorted and suggested ways that the existing system could be speeded up and ways that the system could have been better implemented. He also made several comments about the possible background and lack of training of the original designers of the database schema from which the whole administration system was run.

Braxiatel was of course just passing the time in idle chitchat. When he realized he was unsettling the woman, he relaxed into silence. The whole tortuous process would be marginally quicker if he let her concentrate on the work, so Braxiatel amused himself by redesigning the university systems in his head. He must talk to the Dean, he decided, and get him to agree to take the mainframe computers down for a day so he could implement his ideas. He was just wondering if he could perhaps manage it in half a day when the operator exhaled loudly in relief and turned round in her chair. She gestured at the flat panel display, where a DNA double helix curled round on its axis in a garish mix of purple and orange.

'A perfect match, sir.'

'Good.' Braxiatel did not look at the screen. He stood and walked to the door. 'Forward me the file, would you?'

'I'm sure our antiquated systems can manage that,' she said quietly.

Braxiatel paused in the doorway. He smiled to himself, and without turning said, 'The more antiquated the system, the better the operators have to be.' The smile was still on his face when he turned back. 'Well done. And thank you.'

Back in his office in Theatrology, Braxiatel checked his

mail. The file was waiting for him, as were the usual requests for advice, after-dinner speeches and sponsorship. He waved most of the mail away, but one item intrigued him. It was from a personal node he did not recognize, and that meant it was from someone who had never had cause to send Braxiatel mail before. Braxiatel opened the file.

'Hello, er, you don't know me Mr Brax– er, Prof– um, that is, er, sir.'

Braxiatel sat back and let the sweaty individual bluster his way through his introduction.

'My name is Newark Rappare. I work in Art History. I, er, also dabble a bit myself. I have something in my possession that I think you might be interested in, and I wondered if perhaps we could discuss it.' Rappare's image looked furtively over its shoulder, and as the head turned, Braxiatel got a sudden impression that he had seen the man before. 'Anyway, er, I'll come over to your office. Now, if I may. I'll wait if you're not there, and I hope you'll pardon the intrusion. But I think you'll agree it's worth it. When you see what I have to offer.' Rappare nodded, a short, sharp gesture of dismissal as the video image faded away.

Braxiatel checked the timestamp on the message, wondering why Rappare had never arrived. An unsettling thought struck him and he opened the personnel file for the murdered man.

'Personnel file 664/9418-OOA,' a husky female voice intoned as a face shimmered into view above Braxiatel's desk. 'Newark Rappare, Professor of Art History, University of St Oscar.'

Braxiatel rested his elbows on the desk and his chin in his hands as he watched the file play past him.

Benny let most of it play past her. She had seen enough to conclude that she was not especially keen to work for Romolo Nusek. He smiled at her, and at the others in the room, his image floating over the table. If Benny leant back and squinted a bit, then the reflection in the glass made it seem as if his neck joined to an upside-down copy of itself. This was rather more interesting than most of what he was saying in the recorded message Kamadrich was playing for them.

Nusek, whose harsh voice suggested he enjoyed chewing gravel, had promised funding and grants which obviously impressed Gilder, Follett and Winston. He had promised an archaeological challenge for Benny and a chance to experience history both in the past and in the making for Nicholas. And now he was droning on in a singularly unconvincing way about the value of impartial and independent research to furthering humanity's understanding of the universe in which it lived. Et cetera.

Benny yawned. She caught sight of Gilder's disapproving look halfway through, tried to turn the yawn into a cough, then decided not to bother and ended up almost choking. The recording ended and the lights came up in time for everyone to get a good view of Benny trying desperately to catch her breath. 'Sorry,' she gasped, her eyes watering.

'Well,' Nicholas said when the recording had finished, 'I can't say I'm convinced.'

'But you'll think about it.' Kamadrich was leaning across the table, her eyes fiery in their intensity.

Nicholas looked round. Gilder, Follett and Winston were staring at Nicholas, seeming to will him to agree. Nicholas, by contrast, was swinging to and fro in his chair smiling.

'What about you, Summerfield?' Follett barked.

'We'll think it over,' Nicholas said before Benny could frame a response. 'Professor Summerfield and I both have some reservations about the integrity of the expedition.'

'Right,' said Benny. 'Reservations.' She looked round at the disbelieving faces of the others. She imagined they could see huge piles of grant and sponsorship money fading into the distance. She thought briefly of her own lack of funds and the generous salary Nusek had promised. 'We will think it over.'

'That's fair.' Kamadrich was putting the puter back into

her briefcase. 'I can assure you, though, that the whole expedition will be completely independent and impartial, a great chance for some serious archaeology. It doesn't really matter where the money actually comes from provided we have control.'

'And afterwards?' Nicholas asked.

'Nusek is motivated by an interest in his ancestor's background and history, nothing more, Dr Clyde. But whatever we do find, Nusek has already agreed to hold an independent – genuinely independent – inquiry to assess and report on whatever we turn up. If anything.' Her hair was a flurry of gold as she stood up. 'We shall need to know your decision by midday tomorrow,' she said. 'Thank you for your time.'

Gilder and Follett both glared at Benny and Nicholas as they left the room. Winston avoided making eye contact.

'So, what do you think?' Nicholas asked when they were alone.

Benny shrugged. 'If this inquiry thing is genuine he must be pretty certain of his ground.'

Nicholas laughed. 'I doubt the expedition will find anything. Nusek can afford to go looking on the off chance. I think the whole thing will be a boring waste of time.' He stood up. 'I got interested in Gamaliel because of the romantic heroism and the stories of his derring-do.'

Benny frowned. 'What's Gamaliel got to do with it?'

Nicholas looked at her in disbelief. 'Well, Nusek of course.' She must have still looked blank. 'You know, descended from Gamaliel and destined to succeed him in glory. All that rubbish. Mind you, I'm more into the Gamalian Dragon Myths than grubbing about in the dirt for days on end.'

'Dragon myths?' Benny tried to sound nonchalant, as if she were suffering from a temporary mindslip rather than complete ignorance. She was going to have to do some background reading if she did go on this expedition.

'You know.' Nicholas was heading for the door. He held it open for Benny and together they walked down the corridor.

'The Knights of Jeneve. All that stuff.'

'Perhaps you had better remind me.'

Nicholas looked sideways at Benny. He obviously thought it odd that she needed telling, but he was good enough not to say so. 'Towards the end of the twenty-fourth century, when he was starting on the series of campaigns that would take him to his eventual position of power, Gamaliel's first major battle was against the Knights of Jeneve at Bocaro, in the Tersalian system.'

'And Gamaliel won?'

Nicholas nodded. 'Big time. Wiped them out, practically, despite their overwhelming advantage. They were never heard of again.'

They had walked through the foyer and were at the main door to the History Department by now. Benny stopped and turned to Nicholas. 'So where did the dragon come into it?' she asked.

'Well, the whole thing's a bit vague. I've studied the period, and there just isn't any more to it than what's in the popular myths. You probably know as much as there is to know.'

Benny doubted it. But she could hardly pursue the subject without arousing undue suspicion. So she tried a different tack. 'I was wondering what historical evidence still exists. What did you actually study if you didn't do any archaeology?'

'There are some texts, popular culture. There's Brahmyn's holovid as well as some oral tradition and the romances of Anton Phelps, of course. And the Gamalian Dragon itself is well enough documented, though I've never seen it in the flesh so to speak.'

'The Gamalian Dragon?' Benny was beginning to feel slightly uncomfortable about the way the conversation was developing.

Nicholas did not seem to notice her discomfort. He held his hands about half a metre apart vertically. 'It's about so high. Wings spread and mouth open. Scales and so on.' He shrugged. 'It's pretty much what you'd expect for a statuette of a rearing dragon made from precious metal and encrusted with jewels. Are you all right?'

Benny was not sure. She felt a little light-headed. She had had a sinking feeling from the moment Nicholas mentioned the Dragon Myths, but she had not really believed that there could be a connection. However, his description of the Gamalian Dragon had dispelled her doubts: a statuette of a jewelled dragon, complete with scales and spread wings. He had just described something she had recently seen for herself, in the flesh, as he would say. And she had seen it late last night, nestling inside a battered Gladstone bag which was now lying with yesterday's dirty laundry on the floor of her bedroom.

ENTER THE DRAGON

It took three large gulps of beer before Nicholas felt relaxed enough to join in the conversation. Until then, Benny was doing all the talking. Or, rather, Benny was asking a lot of questions. But after three gulps the evil beer, which Benny had bought Nicholas when he seemed unable to decide what he wanted, started to have an effect. He was still mentally numbed by the shock, but he was beginning to feel in control of himself again.

'So, what do you think?' Benny asked for about the fifth time in as many minutes.

Nicholas considered. He held the pint of Captain's Ruin up to what little light there was in their corner of the Witch and Whirlwind. 'I think you're right,' he said at last.

Benny frowned. 'About what in particular?'

'About the clean dry finish. It really is remarkably good.'

'That wasn't what I was most intrigued by, actually.'

Nicholas nodded. 'No. Nor me.'

After they had left the History Department, Benny had taken Nicholas back to her apartment. He had initially been slightly unsettled by her suggestion that she might have something he ought to look at. But when it turned out not to be etchings at all but rather a battered black Gladstone bag, he felt slightly relieved. But not for long.

There was no doubt in Nicholas's mind, despite his reticence, that the statuette Benny had found was the Gamalian Dragon. The main problem though, as he had explained to Benny, was that the Dragon was not actually lost. Most members of historical and archaeological academia knew exactly where it was. He would have said 'all' had Benny not been an obvious exception. It had remained in the possession of Gamaliel's descendants, and now Romolo Nusek had it. The same Romolo Nusek who was offering them gainful and allegedly honest employment.

Benny suggested it might be a copy. A very good copy. But now that the beer was loosening his numbed brain, Nicholas was explaining why a copy was unlikely to exist.

'One problem we have,' he said between gulps, 'is that Nusek is fanatically paranoid about it.'

Benny smiled. 'What other sort of paranoia is there?'

'Are you getting at me?' Nicholas asked mock-seriously.

'So why is that a problem?'

Nicholas leant forward over the table, positioning his elbows carefully on dry islands among the spilt beer and suspicious stains. 'The Dragon is kept carefully guarded. There are records, still photographs even. But the Dragon itself is never removed from the archives on Tharn, and hardly anyone is ever granted permission to see it in the flesh. And then only through the blastproof glass and counter-intrusion systems.'

'So you know all about it.'

Nicholas laughed. 'Are you kidding? It's my life's study.' He took another gulp of beer. 'Well,' he admitted, 'I know a bit about Gamaliel. To tell you the truth, I chose the period because there's so little proper documentation. Makes it easy for a historian as there's so little to study.'

Benny snorted. 'Archaeology students dream of getting assigned a period that's completely documented. That way they know the answers before they start. So what's the other problem with it being a fake?'

'The material. I'm not an expert, but working with bonded barolium is notoriously difficult. And giving the metallic glaze that aged sheen must be well-nigh impossible.'

They drank without speaking for a while. The business of the Witch and Whirlwind went on around them as they sat oblivious to it. They finished their drinks, and Nicholas got more. He was getting used to the beer now, and found that he actually liked it.

'Maybe it's been stolen,' Benny suggested as he returned. 'After all, if it's never seen nobody would know.'

'Maybe.' Nicholas was not convinced though. He smiled. 'You reckon the Cat's Paw called in on Nusek and lifted it at dead of night?' He shook his head. 'Benny, it's one of the best-guarded artefacts in this part of known space. And I can't see Nusek sitting around organizing archaeological jollies if his prize historical relic has just gone walkabout.'

'Well,' Benny said, 'that's another thing. From what you say, I can't see him sponsoring the expedition anyway. Hardly sounds his style.' The beer left a pale film on her upper lip as she drank. 'But whatever his motivation, and wherever my dragon came from, it's a huge coincidence that Nusek should make us this offer just now.' She wiped her mouth with the back of her hand. 'Don't you think?'

Nicholas nodded. 'So, you still think we shouldn't go?'

'On the contrary. I think we should accept the man's kind offer.'

'Good,' said Nicholas. 'Let's drink to that.' And they did.

'What will you do with all this?' Braxiatel gestured round at the contents of the studio. The white walls were almost covered with famous paintings, and various statuary and other artefacts stood on white plinths around the room. Each of the pieces was lit by its own halogen discharger: a sketch by Leonardo here, a Ming vase there, a Potharnio figure on one plinth, a fragment from Lessing's *Arcturan Doom* painting on the wall behind. Classical rubbed shoulders with rococo and impressionism faced off Dada in an amalgam of styles, periods and cultures.

Anton Rastian, senior professor of Art History, shrugged what passed for his shoulders and grunted. 'I suppose we should put them on display and incorporate them into the curriculum.' He shook his huge head, the veins on his grey neck standing out as he did so. 'I had no idea he'd done so much. None of us had. We never came here of course.'

'Really?'

'Well, he called it a studio, but Rappare never actually encouraged visitors. The assumption was that it was a sort of retirement fund.' He picked up a small ornate box made from stalsor wood, holding it surprisingly delicately between talons. 'I knew he sold some pieces for a lot of money, but I really had no idea his work was so good.'

Braxiatel nodded. 'I was looking at the *Mona Lisa* just now. Quite exquisite in my opinion. And the statues are if anything more authentic.'

'Yes, statuary was his speciality, I gather.'

They wandered among the collection for a while. Braxiatel asked Rastian about Rappare, but learnt little. He had been a hopeless lecturer, but his reputation was enough to keep him secure in his position as the Art History Department's Artisan-in-Residence at St Oscar's. The workmanship on the pieces of art in the studio was outstanding.

'You know,' Braxiatel remarked at one point, 'if there was one genuine article here, I'm not sure even I could spot it.'

Rastian bared his teeth in what might have been a grin. 'The first thing we'll do is engrave some distinguishing mark on everything. The last thing we can afford is for these to go astray and turn up as genuine somewhere.'

'Did he ever sell his work as genuine?'

'I don't think so, no. Mostly it was for his own collection here, or special commissions. Mind you, I can't attest to what happened to the stuff after Rappare sold it on.' He barked a laugh. 'Could be anywhere now. You might even have a piece or two yourself.'

They had completed their circuit of the studio now and returned to the entrance. 'I'm not sure that's very funny, actually,' Braxiatel said with a trace of a smile. He looked once more round the room, wondering what he might have missed that was of significance. The wall safe concealed behind the *Mona Lisa*; the faint mark on the floor where something had broken and then been cleared up; the Ming vase (second dynasty) standing slightly off-centre on its plinth.

As they left, Braxiatel said to Rastian, 'This mark you intend to engrave – do you have any idea what you might use?'

'Not really.' Rastian locked the door behind them. 'Maybe the university coat of arms or something.'

'Why not Newark Rappare's signature? Faked of course.'

Rastian laughed again, an explosion of coughing sound. 'Yes, very appropriate,' he said between barks, 'and I think that would appeal to him.'

Braxiatel sat alone at his desk. In front of him was a printout of the computer access log for the Theatrology Building on the previous night, and Newark Rappare's file played through in a loop on the wall in front of the desk. In his mind, Braxiatel could see Rappare's brightly lit studio as he went over what he knew in his mind.

Since he was a prominent collector of... well, of just about everything, it was hardly surprising that Rappare had eventually contacted Braxiatel with some sort of proposition. But why so late at night? And why was he killed? And what had he been offering or asking for?

Certainly Rappare had been distracted, the computer log told him that. And something had happened at the studio – the mark on the floor, the vase not quite positioned properly, and the painting not quite flush to the wall so that the safe was just visible behind it were all evidence of this. And then there was the money.

Braxiatel picked up the computer access log again and checked it for the third time. They had been right to bring it to his attention: it was certainly significant. He was not sure what it meant, but even an idiot could conclude that the card incorrectly swiped just seconds before Rappare's access code was recorded was a mistake made by Rappare himself. The computer had read the information on the card's chip, and quite rightly refused access. All the computer knew as it slavishly recorded the card's ident number was that it was not a valid access code. But Braxiatel, after some basic research, knew from the recorded ident number what was on that card. It was a proof of transaction, a digital IOU. It was a guarantee that a sum of money had been paid into an off-world account in Newark Rappare's name. A sum of money in excess of ten million shillings.

Some rather more sophisticated research, coupled with a favour he was owed by one of the bank's governors, had enabled Braxiatel to discover that the account was indeed valid and was indeed Rappare's. And it had been closed remotely through a clearing house early this morning. It had been closed in such a clumsy and unsophisticated manner that it suggested at least suspicious circumstances if not actual fraud. And that was before one considered the fact that the account's owner had been lying dead at the time.

It was while describing to Nicholas for the third time how she had come by the bag containing the Dragon that Benny recalled where she had seen the man again. Or, rather, where she had seen a holograph of his dead body. The level of interlocking coincidences, Benny felt, was now well past a plausible threshold. To his obvious disappointment, she declined Nicholas's offer of dinner and a discussion about the impending expedition. Instead she called Braxiatel.

They met at Benny's apartment, since she had to pack. Braxiatel brought an incredibly rare and palatable wine (which he claimed to have several cases of), and Benny arranged for a takeaway to be delivered. Then she told Braxiatel what had been happening to her.

If Braxiatel was surprised by any of the events he did not show it. He asked to see the Dragon, and agreed that it seemed identical to the Gamalian Dragon. He asked Benny to repeat word for word what Nusek had said in his holographic address. He frowned slightly at Benny's description of Truby Kamadrich and mentioned in passing that he had read some of her papers and had imagined her to be older than she seemed. Benny had remarked that she thought Braxiatel was probably older than he seemed, and he had nodded his agreement. Then he had listened with interest as Benny described Kamadrich's obvious delight when Benny and Nicholas accepted the invitation, and he smiled when Benny gave him 'the bad news'.

The bad news, so far as Benny was concerned, was that Follett had insisted that she be accompanied by another member of the Archaeology Department – Mappin Gilder. Braxiatel laughed out loud as Benny described how she had told Follett exactly what she really thought of Gilder, and how Follett had then explained that he wanted Gilder to have some actual field experience and appreciation for the rigours of the science. After her protestations that Gilder was merely a jumped-up accountant with no experience or appreciation of the rigours of archaeology, Benny's arguments had rather fallen apart.

'So tomorrow we're off on Kamadrich's ship to this planet Tharn to see Nusek,' Benny finished. 'Kamadrich says he wants to give us a pep talk and officially approve the expedition, but I think he really wants to look us over and see what he's getting for his money.'

They had finished eating, and Braxiatel poured more wine. 'I agree,' he said. 'And I think you're doing the right thing by going along. We've learnt a lot today, but most of it only enables us to ask more precise questions.'

'Like is the Dragon I have the original, or a copy?'

'Oh I think it's a fake.' Braxiatel leant back in the chair, seeming completely relaxed. 'Let me tell you what I've been up to since we last spoke, and what I've discovered about the dead man.'

Braxiatel told Benny how he had identified Rappare, and about his background and talent for manipulating materials and faking pieces of art. He was to the point and objective. Benny listened carefully and wondered how her rambling description of her day had seemed to him.

When he finished, Braxiatel drained his glass and stood up.

'Now, I must be on my way. You've got packing to do, and I still have the day's work to deal with.'

'You work as well?' Benny feigned surprise. 'I thought you'd have people to do that for you. While you get on with whatever schemes you're really here for.'

'Schemes?' He raised an eyebrow. 'I work here because it's good for the soul.'

'Not so as you'd notice.'

'Let's just say that helping out here on Dellah I feel closer to God,' Braxiatel said. He smiled. 'Though between you and me, I could have done without this little diversion just now.'

'Oh I like a little diverting,' Benny said as she walked him to the door.

'Mind you don't get too diverted, Benny.' Braxiatel's voice was more serious as they stood by the door. 'I know something about Nusek – he's a nasty piece of work.'

'Anything in particular I should know?'

Braxiatel considered. 'As your friend Nicholas may have already told you, he's recently started a propaganda campaign proclaiming himself to be the successor of Gamaliel. Which genetically if not idealistically he is. Gamaliel had a huge following when he broke away from Earth's control and built up a small power base in the region. Nusek wants to resist Earth's renewed grasping, and build up his own power base opposed to any future centralization Earth might want to impose. Earth, of course, is unhappy with this, but can do little, being so far away.'

'Will he succeed?' This was beginning to make some sense of the change of mood at the briefing when Nusek's name was first mentioned.

'There are several warlords interested in controlling the system,' Braxiatel explained. 'If any one of them can establish a valid claim to Stanturus Three, the oldest of the inhabitable biospheres, then he can claim the whole system. At the moment, the Gang of Five, as they are called, are beating each other's diplomatic heads together trying to decide which of them is best placed to lead their consolidated forces and establish some territorial rights in this area.'

'And Nusek's the frontrunner?'

'Well, the other local warlords aren't wild about Nusek, but they are sympathetic to his cause. If he can win their approval and gain some credibility by successfully claiming Stanturus Three, Nusek will have overcome his biggest stumbling block. I can only assume that he thinks you will find evidence that Gamaliel once controlled Stanturus, giving him a claim on that strategic bit of space. It would be a huge boost to his position and his plans. Nusek is invoking Gamaliel's memory as a rallying point for his own ends. And somehow you're being drawn into that.'

'Terrific. And what's he like as a person?'

'I'm afraid he's probably best described as a psychopathic megalomaniac. His only saving grace is that he isn't as sadistically unpleasant as Mastrov, his *éminence grise*.'

'I'll watch out for him, then.'

'Do. Mastrov provides a lot of the power and brains for Nusek. But nobody other than Nusek and maybe some of his inner circle know anything much about Mastrov. I'd be interested in your thoughts if you do meet him.'

Benny opened the door, and the night air crept into the hallway, making her shiver. 'I can see this whole thing's going to be a bundle of fun,' she said. 'One last thing,' she added as a thought struck her.

Braxiatel paused just outside the door. His collar was turned up against the cold, and the wind riffled through his hair. Somewhere in the distance a shuttle's retros fired.

'Was Gamaliel really the Robin Hood character he's made out to be? You know, helping the poor starving colonists break free of the nasty imperialist Earth government?'

Braxiatel chuckled. 'You probably aren't supposed to know this, so keep it to yourself. Gamaliel was a corporate boss who realized his corporation's best interests would be served by breaking from Earth and stopping paying the huge taxes. Earth levied taxes to enable it to keep control both by keeping the corporations underfunded and Earth in liquidity. The fact that some colonists might benefit from Gamaliel's unilateral declaration of independence probably never occurred to him, though he certainly capitalized on it afterwards.'

'Oh.' Benny's disappointment was evident. Another potential ideal dashed, another hero gone.

'Sorry.' Braxiatel raised his eyebrows in sympathy. 'I'm afraid he was closer to your colleague Gilder than to Robin Hood.'

'Thanks. That makes me feel much better.'

They both laughed briefly. 'I'll send you a digest of whatever I can find relating to Gamaliel. If nothing else it's something for you to read of a cold lonely evening,' said Braxiatel. Then he turned and walked into the night. 'Watch yourself,' his voice floated back over his shoulder, 'and good luck.'

Benny stood in the doorway, watching him until he was almost out of sight. He didn't look back, and she closed the door.

THE CASTLE OF ICE AND FIRE

With little else to do on the journey, apart from avoid Gilder and get drunk with Nicholas, Benny read up on Romolo Nusek and his homeworld of Tharn. Braxiatel had provided her with a floptical disk containing digital copies of all the extant materials he could find relating to Gamaliel. There were hundreds, needless to say, some of them containing the slightest reference or footnote. She had spent a little time going through it all, with the help of a software agent called Mike, which Braxiatel had included on the disk. Most of Benny's research was merely to satisfy herself that Gamaliel did indeed have a corporate background – a Hugo Gamaliel was chairman and chief executive of a company called BrokTek, though a cursory glance at the other documents suggested nobody but Braxiatel had ever made the connection. BrokTek's entire financial history was also included on the disk, and it was after wading through some of it that Benny decided to turn her attention to more immediate topics.

On the subjects of Nusek and Tharn, however, she felt she had learnt quite a lot. It was something of a disappointment, therefore, to discover that they were scheduled to spend only one day and night as Nusek's guests before setting off again. Tomorrow they would depart for Stanturus Three and the expedition proper would begin. But tonight they would be staying in Nusek's palace at Omensk.

'Palace' was a bit rich, Benny decided. Watching it

loom closer on the vis-screen as they made their final approach in the shuttle, she could not help but be impressed. It was more like a medieval fortress, both in its architecture and its amenities. It was a huge structure of blast-retarded stone, complete with towers and ramparts. It rested massively on top of an ice-covered mountain in the middle of a sea of unbroken cold white, as if the top of the mountain had been sliced off and the castle placed on the resulting shelf.

Benny could see that it was set well away from any centre of population – there was nothing else but ice for as far as the sensors could see. Ostensibly this was a security measure, but Benny knew from her superficial research that it was because Nusek wanted to be far away from the downtrodden tribes and villages that littered his planet.

She returned to the disk-reader. Mike was waiting patiently at the edge of the screen, pouting and flexing his muscles when he thought she wasn't looking. If he knew or cared.

'While the planet's initial wealth and power was based on its valuable ore deposits, most of this is now mined out,' Mike explained in reply to her prompting. 'Whatever wealth remains or came into the planet is squandered by its ruler on his expansionist crusade.'

'Squandered?' Benny interrupted. 'That doesn't sound very objective to me.'

Mike frowned, the screen shimmering slightly over his forehead. 'I merely repeat what is in the source documents on this disk,' he said with a hint of huff. 'If they are subjective, then so is the manner in which I repeat the information they contain. May I continue?'

'Oh, please.'

'Predictably, Nusek spends the money on weaponry, mercenaries, military training, command and control systems, and the upkeep of his navy. Whatever little remains is spent almost entirely within the walls of the palace.'

'From the look of it, that's hardly anything,' Benny muttered.

'I can check the exact figures if you wish.'

'No, thank you.' Benny had peeked at a couple of the balance sheets and financial reports on the disk. They were huge, boring and unintelligible.

The people, Benny was not surprised to learn from Mike, resented Nusek's budgeting. Given the chance – a little more cash to buy some arms and expertise, a little time away from the grinding, backbreaking work in the ore mines and munitions factories, and some way of getting at their leader – they would rebel. As it was, most of the people were old peasant farmers or labourers trying to scratch out an existence.

'So why do they stand for it?' she asked.

'The younger men and women, those who might be able to resist, do not want to. The reason for this is simple. The young people are drafted into the military as soon as they are old enough to think for themselves, and, once in the armed forces, are well fed for the first time in their lives. When this is coupled with a new sense of purpose and belonging, they have very little desire to rebel. Another factor is that Nusek's expansionist ambitions are better suited to the idealistic, adventurous young – to the optimistic idealists rather than the old realistic cynics.'

Benny wondered which of the two camps she might fit into. She doubted she was young and idealistic, but she resented the suggestion that her cynicism implied she might be old. She was sure she was not about to ask Mike for his opinion.

'Those left behind on Tharn,' Mike continued, 'are the old, the infirm, the dropouts and those too stupid to pass the less-than-challenging army intelligence tests. The only intelligent able-bodied people are the few visiting off-worlders, mainly from determined relief agencies, and those who have worked out how to make more money from criminal activities in the black market, the illegal arms trade, drugs, prostitution and creaming off the decrepit civil-service system.'

So, Benny reflected as she stared at the vis-screen and turned down Mike's volume. The imperial palace was sited well away from the general populace. A huge, impressive, Bavarian fairy-tale type of castle-fortress built from blast-retarded stone on the top of a semidormant volcano in the middle of the impenetrable ice region. Perhaps, Benny decided as she looked round on a VR walk-through the Spartan sleeping quarters she had been assigned for the night, it was as well they were not stopping for long.

The shuttle touched down on the imperial landing pad mid-morning. With very little ceremony or delay, Benny, Nicholas and Gilder were shown to their rooms. Kamadrich wandered off on her own. She already had an office and quarters in the palace, she had told them.

When she had finished unpacking, which involved searching out a toothbrush and a clean set of clothes for the morning, Benny went in search of Nicholas. They had waved to each other as they went into their rooms, situated off the same corridor. Now Benny hoped she had the right door and was not about to come face to face with the oily Mappin Gilder clutching his own toothbrush in one hand and goodness only knew what in the other.

'It's open,' came Nicholas's voice in response to her knock. Relieved, she went in.

Nicholas's room was all but identical to Benny's. The walls were bare stone, and a curtained archway led, presumably, to what served for a bathroom. There was a convoluted and inexplicable but obviously lethal antique weapon hanging on the wall over the bed where in Benny's room there was a rather unpleasant painting, but otherwise it looked pretty much the same. Nicholas was sitting on the shelf that seemed to be the bed. He was examining what looked like an old computer input keypad, and as Benny came in, he tossed it into his bag.

Benny glanced into the bag as she sat down beside Nicholas. 'All the trappings of home,' she said, and he laughed. It was a numeric keypad, partly hidden by the shirt it had landed on. 'What's that?' Benny asked. It was obviously antique, perhaps a couple of hundred years old.

'Oh, nothing much.' Nicholas picked up the bag and slung it out of the way, and out of Benny's line of sight. 'Lucky keepsake.'

'Strange choice.'

'Sentimental value. It was the first relic I ever unearthed myself.' Nicholas sat down again next to Benny. 'Do you remember your first relic?'

Benny smiled, deciding to indulge him rather than point out the obvious contradiction. Maybe her comments about history and archaeology had made more of an impression than she had realized. 'Yeah, he was one of the lecturers. They dug him up every week to splutter at us for an hour, then put him back in his box afterwards.'

A loud knock at the door interrupted them. It was one of the palace staff. Romolo Nusek would be pleased if they would join him for lunch.

The dining hall was slightly less stark than the accommodation only because it had more in it. The walls were hung with antique weaponry, and suits of space armour stood in the corners and alcoves. Halfway along one wall was a huge fireplace, gas burners powering the fire, which danced and roared but provided precious little heat. Another wall was hung with faded and threadbare tapestries depicting acts of tarnished heroism. But despite these adornments, the dark roughness of the stone walls was not concealed enough to disguise the utilitarian nature of the room.

Romolo Nusek savoured his wine as he watched and listened to his guests. Mastrov had long ago taught him that observation was more instructive and useful than trying to make a good impression. So he observed them closely, as he knew Mastrov was also secretly doing.

They were a strange combination. Gilder, the logistics man, was quiet. He seemed out of his depth and was obviously not enjoying his experiences so far. Nicholas Clyde seemed intelligent and well informed. But his reserve suggested some level of uncertainty if not actual disapproval.

Professor Summerfield was a strange mixture. She was attractive, though not actually beautiful or even conventionally pretty. She seemed happy and amused, yet projected irony, sarcasm and cynicism. She certainly knew her subject area, and spoke with authority. Yet she had deferred to Nicholas Clyde on several very basic historical points.

The other woman was, Nusek already knew, as beautiful as she was efficient and dependable. But of all of them, Nusek decided, Summerfield presented the greatest threat.

Lanslot Webbe was the only other person at the table besides the archaeological team and Nusek himself. Webbe was Nusek's Head of Internal Security and did nothing to conceal his boredom. He pushed unwanted food round his plate, left his wine untouched and tugged repeatedly at his short dark beard.

'So what do you think of this fortress?' Nusek asked Nicholas Clyde as the plates were cleared away. 'It was designed for your hero Gamaliel, though he spent very little time here. Always so busy campaigning.'

'It's certainly impressive. If a little cold.'

Nusek laughed. 'Gamaliel's brilliance. But you can't build a structure like this on top of a glacier and expect it to keep warm in winter.'

'The lower floors are somewhat warmer.' Webbe gestured for the waiter to take his plate, tossing his napkin on to the table.

Nusek responded without looking at him. 'And you can't build in an active volcano without getting some heat.'

'So how does it work?' Benny asked. Nusek motioned for Webbe to answer her. If he was taking an interest in the conversation he might as well join in properly.

'It's an accident of nature. A form of symbiosis. This palace is situated on the edge of a volcano which is itself in the middle of the largest area of ice on the planet. The massive glacier is held in check by the heat bubbling up from the volcano.'

'And the volcano is kept dormant by the cooling effect of the glacier?'

'Semidormant,' Webbe corrected. 'We have occasional rumblings. The lowest level is, as I mentioned just now, a little warm for comfort at times. The older soldiers will talk of lava flowing into the guards' sleeping quarters, but pay them no heed.'

Nusek held up his empty glass, and it was at once refilled. 'You should not listen to old soldiers, even Webbe. These are the same troops who will tell you how they got frostbite in those same quarters when the glacier edged forward an inch. Any story, any topic, for the modest cost of a jug of ale or a round of shamlik. Rather you should see for yourself, Professor Summerfield.'

She nodded, holding her glass up for replenishment. 'I'd like that.' The service was somewhat slower this time.

'Webbe?' Nusek raised his glass to his captain, as if for a toast.

'I should be more than happy to give you a short tour of the palace,' Webbe said, his voice at odds with his words.

'Oh goody.' Benny clapped her hands together in exaggerated delight. Then, more seriously, she said, 'Can we see the Gamalian Dragon? I've heard and read so much about it.'

Webbe's mouth dropped open. He looked to Nusek for an answer. For a long moment Nusek said nothing, undecided. Then he leant back in his chair, his elbows on the armrests and his fingers steepled. 'I don't see why you should not visit the palace archives. They are usually open to interested members of the academic community, though they have been closed for renovation and refurbishment. However, if the work is now close enough to being complete . . .' He tapped the points of his fingers together. 'Kamadrich?'

If she seemed surprised that he was asking her, it was only

for an instant. 'I believe the work is practically complete. There should be no problem.'

'Good. Then Webbe will show you round this afternoon.' Nusek stood up. 'I doubt I shall see you again before you leave for Stanturus Three, as I have other duties that command my attention. But I wish you a stimulating and successful expedition.'

The archives were in the lower levels of the palace. Since the building seemed to have no lifts or travel tubes, Benny, Nicholas and Gilder got a tour of a large part of the palace thrown in for free. Benny was annoyed that Gilder had invited himself on 'her' tour, and his insistence on knowing how much every tapestry, painting and carved balustrade was worth annoyed her still more. Nicholas seemed oblivious, but Webbe became increasingly irritated with each question.

Before long Benny found her interest in the stark architecture crumbling like some of the flagstones. The sooner they reached the archives the better.

They paused in a corridor while Webbe stood slightly apart from them and mumbled something into the communicator on his wrist. When he finished, he apologized for the delay, and led them to a large wood-effect blast door.

'Yes,' said Webbe as they passed through and entered another chamber. 'I think this will interest you.'

Benny was ready to comment on just how interesting it was to be in yet another dimly lit stone room when she crossed the threshold. It was staggering. They were standing on a narrow balcony near the top of a huge circular chamber. The walls, floor and ceiling, as everywhere else, were made of large blocks of stone. But instead of being broken up with tapestries and holograms, the walls of this chamber were set with alcoves and recesses. Several were empty, but most contained statues.

At least, Benny hoped they were art imitating life and not the real thing. Each was a portrayal of suffering, of pain, of death. A humanoid skeleton was chained in bas-relief in one alcove, a decaying body hung in a cage in another. Several of the tableaux were so gross that Benny could not bring herself to look too closely. She was not at all sure that the pallid stone from which the images were carved was better than full colour, or whether it just made the tortured figures seem drained of blood.

They all stood staring down into the room for a while. Gilder was as silent as Benny and Nicholas, too shocked to enquire about value and cost.

Despite the emotionally numbing effect of the statues and carvings, the main feature of the room still impressed. The circular floor sloped slightly down towards its centre, and set in the middle of the floor was a circular dais. The dais was raised several feet above the floor, with steps up to it running all round. In the centre of the dais was a large, deep hole. From the balcony they were high enough to see over the lip and down into the volcano beneath. Sulphurous yellow smoke wisped out, mistily obscuring the view into the heart of fire. But even from where she stood, Benny could feel the heat and hear the lava spitting and rumbling inside the mountain. As they watched, a sudden tongue of flame licked up through the hole, black smoke billowing out from it. Benny and the others all took a step backward. Then, as abruptly as it had appeared, the flame was gone.

Webbe was the only one of them still standing in the same place as when they had arrived. There was the first hint of a smile on his face as he watched their reactions. 'Execution chamber,' he explained matter-of-factly. 'We maintain it as it was in Gamaliel's time. There is force shielding that is automatically generated from projectors in the roof if the volcano gets too excited, but the glacier keeps it in check. Usually.' He gestured along the balcony. 'Now, we can cut through to the archives just along here.'

The heavy balcony door clanged shut behind the visitors, the noise echoing round the execution chamber. For a moment the room was still apart from the hazy reflections of the flames against the walls. Then another door opened to allow a group of soldiers into the main room.

The man they half carried, half dragged, struggled fiercely and bit at the gag which kept him all but silent. The fire flickered in his terrified eyes as they pulled him up the steps of the dais. He seemed to lose his energy as he stared down at the glowing hole in the floor, the chains hanging loosely from his wrists and ankles. He was silent with fear as one of the guards pulled the gag down round his neck.

'We shall want to hear what you have to say,' the guard hissed, and his colleagues laughed.

The man whimpered quietly at first. Then his sobs grew louder and more frantic as his captors pushed him towards the edge.

On the balcony high above, Nusek licked his thin lips and watched, fascinated. He was always fascinated. In the back of his mind he replayed his conversation with Mastrov from just after the lunch.

'You don't foresee any problems?' he had asked Mastrov.

'None we can't deal with.'

'The Summerfield woman?'

'She is ideal. A credible ally, or a discredited scapegoat.' Mastrov had shrugged. 'It's up to her.'

Disappointingly, the archives were housed in rooms of the same structure and design as the rest of the palace. Benny was not quite sure what she had expected, but the entrance way was as dreary as almost everywhere else, albeit with various relics dotted about on plinths and in display cases.

But as soon as they were through the entrance, it was a different story. The architecture remained unchanged, but in the first main room of the archives stood a glass display case. There were other displays, other antiquities, but this particular case was in the very middle of the room illuminated from above by a powerful halogen spotlight. Inside, resting on a sheet of purple velvet, stood the Gamalian Dragon.

Benny and the others stared at the Dragon. It was rearing up, wings spread and mouth open ready to spew fire past the forked tongue that licked out. The statue was made of a bronze-like metal, gleaming under the spotlight, shimmering from the reflections of the fake gaslight flambeaux fixed to the castle walls. Its eyes were sparkling emerald, and its wings encrusted with jewels and precious stones. The statuette was about eighteen inches high and twelve inches across. It looked robust rather than delicate. And in every way, it appeared absolutely identical to the dragon that Benny had packed in her rucksack a few days previously.

'The Gamalian Dragon,' said Webbe unnecessarily. For the first time Benny could hear something other than bored amusement in his voice. He too was in awe of the thing. 'Protected by the most state-of-the-art systems available two hundred years ago.' He glanced at Gilder. 'Available only as a special bid from the Ormand-Seltec corporation. Even now, two hundred years later, it's doubtful we could have it better protected. If you look closely at the casing, you can see the laser chain woven into the blastproof glass. Not that there has ever been any attempt to steal the Dragon.'

Benny peered at the glass. She could just make out the faint tracery of red at the edges of the case where the light was slightly more diffused.

'For over a century the Dragon has been in these archives.' The voice was husky and unexpected. They all turned at once towards the archway it had come from. 'And in all those years, it has never left that case.' The old man shuffled slowly towards them. His face was lined and wrinkled, and a long grey beard shook and exaggerated the movement of his head. 'Greetings,' the man said. 'I am Moxon Reddik, Keeper of the Archives of Tharn.'

Reddik was, not surprisingly, a more informed and enthusiastic guide than Webbe. While Webbe made occasional comments about Gamaliel's accomplishments and his bravery, Reddik was more balanced in his opinions. If neither of them expanded on any mention of the mysterious Knights of Jeneve, it seemed to be because so little was actually known about them anyway.

Eventually, in answer to Benny's repeated questions about Gamaliel's greatest battle, Reddik led them out of the main relic room, back past the Dragon, and through an archway. They entered what seemed to be a small chapel. The vaulted ceiling and low lighting from artificial candles was enough for Benny to turn a complete circle looking for an altar. But there was none. Instead the room was dominated by a tomb.

The tomb was about the size of an altar, which added to the confusion. But while the top of an altar would be flat, the tomb was a large stone box sealed with a carved lid. The carving was a supine figure, every bit as lifelike as those in the execution chamber, but far more peaceful. The figure was dressed in full ceremonial combat armour, laser sword held at his side and blast-absorber across his chest. The visor of his helmet was up, so the features of the man could be seen. His face was grim and determined. The slight corrosion gave only a hint of the decay and corruption that must have long since claimed the body inside the tomb.

At the soldier's feet nestled a small animal. It was the size of a small dog, but it was posed as if it walked on its hind legs. Its face was more round than a dog's, with large eyes and framed by a ragged collar of hair. It seemed less finished than the rest of the carving, the detail not completed and the definition lacking depth. It also lacked the warmth that made the main figure seem so lifelike. Almost, Benny thought, as if the sculptor was not interested in the animal, or was carving from a picture and not from life. Or, rather, from death.

'Henri of Bosarno,' the old archivist said quietly. There was something about the place which encouraged conversation only in hushed and reverent tones.

'Really?' Nicholas was impressed. 'The legends say they brought him home and buried him with full honours.' He shook his head and gestured at the tomb. 'But this is incredible. And so well preserved.'

'The acidic atmosphere takes its toll,' Webbe said. 'The

familiar at his feet is somewhat corroded by the fumes from the volcano, but generally it is in good condition. Atmospheric balancers help now, of course.'

'Er, excuse me.' Benny held her hand up, shy schoolgirl for a moment. 'I can tell it's all very exciting, but who was this Henri of wherever?'

Only Reddik's slight pause before answering suggested he was surprised by the question. 'He was Gamaliel's right hand in battle. The architect, according to some, of the victory at Bocaro against the Knights of Jeneve.'

'He was killed in a skirmish just after the main battle was over,' Nicholas explained. 'The stories say that he was desperate to get back to Gamaliel after the victory, and cut across an area outside the battlefield where there were still some retreating Knights or a command post or something.'

Reddik continued the story. 'They say he put up a spirited fight, dispatching several of the Knights and routing the rest. He took what trophies he could carry, and resumed his journey. He reached Gamaliel, and collapsed in his arms. Henri died of his wounds soon after. Gamaliel awarded him as many posthumous honours as he decently could, and he is always referred to as Henri of Bosarno.'

'I thought the battle was at Bocaro.' That much Benny did know.

Nicholas shrugged. 'Bocaro is the local name, the one we historians use. Gamaliel and his people always called it "Bosarno".'

'History is so confusing.' Benny smiled. 'What do we see next?'

Reddik smiled back, a sudden lifting of his grim features into warmth. 'History books,' he said quietly.

The main library was a huge room in the middle of the archives. The other rooms they had seen so far encircled it, although there was only one door in. This gave on to a corridor which ran inside the circle of relic rooms. The result was an impressive lead-in to what was a room made warmer than the others by the wooden bookshelves which lined every wall. Even the back of the door was shelved.

Benny could imagine being trapped inside the room, unable to find where the bookcase opened to let you out again. She looked round for a landmark, a feature that would help her keep orientated. It was not difficult. A huge painting hung in one of the few spaces on the walls. It was a portrait, the subject staring out towards the door, though his eyes followed Benny as she made her way through the document cases and reading tables to get a closer view.

'Weird,' Benny said when she was standing directly in front of the picture.

Nicholas was standing next to her. He nodded. Then frowned. 'What's weird about it?'

Benny shrugged. 'I don't know. It just seems...' She struggled to work out what did seem so odd. 'It just seems a bit out of keeping, I guess. Sort of disturbing, almost.' She considered for a while longer. 'Disorientating. I don't know, but there's something. Who is he, anyway?'

'Romolo Nusek's father.' Webbe's voice was quiet behind Benny. She had not heard him approach. 'As a young man.'

'There is some family resemblance,' Benny admitted, looking back at the picture. The figure was standing in a doorway beside one of the bookcases in the library. Perhaps that was what was unsettling about the picture, the fact that the background was so obviously the room they were actually in. She could read some of the titles on the spines of the leather-bound volumes in the two-dimensional shelves.

Nicholas wandered off, more interested in the books than the painting. Benny noticed Reddik intercept him by a document display case, and they struck up a quiet conversation. Benny could not hear them as Webbe had started talking again. Gilder was standing just inside the door, examining a large book on a reading table in front of him. For once he did not seem bored.

'Coplan Nusek spent much of his time in this library,' Webbe was saying quietly. 'He was an academician and a historian. He collected a good deal of the stuff in these archives. He restored large parts of this palace and he let his people get on with their lives with the minimum of fuss and interference. He was a quiet, good man.'

Benny turned to look at Webbe. He was staring at the painting, talking quietly as if to himself. 'A good man,' he repeated, even more quietly. A nerve ticked under his left eye. Then with a sudden movement of the head he was looking back at Benny. The bored half-smile was back and his eyes seemed somehow less lively than they had a moment earlier. 'Family resemblance?' The sarcasm was back in his voice. 'As much as you can see is as much as there is.'

Benny left Webbe staring at the portrait again, and went to join Nicholas and Reddik. But before she could ask them what they were talking about, Gilder joined them. He was frowning, the first overt emotion other than boredom that Benny could remember from him since they arrived.

'It's incredible,' he said.

'Really? I wouldn't have thought old books were your sort of thing.'

'What? Oh no, not the books. No, this.' Gilder waved back at the table he had just left. 'The account ledger contains the financial data and running costs for the archives. They charge off-worlders a fortune to visit, and send out time-expiring holo-copies on a subscription basis. There are even virtual tours. They make a fortune.'

Nicholas shrugged. 'Makes sense.'

But Gilder was shaking his head. 'So why stop?'

'Sorry?'

Reddik answered. 'During the refurbishment, we have suspended all tours, all subscription information, all holo-copies. They are all created to order at source, and the source – the archives themselves – have been closed. To everyone.'

'Even to you?' Benny was surprised.

'Even to me. Only Nusek's refurbishment team have been permitted access for the last month. I was only allowed back today because you were here.'

'And during that month, there has been no direct revenue from the venture, only some slight costs for refurbishment,' Gilder said. 'It's an incredibly inept way for Nusek to run a business of this kind with the sort of margins it has.'

Benny and Nicholas both smiled at Gilder's sense of priorities. 'You tell him,' Benny said.

As they were shown out of the library, Benny asked Webbe what had actually been done in the refurbishment.

'Infrastructure, mainly,' he said. 'Conduit rationalization and atmosphere cleansing. That sort of thing. Nothing you can really see, but essential nonetheless.'

They passed the Gamalian Dragon again on their way out. By unspoken agreement they all paused beside the case and looked again at the statuette. After a short while, Webbe led them to the door. Reddik left them to return to the library, and Gilder was first to follow Webbe. So Benny and Nicholas had a few moments together beside the display case.

'You realize, I suppose,' Nicholas whispered across the display case, 'that since nobody has been in here or seen it for a month, this Dragon could actually have been anywhere?'

'Oh, I'm sure it has,' Benny whispered back. 'Come round here.'

Nicholas walked round the case to stand beside Benny. She nodded towards the base of the Dragon. There was a faint line around part of the base, a slight darkening of the cloth on which it rested.

'You can see where the velvet at the base is slightly compressed and less faded.'

'It could have slipped a little.'

They made their way to the door where Gilder and Webbe were waiting. 'Oh yeah,' Benny said quietly. 'Perhaps it just wobbled a bit within the controlled atmosphere inside the Ormand-Seltec laser lattice which not even a molecule of dust can penetrate. Or perhaps, just perhaps, someone took the Dragon out. And wherever they took it and whatever for, when they put it back, they didn't quite position it exactly where it had been for the last couple of hundred years.'

'There's some odd things in the library, too,' Nicholas said as they made their way back to their rooms. 'I wouldn't mind another look.'

Benny smiled. 'Are you suggesting we sneak in tonight, past the guards and the security systems and goodness knows what else, for another look round? Because if so, I'm right with you.'

DEAD OF NIGHT

The Dragon stood in the centre of the equipment. A lens on an extended arm swung slowly round the statuette, the laser making its delicate way across the surface, traversing every crevice and imperfection, mapping the three-dimensional space in infinitesimal detail. The hammering on the door was loud, growing more insistent. The voice calling for attention became more worried and urgent.

There was a click as the holographic imager completed its task, and the lens swung back to its parking position. When she was sure that the operation had been completed satisfactorily, Benny switched the room lights back on. Only then did she open the door.

Nicholas shook his head in relief. 'You could have answered, at least. I was worried sick.'

'Sorry.' Benny waved him into her room. 'I was busy.'

Nicholas stared in puzzlement at the holographic equipment hunched over the Dragon. 'So I see.'

'I borrowed it from the survey manifest. Said I wanted to check it out.' Benny retrieved the Dragon from the tangle of technology and returned it to her rucksack. 'Just messing about. I thought a holographic model of our dragon might be useful.'

'You mean in case we lose the real one?'

Benny shrugged. 'Just useful. Insurance if you like. Forward planning.'

Nicholas slumped on the bed. 'Yes, well it was forward planning I came to talk about.'

'Tonight?'

He nodded. 'I don't know how easy it will be to get in, or how much time we'll have. But we ought to plan exactly what we want to do and see.'

Benny agreed. She wanted to take another look at the Dragon, she said. Nicholas was keen to see inside the library again. 'There are strange omissions and gaps,' he explained. 'Sometimes there's just a book or document missing, which you could reasonably expect to find. Other times it's more obvious, like the fact that volume four of Sturgey's *The Aspirations of Empire* is missing. The other seven volumes are there, but not number four.'

'So what's volume four about?'

'I don't know,' Nicholas admitted. 'That's why I want to go back. Looking at volumes three and five might give us a good clue. Or there may be an overall introduction or summary in the first or last in the series.'

Benny nodded. That made sense. They talked some more about what they each wanted to check up on, and agreed to meet several hours after dinner.

'What are you doing in the meantime?' Nicholas asked.

'I'm expecting a call,' Benny told him. 'I hope an old friend can provide me with some information.'

'Oh?'

'And,' Benny went on before he could enquire further, 'I want to write up my diary.'

The palace was surprisingly quiet. Perhaps, Benny wondered, its position made it unnecessary to post many sentries or patrol the darkened corridors. Or perhaps, Nicholas suggested, there were places more important to guard than darkened corridors. But whatever the reason, they managed to make their way to the archives without being seen. In fact, the first sentry they saw was posted at the main door to the archives.

He was slouching against his laser-staff and looking more bored than Gilder with the whole deal. Benny was unsure whether they should wait for him to doze off or just walk past and see if he noticed. In the event, they did not need to do either. There was a sound from away down the corridor, and the guard took several paces towards it. In doing so, he left enough space and enough time for Benny and Nicholas to dash quickly and quietly through the doorway and hide behind it.

'That was easy enough,' murmured Nicholas.

'Hmm. Too easy.'

As if in answer to Benny's whisper, the guard returned to the doorway. There was another soldier with him – the source of the noise. Benny strained to hear what they were saying.

'I should close it up,' the newcomer was telling the sentry. 'They've sent in a cryvok.'

The sentry evidently needed no further encouragement. The heavy doors swung shut leaving Benny and Nicholas alone in the room. Ahead of them they could see the Gamalian Dragon illuminated by its spotlight. A shining beacon in the near-darkness. They both headed towards it without making a sound. The sounds they weren't making started as they crossed the threshold into the Dragon chamber.

They both stopped and looked round, peering into the darker corners of the room and the corridor they were just leaving. Silence.

'Er,' Benny hesitated. 'What exactly is a cryvok, do you suppose?'

There it was again. A snuffly, scratching sound. Like the growling of a dog pawing at a closed door.

'I'm afraid we may be about to find out.'

The noise was getting louder, echoing round the room so that it was impossible to tell quite where it was coming from. Nicholas made to say something further, but whatever it was died on his lips. The sounds resolved themselves, as the volume rose, from growls to barks. The scratching became the sound of sharp claws slapping into the flagstones of the floor as the creature ran at full pelt towards them. It launched itself towards Benny and Nicholas as they stood frozen in the gloom. As it leapt, it passed through the light of one of the flambeaux. A glimpse of death in the darkness.

It was a cross between a large dog and a wolf. Or, rather, a cross between a dog and a wolf that had been genetically and cybernetically enhanced by someone with lots of high technology but no aesthetic sense at all. The metal teeth, stained with something unpleasantly dark in colour, were clamped into the creature's organic head below the video-camera eyes; armour plating was grafted into the beast's hide; and the legs were surrounded and strengthened by an exoskeleton of tarnished metal.

It was just a glimpse, but it was enough. Benny and Nicholas both ran. In different directions. The creature hesitated for as long as it must have taken for the augmented brain to determine which target to follow. Then it skidded round and charged after Benny. She shrugged off her heavy rucksack, letting it drop to the floor, and increased her speed.

'Bring it back round the block,' Nicholas called after her, scooping up her rucksack as the beast leapt past it.

'If I get that far,' Benny gasped as she ran. 'Nice doggy.' She sprinted through the door and along a corridor, looking for another door to her left. She needed to bring the beast back past the tomb of Henri of Bosarno. 'Home boy?' she suggested hopefully as the wolf-dog's teeth glanced off her heel. She grabbed the edge of the door as she went through, and slammed it behind her. But the creature jumped through the closing gap easily and continued its relentless pursuit.

It was close now. Terrifyingly close. Benny could hear its short breaths, could smell its sweat and oil. She looked back, a quick twist of the head. But enough to encourage her to make better speed. The manic gleam in the glass lens eyes was enough to hurry a dead snail on its way.

She shot past the tomb, aware of Nicholas standing in the doorway in front of her, rucksack raised. He stepped back to let Benny through, but she was unsettled and scared. She caught her foot on the raised edge of a flagstone and went headlong. She twisted as she fell, faced back at the doorway through which she had tumbled.

And saw the creature launch itself towards her.

Nicholas swung the rucksack, both-handed, with all his strength. It connected with the wolf-dog in mid-flight, smashing into its face and knocking it into the door frame. The beast's neck caught the corner of the frame; the head snapped round. An unholy howl echoed through the room, and the creature smeared its way to the floor. Its eyes were crazed and shattered, a dark viscous liquid oozed from the exposed neck joint. The jaws snapped shut as a whining groan was squeezed through them. Then the head twitched, once, and was still.

'This thing's heavier than it looks.' Nicholas held the rucksack by a strap for Benny to take.

She unzipped it and reached inside, rummaging through various clothing and pulling out the heavy statue. 'Thank goodness for that,' she said as she checked that the Dragon was undamaged.

'I think we'd better get a move on,' Nicholas suggested. 'Meet me in the library when you're done here.'

The insistent bleeping was a depressingly familiar sound. Webbe teetered on the brink of sleep for a moment, then reached out and jabbed inaccurately at the answer button. He fumbled for the lights as he listened to the nervous voice coming through the bedside speaker.

One of the cryvoks, the archive guard, had gone down. Probably it was nothing, the things were notoriously unreliable, but he had better check.

'You'd better send in another one to replace it. We'll recover the one that's malfunctioned.'

'We only have the backups spare. They're old models, sir. No visual relays or recording, less sophisticated –'

'Then send in two,' snapped Webbe. 'And make sure they know who's on duty. The last thing we need is one of those things taking chunks out of the men retrieving the other one. Their pattern-recognition leaves something to be desired at the best of times.' He ended the conversation with a push of a button and reached for his uniform.

Benny reread the printout of Braxiatel's message. It had arrived only minutes before she had met Nicholas for tonight's outing, a coded squirt package beamed directly, and painfully slowly, to her palmtop. But Braxiatel had provided the information she needed. As soon as she had heard that the alarm systems were designed by Ormand-Seltec she had guessed that Braxiatel would know how to subvert them. She knew he collected – or perhaps would collect – examples of their precision engineering, and she reckoned he probably knew all about them. And his information might well be first-hand.

'Like many great designs,' the message said, 'this one is simple and elegant. It relies on well-known and proven techniques implemented to the highest quality. And like many elegant and simple designs, the way round it is childishly straightforward.'

Benny read through the childishly straightforward bit several times. She was not at all sure she understood it. But then she looked at the mangled remains of the creature that had just tried to kill her, and thought: What the hell.

A few minutes later, the side of the glass display case swung smoothly open. There was a faint hiss as the controlled atmosphere mixed with the air outside. Benny stared at the Dragon for a while. Without the intervening glass and laser beams, it seemed to shine even brighter, even more impressively. It was beautiful. And it looked identical to her Dragon.

Benny's hand was actually inside the case, closed on the Dragon, as she peered at the faint indentation in the velvet beneath it, checked the alignment. A flicker of movement unsettled her for a moment, a sudden shimmer in the open glass door. Benny glanced sideways at it, distracted. Then she looked back. Reflected in the glass was the doorway behind her, the archway leading to the tomb.

And in the doorway, padding slowly and softly closer, was another of the wolf creatures. Benny watched, transfixed, as it paused beside the remains of its predecessor. Then it turned towards her, a metal snarl forming on its face.

Benny slammed the display case door shut, barely registering the hum as the alarm system clicked back in. She was already racing as fast as she could towards the library, rucksack dangling from her hand by a strap, bumping along the floor as she ran.

Nicholas looked round in guilty surprise as the door was pushed open, caught in the middle of digitizing a page from a document with a tiny scanner. He breathed a relieved sigh as Benny appeared. She was out of breath, and had barely cleared the doorway when she slammed the door shut behind her. Her lungs were aching as she struggled to suck in enough air to speak. 'Another creature,' she managed to gasp. 'Dog thing. Right behind me. Sorry.' She searched for a way to lock or bolt the door, but there did not seem to be any.

Nicholas swore, and hurried to help her drag one of the heavy reading tables across the door. Then they piled books on top of it. Outside there was a scrabbling of metal on wood and stone accompanied by a frustrated growling.

'So,' said Benny after a short while, 'apart from being trapped in here by a cybernetic mongrel out for our blood, how are you doing?'

'I've been better.' Nicholas showed her his notes. 'Actually I've made some good progress.' He glanced at the door. 'Up till now.' The sounds were louder and more insistent. 'The missing documents and volumes –' Nicholas was talking louder now, above the noise, '– seem to be those that refer to Gamaliel in anything less than glowing terms. But where they are, if they still exist, I don't know.'

'You're sure they were ever here?' Benny asked. 'I mean, given he was a relative, they might just never have got those books and papers.'

Nicholas shook his head. 'Oh they were here all right. Look

at the picture.' He pointed at the portrait of Nusek's father.

'What about it?'

'It's very good. In fact the detailing is very impressive. If you look closely you can read the titles on most of the books in that bookcase behind him.'

Benny could guess where Nicholas was going. 'And there are books in the picture that aren't here now?'

'Exactly. He's standing beside this bookcase.' Nicholas pointed to the wall left of the door. 'And most of the books are still in the same positions on the shelves. But several of them have been removed.'

Benny frowned. The sound of the beast seemingly throwing itself against the door was thumping in her ears, distracting her. There was something on the edge of her realization. Something important. Some half-conclusion. 'Are you sure?'

Nicholas gave a short laugh. 'Well, it's easy enough to check.'

'No, no. I don't mean the books.' Benny moved closer to the portrait for a better view. 'I mean, are you sure it's that bookcase?'

Nicholas joined her. 'Oh yes. Apart from the books being pretty much the same, you can see where the design in the carved wood matches at the edge. None of the others end in quite that way with the curls. And you can see the edge of the main doorway just there.' He pointed to the side of the picture, then turned away. 'But right now, I think we'd be better off trying to decide how we get out of here in one unbitten piece.'

As he finished speaking, as if to punctuate the thought, there was a loud crash from the door. The table against it shifted back slightly, a book toppling from it and landing with a thump on the floor. Another crash, and the table shifted slightly again. Several of the books fell from the shelves on the door as the wood splintered behind them.

It took Webbe only a moment to assess the situation. Two of the guards were swinging a long wooden bench at the door. The wood was cracking and breaking under the onslaught, but the door had hardly moved. The cryvok sat quiet but alert beside the door watching. Its tail twitched slightly and its ears were pricked up. It was growling quietly.

'You're certain there's someone in there?' he asked. 'The door isn't just jammed. Again?'

'The cryvok thinks so, sir. It was hurling itself against the door when we arrived.'

Webbe nodded. 'So why are you pissing about with bits of furniture? Get a high-energy blaster down here. Now.'

'It's not the bookcase I'm interested in, actually.'

'I'm glad to hear it.'

Benny turned to look at Nicholas. 'He's standing in a doorway.'

'So?'

Benny went through it slowly, as much for her own benefit as she worked it out. 'The artist went to great lengths to get everything accurate. Even down to the book titles and the bezier curves on the bookcase there. We can tell exactly where the guy is standing. And he's standing in a doorway.' She paused to let this sink in.

'And it isn't the main doorway,' Nicholas said quietly, 'because that's shown as well, off to the side.'

Benny nodded. 'Exactly.'

There was a commotion from outside the door. A lot of noise followed by a steadily building hum of power. Benny and Nicholas exchanged glances, then ran to where Nusek's father stood in the picture. They clawed at the bookcase that was where the doorway had been, pushed and pulled at it, trying to drag it aside. But it refused to budge.

Benny kicked it.

And the bookcase clicked open, swinging slowly away from the wall to reveal the arched doorway concealed behind. The noise was becoming almost unbearable as they squeezed through the gap and pulled the bookcase-door shut behind them.

* * *

Just as the bookcase clicked back into place, the main doors of the library exploded inward in a shattering blast of wood, paper and leather. Webbe walked calmly though the falling snow of torn pages. He stepped over the broken remains of a reading table just inside the door and surveyed the empty room.

The guard commander was close behind Webbe. He too looked round at the deserted library. 'Sir,' he stammered, 'I don't understand.'

Webbe patted him on the shoulder as he left. 'Then I think we shall have to arrange for some education for you,' he said.

The short corridor behind the hidden door ended in a flight of worn stone steps. They spiralled down seemingly for ever, and Benny could smell the increasing sulphur content of the air, thick and pungent. Eventually the steps ended, and they found themselves in another short corridor. At the end of it was an archway. An orange glow spilt through it into the corridor.

Hesitantly they made their way along the passage, paused at the archway, then went through.

They were in a huge cavern, hollowed out of the living volcanic rock either by man or by nature. The cavern stretched for as far as they could see. Lava was bubbling up in various small pools along one side. Along the other, ice coated the floor and icicles dripped slow and steady water from the vaulted roof. In the centre of the cavern, just visible through the glowing sulphur haze, was a single table. The figure sitting in the lone chair beside it looked up as they entered, and beckoned to them.

Getting to the table was like navigating a maze. The floor of the cavern was smooth and paved, but it was dotted with piles of books. It was as if they had been carried there in armfuls and deposited in the first empty spot, never to be touched again.

'Incredible,' Nicholas murmured as they made their way

through the jungle of literature. 'These are the books missing from the library. And others, too, which I never realized had gone.'

'There must be thousands,' Benny agreed.

They had almost reached the centre now. The man seated at the table had returned to his work, scratching notes on a flat panel display with what looked like a quill pen. He turned towards them, and they could see that it was Reddik, the Keeper of the Archives.

'There you are at last,' he said. 'I've been expecting you.'

Nobody but himself, Reddik told them, knew of the cavern's existence. 'Even Nusek and Webbe have long since forgotten, or given up caring. Certainly he does not know that it is used for anything.'

'And what is it you use it for?' Benny asked.

'Books,' he answered, looking round. 'As you can see.' He smiled. 'Books and papers, information that Nusek has decided should no longer exist. He has become fanatical that Gamaliel was a great hero and his name must not be besmirched.'

'Part of Nusek's propaganda campaign,' Nicholas said.

The librarian nodded. 'Gamaliel's good reputation is essential to Nusek's plans and aspirations – it is Gamaliel's memory rather than Nusek that the warlords will follow. So he ordered these destroyed as fakes. But I could not bear the thought of destroying the texts I have spent my life amassing and cataloguing. So I hid them instead. So long as they are not found Nusek does not seem to care what has actually happened to them.'

'But why?' asked Benny. 'What do these books reveal that Nusek can't bear to have made public?'

'These are part of the most comprehensive information archive about Gamaliel. Nowhere else is there a body of data so complete. Or so revealing. Only here, gathered by his descendants, survive the texts that truly explain Gamaliel's character and motivation.'

Nicholas's eyes were bright. 'So he wasn't quite the hero of legend, then?'

Reddik shook his head. But before he could reply, Benny interrupted. 'Let me guess, he was a corporate boss who realized his company's best interests would be served by breaking from Earth and stopping paying the huge taxes.' She smiled at the astonished look on Reddik's face. 'Right?' He nodded dumbly. 'A corporate cheat, not a brilliant tactician. He ran a company that produced virtual-reality kicks and bio-experiential games, specializing in the dodgy, the sleazy and the outright pornographic. They were twice indicted for indecency, and that's back when even decency had a bad name.' She shook her head and clicked her tongue. 'I ask you, what a role model.'

For a moment nobody spoke. Benny began to wonder if her attempt at gaining credibility had backfired. Or maybe she had just gone too far.

'He was a brilliant tactician as well,' Reddik said, recovering his composure. 'And once he had the Dragon, nothing could stop him.'

'He thought it brought him luck,' Nicholas said. He was still looking at Benny with a kind of fascinated awe. She smiled back, knowing that he was dying to ask how she had known the truth. She hoped she had not shattered his hero's image completely. She knew he would already be shocked at having his own research superseded if not invalidated by her flippant comments.

'Dragons are interesting,' she said by way of changing the subject. 'There's a sort of duality there too, a dichotomy between mythical interpretations. A bit like the difference between reputation and reality, I suppose.'

'How do you mean?' Reddik was suddenly attentive again.

'Well, it's almost like the Eastern and Western Earth cultures just hit on the same name for different beasts. The Western image is fierce, fire-breathing and aggressive with wings and scales. The Eastern dragon is more benign and closer to a mammal.'

'I don't see what that has to do with Gamaliel's beliefs.' Nicholas picked up a book and flicked through it.

Reddik drew Benny to one side. 'Your friend is a little peeved, I think. I will show him some of the books – he will soon recover his humour.'

Benny left Reddik to examine the book with Nicholas. They huddled together over the table, talking in urgent, hushed whispers. She wandered through the piles of books, thinking of what they had done tonight. And pondering on the events of the expedition ahead.

THE GRAVE ROBBERS

The smell of sulphur abated slightly once they were out of the cavern. But it was still there, lingering in the air and on their clothes. Reddik had led them to the back of the huge cavern, and then out into another passageway. It sloped gently upward as it twisted and turned. The floor was uneven, and the walls were rough-hewn out of the mountain.

There were lights strung up along the way, but there was also light from the volcano itself. Periodically, one wall of the passage would end, and they could look out over the abyss, could see into the heart of the trembling mass of lava that was the core of the volcano. Sometimes there were breaks in the other wall too, and glistening rivers of sheer ice inched across the floor of the corridor. They picked their way carefully over the slippery surface, alternately shivering in the cold or gasping from the heat.

Eventually they reached what seemed to be the end of the passageway. It stopped in a smooth wall of stone. Benny and Nicholas turned and waited for Reddik to catch up with them.

'Now what?'

The old librarian smiled. 'It is not as solid as it appears,' he said, fumbling with a particular piece of rock jutting from the passage wall. He twisted it, and the smooth wall in front of them slid quietly aside.

Benny could see immediately where they were. The wall that had opened was the back of one of the alcoves surrounding the tomb of Henri of Bosarno. They emerged beside the tomb, the Gamalian Dragon framed in the doorway to their left. There was nobody in sight, and all was quiet as the wall slid silently shut behind them.

'Thank you,' Benny and Nicholas both said quietly to Reddik.

'I think we can find our way from here,' Nicholas whispered.

The old man nodded. 'I would just ask one small favour,' he said. 'It is only a matter of time, I think, before Nusek decides that the memory of the valour of Henri of Bosarno detracts from or even eclipses that of Gamaliel. A foolish notion, I know. But I think he may destroy this tomb and try to erase the memory of Henri.'

'What do you want us to do about it?' Benny asked. 'We can hardly carry the whole tomb back to your secret cavern.'

Reddik shook his head. 'But you can help me to move the lid of the tomb. There may be something inside that I can recover, that I can save for the future.' He shook his head sadly. 'One of my ancestors fought in the same engagement that led to the death of Henri of Bosarno. He was a brave man, committed to his beliefs. He should not just be wiped from our history.'

Benny was not too keen on grave-robbing, but Nicholas and Reddik managed to persuade her that it was a better option than letting everything be destroyed. 'And if Nusek does not destroy the tomb,' Nicholas pointed out, 'Reddik can always return whatever we remove later.'

With Benny's reluctant agreement, they put their weight to the carved top of the tomb. As Reddik had surmised, it was held in place only by its own weight, and with considerable effort they managed to shift it far enough to peer inside.

The inside of the tomb was dark and the smell of decay was sickening. Benny could just make out the skeletal figure stretched out inside, his battle armour rotted by age and the sulphurous atmosphere. A skull-head behind a cracked blast visor stared back at her with hollow eyes.

There was a hint of movement behind the visor – a trick of the light? Or perhaps a worm or insect crawling through the brain cavity. Benny and Nicholas both recoiled from the sight and the smell, but Reddik gritted his discoloured teeth and reached inside.

'At my age,' he gasped, 'the senses have become dulled.' He pulled at something from towards the lower end of the huge casket. 'But even so . . .' He lifted out a stone shape, placing it carefully on the floor. 'That, I think, will do.'

They heaved the lid back into place. But the smell of death still hung around them. Benny examined the thing that Reddik had recovered. It was a stone carving, a statue. It was an animal, a sort of cross between a lion and a dog, its eyes large and its nose ending in a rounded button. 'A carving of a carving,' she said quietly. 'The animal at the guy's feet isn't an animal or a pet at all. It was this statue.'

Reddik nodded. 'So it would seem. A fitting souvenir, I would think.'

'Well, it obviously meant something to him,' Nicholas agreed. 'Now, I think we should be on our way.'

Benny was about to agree when she heard a noise in the distance. Nicholas turned towards the arched doorway – he had heard it too. Reddik looked at them puzzled, his old ears not seeming to pick up the sounds as quickly. Then he nodded. 'Yes, we should leave.'

The sounds were getting closer now. And they were distinguishable as the ringing of boots on the stone floor.

'Are you up to running?' Benny asked the old man.

He smiled. 'I don't have to. I live here.'

Benny nodded. 'Thanks again. And please excuse us – we have to dash.'

Nicholas shook the old man's hand, but as he turned to go, Reddik held on to him. 'I can explain what I am doing here,' he said in an urgent whisper, 'but I cannot explain this.' He picked up the stone creature and handed it to Nicholas. 'Look after it.'

Their eyes locked for a moment. Standing near the door,

Benny was getting worried and impatient. 'Come on,' she hissed. The echoing footsteps were louder still now, somewhere in the next corridor.

Nicholas took the stone carving. 'Thanks again,' he said. Then he joined Benny at the door.

She turned and waved to Reddik.

'Knowledge above all,' he whispered just loud enough for them to hear.

Nicholas nodded.

'Whatever,' Benny agreed. Then they ran.

The sun was just edging over the horizon as Nicholas Clyde packed his things back into his bag. He paused for a moment to watch the pale light stream across the ice plains, reflecting back off the frozen ground and redoubling its glare. When he could no longer watch without shielding his eyes, he turned away.

He was holding the stone animal which Reddik had entrusted to him, cradling it with both hands. He laid it carefully inside his bag, next to his antique keypad. They lay together, cracked and ragged stone next to brittled plastic; art next to technology. Then he threw a shirt into the bag, covering up the relics. Burying them again.

Nusek did not join them in person on the ship. But his voice, whether recorded or live, was played through into the cabin as Benny, Nicholas, Kamadrich and Gilder sat waiting on the launch pad.

They were using an old passenger shuttle, modified to make the relatively lengthy journey to Stanturus. The four of them were in the main cabin. Benny and Nicholas sat in a group of three seats, an empty seat between them. Gilder was across the aisle and a row in front. Kamadrich was near the front of the cabin, closer to the flight deck. Behind Benny, most of the rest of the seats had been ripped out to make space for the expedition's equipment. There was still a lot of it despite the fact that the advance party had actually been working on Stanturus Three for a while now.

Once in flight, they were shown several smaller cabins where the passengers could make themselves at home. Each had been allocated a room with a bunk, sanitary area and living space. In addition there was a medium-sized open-plan area set aside for group discussions and meals.

'You are embarking,' Nusek concluded his pep talk by saying, 'on an enterprise which could have great import for our systems. You are setting out on a journey to unearth our noble past.' There was a dramatic, if static-filled, pause. 'Let us hope,' the overearnest tones continued, 'that you are worthy of the task.'

Benny snorted. 'Not *us*, I notice.' Gilder glared at her across the aisle. Nicholas laughed. Kamadrich, seated further forward, seemed not to hear. Before anyone could comment further on Nusek's rousing words of encouragement, the pilot's rather less oratorial voice advised them to prepare for liftoff.

A few moments later, all opportunity for conversation was removed by the steadily building noise of the engines. Benny felt the familiar unpleasant pressure on her body as it was forced down in the seat. She closed her eyes and tried to ignore the deafening roar. A few minutes later she breathed a sigh of relief as they left Tharn's atmosphere. The planet was a receding crescent of yellow outside the cabin window; ahead was the blackness of space.

The remains of the cryvok lay across the workbench. Two engineers, lab coats spotlessly white, carefully prodded at various parts of the creature's innards. At one end of the bench, the broken head lay apart from the neck. The smashed glass eyes gazed up into space towards Webbe as he stood watching from the glassed-in observation gallery. He stared back, his mind full of questions.

That someone had been in the archives the previous night was clear. Despite the protestations of the engineers that it was too early to tell whether the beast had been deliberately attacked or simply malfunctioned and run into a wall, Webbe was certain what had happened. The cracks round the head, the way the lenses were crazed, the set of the jaw into a vicious snarl convinced him that the creature had been in pursuit of someone. He had spent enough time with the cryvoks to know they did not snarl like that at anything other than a targeted intruder. And whoever had been in there had moved the table in the library up against the door.

Somewhere in the creature's enhanced brain, before it had been turned to jelly and metal, had been the recognition pattern and pheromone imprints of the target. If only it could talk, Webbe thought with a slight smile. The notion of one of these unholy and vicious creatures actually speaking was somehow comical.

Webbe could remember the first crude models being delivered from the genetic enhancement labs on Pogodus. They were little more than dogs with a remote-control unit. You had to be there, had to see what was happening, and then if you were lucky you could steer the dog after its target. But just as often the thing would break loose from the implanted programming, and turn on the controller. It became an art, controlling a mark-one cryvok with one hand on the remote and the other on your gun. If the mark-two model had not arrived on schedule and had not included a video link they would have gone back to old-fashioned methods. Training guard dogs was a more lengthy process than sticking electrodes through the motor centres of their brains, but it was more reliable. And more humane.

Not that humaneness was much of a consideration on Tharn these days. A reversion to the norm after the more lenient regime of Romolo's father. Romolo Nusek had steered his planet's rule back on to the course it had been set on before. Perhaps he had overcorrected its course.

Webbe did not think openly, consciously, about these things. Rather it was an undercurrent to his thoughts. Nostalgia, of a sort. The young men now joined the armed forces to get fed, to get trained, to escape the squalid existence they would otherwise endure. In Webbe's day it had been subtly different. There was still the notion of escape – but escape to a more glorious and honourable life rather than simply because there was nowhere else to go. He could have emigrated with the thousands who escaped in those few short years. He could have gone with his parents and sought work on the outer rim. He could have traded out of Xanta with his brother and become rich and lazy.

But instead he stayed. He had risen through the ranks, kept his head and his silence during Nusek's reinstitution of central rule. And now he was Head of Internal Security. An honourable profession. A noble aspiration, but in ignoble times. If he took time to rationalize his internal thoughts, Webbe might conclude that he was not proud of what he did. But he took pride in doing it well.

It took an hour for the engineers to isolate the flash memory. The internal power supply was still leaking current into the burnt-out circuitry and the chipset which buffered the video output from the eyes was still active. They ran a cable from an external transformer to keep the memory from fading away with the power. Webbe watched them work delicately on the inside of the cryvok. In their white coats, clean-room masks and skin-tight, skin-coloured plastic gloves they looked like surgeons operating on the creature. The cables running into the carcass were life-support. Or, rather, memory-support. Aides-mémoire.

Nusek joined them just as the engineers removed the chipset. One of them carried it carefully, delicately, to the door. They had linked in a power supply to keep the lifeblood of current swimming through the pathways.

'I want to see what happened,' Nusek said quietly to Webbe. 'I want to see it now.' His voice was quiet, but the reddened spots high on his cheeks and the curl of the lip were signs that Webbe knew well. Nusek was angry.

* * *

The room was full of equipment. So full that Nicholas could hardly move from the doorway.

'Stay there,' Benny said. Not that he had much choice.

The Dragon was linked into the middle of the mass of cables and laser probes. It sat on a metal plinth as lasers washed its surface. It was a similar arrangement to the setup that Benny had used to create her holographic model of the Dragon back on Tharn.

'So, what did you want to show me?'

Benny touched a button on a remote control and the Dragon flickered and disappeared. Nicholas realized with a shiver that he had been looking at the computer model, not the real thing. 'Is that it?' he asked, partly to cover his surprise.

'Sort of. Yes.' Benny pulled the Dragon, the actual statuette, from her rucksack and leant forward so as to be able to reach into the mass of equipment. She struggled with the weight of the statue as she tried to position it on the plinth where the image had stood. Nicholas reached in from the other side and helped her to lower the statue into place.

'Thanks.' Benny stepped back, then picked her way through the tangle of wires to stand next to Nicholas by the door. 'They look identical, don't they?' she said.

Nicholas nodded. 'So?'

'So, I did a little test just now. I thought you should see it too.'

'You're not going to tell me that the Dragon isn't on Tharn at all, I hope. That what we saw was a holographic projection and not the real thing.'

Benny laughed. 'Oh no. It was real all right.' She tapped a sequence into the remote, and the hologram flared into view again.

It was offset from the statue, and Nicholas tried to blink away the double vision. 'Ooh. That's bad for the eyes.'

'Hang on just a second.' Benny tapped in more instructions and the image gradually moved so that the Dragons coalesced into a single focused shape. It was impossible to tell that there were actually two Dragons, and only the slight hum of the machinery and the faint glow from the image were clues that the statue was not alone on the plinth.

Benny turned to Nicholas 'As I said, identical.'

Nicholas nodded. 'Certainly looks that way,' he agreed. 'So what?'

'Was anyone in the library?' Nusek's attention was on the monitor. It displayed a snow of static and noise.

'Not when we got there.' Webbe adjusted a control on the side of the chipset. 'But the cryvok thought there was, and the table didn't move on its own. Maybe they gave it the slip and got out before we arrived. Whoever they were.'

'Maybe.' Nusek did not sound convinced. 'Or maybe the damn things are playing up again.'

'We'll soon know. I've had a camera put in the library, anyway. Just in case they come back.'

The blizzard on the monitor resolved itself into a fuzzy picture.

'It's not very good.'

'Low power. We're lucky to retrieve anything.'

The picture was of a figure. The figure was seen from behind, and almost from ground level. The figure was running. The stone walls of the corridor streaked past the camera in a blur of motion. Across the bottom of the screen distorted text and digits flashed. Speed, relative distances, pheromone composition and estimated time to contact scrolled rapidly across. A date- and timestamp flashed in the top left corner. A green target outline swam in and out of focus against the figure's blurred back.

'Definitely not a malfunction,' Nusek snarled. 'Who is it?'

An archway appeared ahead of the running figure. Still there was just a distorted view of the person's back and legs. They did not look round, and the image was not clear enough for more than a rough outline of the shape of the lower body to be seen.

'Could be anyone.' Webbe considered. 'We could run

the pheromone through the records, see if we get a match. But the distortion is such we can't be sure the readout is accurate. Even if the cryvok's sensors got it right in the first place.'

The figure reached the archway, the camera close behind. Just as it passed through, the figure seemed to trip, and fell. The perspective changed as the camera leapt forward, the cryvok sensing the kill. A confused image of waving limbs, raised to fend off the beast, and then a large black shape rushed towards the camera. Nusek and Webbe both flinched as the shape seemed to smash into the monitor. A crack appeared for an instant across the image. Then a moment's blackness before the static and noise snowed over again.

'Two of them.' Nusek's anger was unconcealed. He stood up and paced the room. 'Two intruders.' He stopped, turned and pointed accusingly at his security chief. 'You missed them, Webbe. You missed them. We don't even know who they are.'

Webbe was watching the sequence through again. 'Maybe not,' he said quietly.

Nusek sat down again, his temper back under control. 'You have something?'

'Perhaps.' Webbe was running through the final sequence in slow motion. 'Just here, look.' He pointed to the shapes on the screen. 'The figure falls, arms up to protect itself. Then the heavy object, whatever it was, swings into view. And just here, just for a moment –' he froze the image, pointing to an area between the black shape and a raised hand, '– we can see a face.' He turned to Nusek, who was now leaning forward and staring at the area of the screen.

'Not much good. We still can't make out any features.'

'But if we can enhance the image . . . It wouldn't need to be much clearer and we can discern enough of the face for an image query to match the pattern to our records. We have facial patterns for everyone in the palace.'

'How long will it take?'

Webbe shrugged. 'I don't know.'

'Do it.'

'I don't even know if it will be possible,' Webbe confessed.

'Just do it.'

The Dragon revolved slowly on its plinth. 'The human eye,' Benny said, 'can spot minor discrepancies quite well. It can judge right angles, can discern perspective. You would see if there was a mismatch of even a millimetre.'

'So what?' Nicholas asked again. 'I can believe that the two match exactly.'

'They do. Down to the last micron. Down to the last angstrom unit, according to the computer.'

'But they would, wouldn't they? If you're telling me that the holographic model that this machine created of the Dragon exactly matches the Dragon it made the model of, then I'm impressed with the accuracy of the model.' He shrugged. 'But so what?'

Benny frowned and rubbed her jaw. 'That's not quite what I'm telling you.'

'Oh?'

'No. I'm saying that this particular model exactly matches this particular Dragon.'

He stared at her. An uncomfortable thought at the back on his mind. 'This particular Dragon?'

Benny nodded.

'Are you saying –' Nicholas hesitated, '– and forgive me if I'm being a bit slow, but are you saying that this particular Dragon is not the Dragon the model was made from?'

Benny smiled. 'Exactly.'

Nicholas considered. He tried to ignore the sensation in the pit of his stomach. 'That is rather more interesting.' He swallowed. 'Can I ask where exactly this particular Dragon came from?'

Benny turned off the equipment and reached in to retrieve the statue. 'Oh I switched my Dragon and the real one in the archives.'

Nicholas looked round for somewhere to sit down. He

settled for the floor. He felt a little faint. 'And you had the gall to complain about Reddik removing a minor bit of statuary from a tomb,' he said quietly.

'Professional etiquette,' Benny replied, sitting on the floor beside him. 'But it's interesting, isn't it?'

'It's criminal. And very dangerous. My God, what if you'd been caught?'

Benny laughed. 'You mean, what if I'd been caught with the real Dragon rather than a copy so exact that nobody can tell the difference? You tell me.' She was serious again now. 'I don't know what's going on here, but I don't like it.'

'Well,' Nicholas said, 'I would have to agree with that.'

The face was blotchy and blurred. But it was recognizable. From the monitor Benny silently cried out as the camera-eyes of the cryvok rushed towards her.

'It changes nothing,' Webbe said.

Nusek was glaring at the screen. His cheeks were a livid red and his lip quivered. A nerve ticked at the corner of his left eye.

'We still need independent validation on Stanturus Three.'

Still Nusek said nothing.

'And we need to keep a potential scapegoat, just in case there's a problem there.'

Nusek spoke without looking away from the screen. 'Get me Mastrov.' The words were forced through clenched teeth.

Webbe felt the colour draining from his own face. A contrast to Nusek's reddened features. 'But –'

Nusek turned sharply, grabbing Webbe by the shoulder. 'Get Mastrov,' he hissed. 'I want this sorted. Mastrov can do it better than anyone.'

Webbe shook his head. 'That cold, inhuman –'

Nusek cut him off with a laugh. His humour was back, either because he had decided on a course of action, or because of the prospect of speaking to his adviser. 'I know you would rather have a decent battle than an assassination, Webbe. There may not be as much honour in our approach, but the ends justify the surreptitious means.' He let go of Webbe and crossed to the door. 'We have both Dr Clyde and the Summerfield woman on Stanturus Three. We only need one of them for validation and damage limitation.'

'I'll get Mastrov.'

Nusek paused in the doorway. He looked back at Webbe, and past Webbe to Benny's face on the monitor. 'Yes. Mastrov can deal with the woman.'

FIGHTING IN THE TRENCHES

Extract from the diary of Professor Bernice Summerfield:

I've been busy. Well, that's my excuse, if I need one. After all, this is only supposed to be the innocent thoughts and innermost secrets of a young lady and consequently intended for publication. Or whatever that quote is. Wilde. I'm also hindered by the fact there's a steggie shoving its snout over my shoulder as I write this. Probably after food. They seem to like me, though they shy away from Nicholas. And they can't stand Kamadrich – get very agitated and then run away. Mind you, I find her a bit scary at times – ultra-efficient. She's even got Gilder sorted out. He's in charge of the geophyz equipment, and has turned out to be quite good at it. It needs his sort of pedantic attention to the minutiae of the settings and to interpret the sonic imaging stuff I suppose.

Wilde. It's been pretty wild here at times too. Busy anyway, as I say. The team was already ensconced when we turned up. Geophysics underway, trenches dug, surveys analysed. More like a battle than a dig. I think Nusek wants Kamadrich to run it like a military campaign anyway – he's got a dirty great cruiser in orbit just in case someone tries to offer us unwanted help. I guess that's why, anyway. That said, our accommodation is more like an old school that's run out of funding than an army digging in. Portacabins and softboard, very functional. Very cheap.

Anyhow, things are progressing. We've unearthed some ruins here and there in the jungle. Not difficult, really. They were poking up through the undergrowth anyway. There was certainly a civilization of sorts here a while back. Hundreds rather than thousands of years. My guess is they were settlers who moved on, so Nusek may have some claim if we prove they were a Gamalian expedition or colony of some sort. Can't say I'm bothered either way.

The planet is mainly jungle. It's blooming hot too. Shorts and T-shirt for the most part. And boots, though the floor of the jungle is pretty soft. Lots of lush greenery. Birds aplenty and small mammals. And the steggodons.

They're a strange lot, the steggies. Tapshorn says he's going to write a paper – he's the bio expert. The steggies are sort of a cross between upright anteaters (complete with snout) and Neanderthal men, with loose leathery brown skin.

Hello, here's that snout again. This one seems quite affectionate. The snout is very versatile. They seem to use it to sniff out food (they are herbivores), and then reach up to retrieve it. They seem to spend most of their time eating. I guess their digestive system is relatively undeveloped. They pull whole branches from the lower parts of the trees and bushes, rather than just leaves. If nothing else, it prunes the trees.

I've seen them suck up water through their snouts and squirt it into the mouth for drinking, or over the body for bathing too. Tapshorn says the muscles in the proboscis radiate outwards or run along it, so it's incredibly flexible. He gave a talk the other evening. Quite interesting, actually. I think he was trying out a draft of his paper on us. During trials of strength between males, one form of combat is snout-wrestling, a bit like arm-wrestling. It's certainly difficult getting my steggie here to move his snout. Must be a 'he' as the females tend to stick together with their young, and the males roam about on their own. Just like humans, chuckle-chuckle.

The humans all seem pretty clued up and professional. They really don't need us at all, so it must just be for appearance's sake that we're here. Nicholas and I get as much time off as we want, though the ruins are fascinating and Nicholas is beginning to appreciate 'real' history, I think. That's why I'm writing this soon after dawn, before the work of the day has really got going. The oddest thing is that while there's no shortage of ruined buildings and even the odd street or paved pathway between them, we've found no evidence of habitation – no bones, no bodies. Not an archaeological sausage. Kamadrich says this supports the theory that they upped and left, and I think she's probably right. Doesn't help us much, though.

Actually, that's not the oddest thing at all. The oddest thing is that both Nicholas and I have suddenly become accident-prone. Just little things. Maybe it's our imaginations. We laughed when Gilder let slip that he'd got the university to insure us. I think he was trying to say that he really did value our expertise, a sort of peace offering. But it came across that we're more valuable to him – considerably more – if we're dead. Death while on university business counts for a lot of shillings into the department's coffers, apparently.

So, when a boulder rumbles down a hill and just misses you as you're kneeling down beside a muddy hole scraping about for pottery shards, you get a bit more worried than usual. And when Nicholas got locked in his quarters with a steggie because the door catch malfunctioned, that worried him too. They get agitated with him anyway, so being stuck in an enclosed space with a hungry one is no fun. And he's got the bruises to prove it.

Paranoia, I expect. You get paranoid when you've had as many people out to get you as I have.

It's even getting to me in my research into Gamaliel and his chums. Nicholas has been going through the documents he digitized in Nusek's library, though he says they haven't told him much yet. I've been studying the stuff Braxiatel gave me. There are a couple of gaps, documents referred to that he didn't include. So I requested them from the various collections and archives where they're supposed to be. And that's when I got worried.

I got Agent Mike to check the indexes first. The University of Praxis Maier, the Musée des Arts d'Antiquites, the Collegiate Archives of Thrast, a couple of others. They all had the documents listed exactly as referred to in the sources I had. So I requested copies of them. Getting an uplink through Nusek's cruiser's comms unit took a bit of haggling, but nothing too untoward. The first two documents got downloaded the next day – a land registry for one of the frontier worlds, and a memo from one of President Baygent's ambassadors which refers in passing to an 'order' which may be the Knights of Jeneve, but probably isn't. Then nothing for a while. So I requested the others again, and got a standard message from the mainframe server at each site. Pretty much the same message from each – no such document, never heard of it, sorry.

I checked the indexes again. Thought I'd copy the entries into a snotty reply. But there weren't any. They'd all gone. And the dates on the index files matched the copies I had started with, so they should have matched. But they didn't. First time I've seen Mike the software he-man stumped for words.

Nicholas says it's just a glitch. Happens all the time. Software error. I'm not convinced. It's a funny sort of error. Never mind that as soon as I get copies of a couple of the documents, the others vanish. As if I'm allowed to see two, but no more – quota filled. Someone's hiding the others. Were they hidden from Braxiatel? What do they think I can discover if I put them together? What are they afraid of? And who are *they*? I've been through the two documents I have over and over again. Nothing. Nothing at all. They don't seem to relate to each other, and are only of peripheral interest anyway.

Nicholas says I'm getting paranoid. But even if I am paranoid it doesn't mean people aren't out to get me.

End of extract

Benny sat back and looked round. She was sitting on the ground in a clearing in the jungle, her back against a tree. The steggodon that had been nuzzling up to her had wandered away and was pulling branches off a nearby bush. Benny could see the stripped bark and scarred wood where the bush had been targeted before.

She was about to return to her diary when movement from the other side of the clearing caught her eye. Another steggie was entering the clearing. The animal stripping the bush stopped and watched as well as the newcomer limped towards them. It was injured, favouring one leg. Benny could see the round foot as it compressed slightly under the animal's weight. They could move almost silently if they wished, the padding on the foot absorbing the sound and moulding itself to the shape of the uneven ground. But this one was breathing heavily, rasping even, as it staggered towards them.

Benny stood up, unsure how or if to help. But before she could come to any decision, the steggie lost its uncertain balance and toppled forward. It lay panting in the thick, short grass. The first steggie, Benny's steggie, walked up to its fallen comrade. It leant forward slightly, prodding at the injured creature with its snout. Then it leant back, its snout rose, and it emitted a loud, trumpeting sound.

Benny dropped her diary in surprise. She had not seen one of the steggies do that before. She had seen them snout-wrestle; she had seen them caress each other's face when they met; she had even seen one dive underwater and then stick out its snout like a snorkel. But calling out like this, never.

A moment later, there was an answering call. Then another, and another. The jungle seemed to erupt into sound. Then the first of the steggies to answer the initial call entered the clearing.

It was, Benny thought afterwards, like a procession. It was almost as if each of the steggies took up a predetermined position according to some rehearsed ceremony. They stood round the prone body of their fellow, about a dozen of them in all. Benny had seen packs of steggies before – females and children led by an older female, a matriarch. But this was a mixture of sexes and ages. They leant forward as if on an instruction, though Benny heard nothing as she watched intently.

She thought they were about to pick up the injured animal, to lift and carry it away for treatment or rest. It was only when the animal started screaming that she realized this was not the case. The steggies were leaning forward, then standing upright again. It was as if they were pulling at something with their snouts and their forelimbs. Benny edged closer, not wanting to disturb or to interfere. Then she stopped dead.

A limb was raised in the air. An arm. But the creature that raised it was not the one that owned it, if *owned* was the right word. The severed arm was dripping and red, the bone shining through the gore in the morning sunlight. A glimpse, then it was gone, hurled back down into the bloody mêlée to be ripped and torn still further. A moment later, the screaming stopped.

Benny watched in silence. Her mouth was dry and open. She stood rooted to the spot as the animals tore at the carcass on the ground, dismembering it and scattering the pieces. She watched in silence as they kicked at the limbs, trampled them into the grass. Yet the creatures did not seem to be acting violently or out of malice. The whole affair had the feeling more of a ceremony, of a ritual, than of a murder. There was a gentleness almost in the animals' movements, an understanding of some sort.

After a while, Benny realized they had gone. The clearing was empty apart from herself, her diary, and the red grass.

Tapshorn was short and stout with thinning dark hair. He insisted on wearing a pith helmet which was a somewhat battered and faded grey. The effect was to make him look rather like a character in a cartoon Benny had once seen. The celluloid version had fallen off a tall building, and ended up as just a hat with feet poking out from under it and tiny beady eyes glinting as they blinked in surprise.

Tapshorn did not blink in surprise, though his eyes were all but hidden under his huge helmet. What credibility this might leave him was, however, undermined by two other factors. One was an inability to pronounce the letter 'r', which he seemed to regard as something of a challenge. So he apparently went out of his way to use words which included it rather than avoiding them. Why say 'shining' when 'relucent' will do? This, Benny decided, must be his motto.

Tapshorn's other peculiarity was a habit of pulling at his ear when he got excited. This made him look, to experts in ancient Earth history such as Benny, like a petrol pump. Just now, as Benny related what she had witnessed in the clearing, she was afraid he might pull his ear right off.

Kamadrich joined them in time to hear Tapshorn's excited, 'Tewiffic, gveatly intvesting.'

Kamadrich smiled, cocking her head slightly to one side so that her long blonde hair hung free. Tapshorn launched into a vivid retelling of Benny's story, allowing her time to nod occasionally in agreement that this was indeed what she had just been saying. Eventually, about halfway through his second retelling, Tapshorn shook his head in excitement, and wandered off to work on his paper. Benny and Kamadrich turned to watch him go, elbow sticking out as he reached under his hat to pull at his ear.

'I don't know,' Benny remarked, 'ten minutes sitting in a clearing and I've given him about three new papers to rush off and work on.'

Kamadrich's smile was still set on her face. 'Talking of rushing off,' she said, and Benny knew she was about to change the subject completely. She seemed able to do that – to dispel one train of thought at a moment in favour of another.

'Yes?'

'I think we're about done here. There's the trench we're

digging across H and J sections at the moment, but after that there's not much more to do, really. Cataloguing, cleaning up.'

Benny nodded. 'That's probably true. Are you saying we're done?' It seemed unlikely. They had not really found anything that Nusek would be pleased with. Pottery, tiles, some primitive glassware. Invaluable archaeological treasures, but not the proof of ownership that they had been not so tacitly charged with discovering.

'I think we may want to move on. Try another couple of sites to see if there's an appreciable difference in the structure of the buildings or the signs of habitation.'

'Or lack of.' Benny nodded in agreement. 'But this is by far the greatest concentration of buildings according to the orbital survey. Nowhere else comes close. Where were you thinking of going?'

'I was thinking of asking you, actually.'

The afternoon sun was in Benny's eyes as she looked at Kamadrich. The woman's face was a blank silhouette, so Benny was unable to read the expression. 'Oh,' she said, trying to sound appreciative and noncommittal at the same time.

'There was another concentration of stonework to the north. It's probably about a day away if you take the groundriders.'

'Ah.' Benny was beginning to see the sort of advice she was being asked for. Still, one part of the jungle would be very like another. Probably.

'So you're off tomorrow, then?'

'Seems like it.' Benny and Nicholas were working at the front of the final trench. It was tunnelled into the side of a small hill, and they had reached the foundations of a stone wall. The plan was to cut through the wall and examine the exposed cross-section to see what they could learn of the construction methods. It was a relief to Benny to be using the most up-to-date equipment for the dig for a change, rather than scrabbling about with a trowel.

'She wants to move on to the northern site when we're done here in a few days. And she wants me to take a small team in advance and start planning the dig. Which will make keeping in touch a bit tricky.' The communications gear, in contrast to the archaeological equipment, was worse than antiquated. Benny assumed that, since there was an obvious military application for communications technology, their expedition was last on the list. The planetary atmospherics didn't help: the jungle seemed to suppress any broadcast signal. In fact, the only way to keep in touch over distances of more than a few kilometres was to send a signal straight up and bounce it down again through boosters on Nusek's cruiser.

Nicholas scraped away at the edge of a slab of stone with a sonic trowel. 'Sounds like fun.'

'Yeah. Great.' Benny lowered her voice. 'She wants me to take Gilder,' she hissed.

They both turned and looked over their shoulders. Gilder was at the edge of the trench, three feet above them. The geophysics scanner was hooked to the wall, probing for signs of what might be behind it. Gilder was staring at the readout screen, jotting notes on a scratchpad built into the side of the display and adjusting various controls. Hunched over the display, tapping at buttons, he looked to Benny like an accountant working through a balance sheet. And in that moment she felt she understood and appreciated more about Gilder than she had until then.

The work was delicate. They needed to identify the best stone to remove first. The last thing they wanted was to damage the very structure they were trying to examine. They both knew that in science in general, but in archaeology in particular, the very act of measurement, of examination, was certain to distort the results. That's Heisenberg for you, Benny thought as she probed delicately at some decaying mortar – the only certain law in an uncertain universe.

Eventually they identified the stone to remove, which was

about a foot square, at shoulder height in the wall. The next stage would be slow and tedious. They needed to remove the cement and mortar that held it in place. Gilder monitored the structural integrity of the wall and any redistribution in pressure from within or behind it. The slightest change and they would know that they had picked the wrong place to make a sonic incision, or had been too enthusiastic with the molecular debonder.

Nicholas glanced over his shoulder, then asked quietly, 'So, how's the *research* going?'

'As slowly as this.'

Nicholas grinned. 'Up against a stone wall, then? Me too.'

They discussed in hushed tones what they had learnt in the last day or so. Occasionally they looked round to see that Gilder was still absorbed in his work. Only once did he call out, warning them of a slight fluctuation in the levels he was monitoring. Nicholas apologized and probed more delicately with his trowel.

Nicholas had been going through his notes from Nusek's library and what he could remember of the books and documents that Reddik had hidden away. He had spent hours going through the scanned images he had taken of some of the more interesting documents. And he had come to only a few conclusions.

'There's practically nothing about Gamaliel before Bocaro in the documents that Nusek has kept in the library.'

Benny chuckled. 'I can imagine.'

'But there's also practically no mention of the Knights of Jeneve either.'

'I've found that too. A few throwaway references here and there. Nothing conclusive. There's one vid-news narrowcast that mentions the Knights and their dragon standard. No detail though.'

Nicholas pushed a debonder probe into a tiny hole he had drilled. 'Any luck chasing down those documents?'

Benny shook her head. She reached for a probe of her own. 'No. It's almost like . . .' She paused while she pushed the probe deep into the wall.

'Like? Like what?'

Benny shrugged. 'Just an idea. I need to think it through a bit more. Probably just a stupid notion.' She stepped back from the wall and dusted her hands on her shirt. 'Ready?'

Nicholas nodded. 'A big moment on my first dig,' he said with a smile. 'What glories lie undiscovered behind this wall?'

Benny laughed. 'None, I should think.' She turned to check with Gilder that they were ready. He gave a thumbs-up, and then activated the debonders.

A tiny trickle of powder from the edges of the stone was the only clue that anything had happened. Benny poked at the stone with a finger. It shifted slightly, and more of the disintegrated cement trickled from the edges.

Then Benny froze suddenly. 'Did you hear that?' There was a faint sound from the wall, a tiny scratching sound seeming to squeeze through the thin gaps round the stone.

Nicholas listened for a moment, then shook his head. 'No, can't hear anything.'

Benny strained to hear the sound again, but there was nothing. 'Strange.' She called up to Gilder. 'Are you sure there's just a hole behind here? No movement or pressure at all? I don't want to take that stone out if the wall's holding back an underground river or something.'

Gilder checked the display. 'No, nothing. Just stale air.'

Nicholas went to the side of the trench, where the exposed wall met the mud of the excavation. 'The scanner connection looks fine.' He traced the cable back along the trench. 'I'll check along, but it looks OK.'

Benny was vaguely aware of Nicholas walking slowly back down the trench. Her attention was focused on the stone in front of her. This was the moment of discovery, the moment when she got the greatest thrill from her work. She levered the tips of her fingers gently, expertly, around the stone. It would be heavy, and she strained to ease it slowly out of the wall towards her.

The stone shifted slightly. Easier than Benny had expected. She pulled again, harder. From back along the trench she heard Nicholas's voice, an urgent call: 'Wait a minute. That's not right. Benny!'

She half turned to catch the words. As she did so, a shower of cement powder hit her in the face as the stone suddenly came forward. She fell back, choking and blinking, aware of the weight of the stone in her hands, and knowing it had moved too easily – something had been pushing from the other side.

The creatures leapt through the hole in the wall. There were so many it was like a liquid stream as they tumbled to the floor of the trench and flowed along it. Their claws and teeth glinted in the light. Their matted fur was caked with mud and grime. Their eyes were beads of pure blackness in the gloom. Segmented tails whipped round as they fell, clawed at the muddy ground, and scuttled away.

Three things had saved Benny for the moment. The first was that she had turned away, so her face had not been in line with the torrent of scratching, clawing animals as they poured out of the hole in the wall. The second was that she had fallen as the stone came away from the wall, and the creatures were tumbling down on to her rather than leaping through the wall at her. The third was that she was still holding the stone. It was shielding her face from the creatures.

She could feel them flopping on to the rest of her body, crawling along her stomach, scratching at her legs, biting at her clothes and skin. She held the stone over her face, aware that she was screaming, aware that her vision was blurred from the dust and getting more blurred with the tears, aware that the tide of animals was flowing up her body and would soon engulf her. She had a distorted vision of herself sinking beneath the creatures, and she knew the heaving mass of fur, teeth and claws would soon burrow beneath the stone. Even if she could continue to hold its weight over her face, she knew the animals would push and wriggle underneath, nipping at her mouth, ripping into her cheeks, clawing at her eyes.

The stone was heaved from her hands. She had time for one muffled scream before a huge dark shape blotted out what was left of the light.

Departures

The mechanical hum was a steady background to her thoughts. The light was so bright it hurt the backs of her eyelids, and when she tentatively opened her eyes for a split second, it spilt in and whited out her thoughts again. Gradually, the hum receded, and the light diffused into a warm glow. A dark shape swept across her vision, regular, rhythmic.

As Benny's eyes focused, the dark shape resolved itself into the blades of the ceiling fan. At the same moment, the mechanical hum settled into the familiar sound of the air-conditioning system. She was lying in bed in her quarters on Stanturus Three, and she was staring at the ceiling.

There was a noise from beside her. For a fraction of a moment, she thought it was the sound of the ceiling cracking open. Cracking open to let through a torrent of the ratlike creatures which had clawed and crawled and bitten their way across her just moments ago. Or so it seemed.

But the noise had come from beside her, not above. She turned her head slightly, painfully, towards the sound. It was Nicholas, coughing quietly and politely. As if he wanted to let her know he was there. She realized with surprise that he was holding her hand, covering it with his own as it lay limp and painful on the bedcovers.

Then everything went black again.

'How is she?'

'Better, I think.' Nicholas stood up to let Kamadrich closer to the bed where Benny was once again sleeping peacefully. 'She was dreaming earlier. Then she woke for a moment.'

Kamadrich leant closer to the bed. 'She seems peaceful enough now. The treatment should counteract the poison in the bites before long.' She watched the sleeping woman for a short while. Then she turned back to Nicholas. 'But not soon enough, I'm afraid. When can you leave?'

'You agree with my terms?'

'You don't give me much choice. Professor Summerfield obviously won't be up to it, and I need one of you there.'

Nicholas smiled. 'You mean to keep Nusek happy.'

Kamadrich nodded. 'If the expedition finds something significant and one of you isn't there to validate the find as an independent observer, he'll kill me.'

'I hope you don't mean that literally.'

Kamadrich smiled. It was, Nicholas knew, a rare occurrence. But he thought it was worth waiting for. Her face lifted and her eyes sparkled as if with an inner light. It was quite a transformation from the efficient, stern woman. 'I hope so too,' she said. Then the smile was gone as suddenly as it had arrived, wiped away in an instant. 'When can you leave?' she repeated.

'As soon as I'm sure Benny is recovering. When she wakes. It shouldn't be long now.'

Kamadrich looked back at Benny for a moment. Then she crossed to the door.

'Why don't you count?' Nicholas asked her as she stood on the threshold. 'As an independent assessor, I mean?'

'You work for your university. Most of the remuneration goes to them, not to you. But I'm reimbursed directly by Nusek for my consultancy.' She smiled again. 'I guess I'm just paid too much to be thought of as unbiased.'

'I resign my independence.' The voice was strong and loud and startled Nicholas. Kamadrich, who had been looking back into the room, was unsurprised.

'Well,' Benny went on, 'I could do with the cash.'

Kamadrich gave Nicholas an hour, and left them to talk.

Benny seemed wide awake now, though she complained of a headache, and the scratches and bites across her face, hands and arms in particular were sore. She remarked immediately on the marks on Nicholas's face. He avoided commenting, and he was glad he had removed the mirror from beside her bed. If she thought that his face had taken a battering, the sight of her own in its present state would be something of a shock.

They spent about half an hour talking over recent events. Nicholas told Benny how he had taken the stone from her hands and dragged her out of the trench. He explained that he was now the preferred, or rather only, choice to lead the offshoot expedition. He admitted that he had to leave in under an hour.

'And what about the geophyz scanner?' Benny asked.

'I'd just found the end of the cable when you screamed. And I mean the end. It wasn't connected. In fact, the scanner was reading the geophysical attributes of a pile of mud the other side of the trench.'

'You mean someone deliberately fed another cable into the thing?'

Nicholas nodded. 'To give a false reading, yes. It's not the sort of thing that can happen by accident. And it would have to be someone who knew there was something behind the wall.'

'Gilder?' Benny suggested.

'The obvious choice. Perhaps too obvious. But I've got Kamadrich to pull him off my expedition anyway. I can't lead that and be watching my back at the same time.'

Benny laughed and her head flopped back into the pillow. 'So you're leaving him with me. Terrific.' She sat up again. 'So what does Kamadrich think?'

'She admits it was sabotage. Not much else she can do. But she suggests we don't let on that we know, but treat it as an accident.'

Benny considered this. 'To avoid panicking the others? Or to lull the saboteur into thinking we aren't on to him yet?'

'Both of those. And also to avoid slowing down the work.'

He took her hand in his again. It felt cooler than it had when she was asleep. 'Take care of yourself.'

Benny smiled, the effort and pain of it apparent. 'And you. We'll catch up with you soon. I'll get on with my reading in the meantime.'

Nicholas nodded. 'Good idea.' He squeezed her hand slightly, turned and left.

Some while later, Benny heaved her protesting body out of bed and limped to the window. Outside several groundriders were lined up, engines idling. Several more were already disappearing into the jungle, laden with equipment and people. She could see no sign of Nicholas – he must have left in the first batch.

The last few groundriders were loaded up, their large tyres compressing slightly under the weight. The remaining archaeologists were gathered round to see them off (about a third of the total complement of the expedition were remaining behind to finish up at the main site).

Benny watched the last of the vehicles set off across the clearing and start into the jungle. She could see the men and women waving from the groundriders as they were swallowed up by the greenery.

It was only a day before the mild poison in the bites had been suppressed enough by her medication for Benny to get back on her feet. But it was a lot longer before she could bear to look in a mirror. It somehow annoyed her more that she was so upset than that her face was criss-crossed with scratches and pitted with tooth marks. She had assumed, had hoped, that vanity was a failing that was long behind her. What was the use of growing older if you didn't grow out of things like that? Perhaps there were new things to grow into, but if there were, she hadn't found them yet.

Of course, the classic attribute that comes with age is wisdom. But as Benny pursued her researches, and found several more potentially fruitful trails mysteriously blocked as documents vanished from their archives, she began to doubt her sanity, let alone how wise she was being. And when she checked her credit balance to see if she had been paid for her consultancy, she decided that ignorance was not only blissful but probably cheap as well. She had indeed been paid for her time. But she had also been charged for the uplink and transfer services she thought Nusek's cruiser was supplying as part of her standard remuneration. In short, she was worse off than when she started, and she had been broke then.

The obvious answer was to go to Braxiatel – both for enlightenment and cash. But she was too proud to beg from him, though she knew he wouldn't see it like that and, God knew, he was rolling in it. Equally, she did not feel inclined to contact him about the progress her research was making until she was sure she had something to tell him that he did not already know. Or at least, could not reasonably be expected to know.

The result, which Benny managed to convince herself was a Good Thing, was that she spent her time going back over what she had already gleaned from various sources and rethinking everything from beginning to end. It became something of a routine after a couple of days. She would have a late breakfast, then find a quiet spot in the jungle away from the excavations. She would read till lunchtime, then check the daily report from Nicholas's team. Having eaten, she would compose a short reply to Nicholas commenting on their (lack of) progress. When Kamadrich expressed concern that Nicholas and his team did not seem to be finding anything interesting or useful, it was an effort for Benny to resist saying that she expected no less from a jumped-up historian with no previous field experience. But she told herself that it was her frustration and boredom coming through. Even if it was true.

Benny spent the afternoons thinking through the implications and ramifications of what she had read in the morning. Often she did this while helping out with a light, menial task about the camp. Cataloguing the various pottery shards, metal fragments and other discoveries was a favourite, though mapping out the ruins was almost as mindless.

It was Tapshorn who gave Benny the clue she was after, albeit inadvertently. They were cataloguing various artefacts in the main cabin, tapping ident codes and locations into the database alongside scanned images of each find. Harker and Menson were doing much the same thing at the next console, griping about how they would rather have gone with Nicholas. Benny and Tapshorn were passing the time by talking about the steggies. Tapshorn was actually doing all the talking, while Benny was only half listening.

'It seems to be an instinctive response to danger,' Tapshorn was saying. He was answering a question about why the steggies suddenly became agitated and even on occasion aggressive. It was a question that Benny had not asked, but this did not deter him. 'I've seen them do it at the water hole when there's a major storm coming in. And the other day when there was a pack of those vat things, like the ones that you, er, met with.'

It took Benny a moment to work out what he meant by 'vat things'. Her immediate assumption was that he was talking about a brewing process of some sort, but she was disappointed when she realized this was not the case.

'Anyway, the steggies got agitated in the same way and moved off before the animals got to them. A response system of sorts.' He paused to read out the ident number tagged to a broken drinking vessel. 'Can't say why they take against some of us so much, though, especially Kamadrich and your friend Nicholas.'

'I think it's mutual,' Benny told him. 'I think they sense that.'

'Perhaps,' Tapshorn said, obviously meaning perhaps not. 'But they are not naturally furtive creatures, although they do cover their tracks pretty well. It's not that they are afraid of us: they'd just rather we didn't know they were here.'

Benny paused, midway through entering a location code.

'Covering their tracks,' she repeated quietly. 'You know, you could be wight. Sorry, *right*.' She made a point of checking the time. 'Well, it's been fun, but I've got to dash. You know how it is.' She paused at the entrance to the cabin. 'Sure you can manage on your own?' She did not wait for a reply. 'Good.'

Benny made her way to the communications room. There was a chance they would transmit a message to Nicholas later that day. If they did, Benny wanted to include a short message of her own. On the way, she tried to think how to phrase it so that Nicholas would understand and nobody else would. But the key phrases and words she had decided upon went out of her head when she saw the excited group spilling out of the comms room.

Kamadrich was standing in the doorway, and nodded to Benny as she approached.

'What is it?' Benny asked. 'What's going on?'

'We've had a signal from the expedition. They say they've found something.'

They set up a real-time link-up that evening, as soon as the cruiser was able to make position. The picture was grainy but acceptable. Just. Kamadrich and Benny sat close to the small screen in the main cabin. Everyone else was further back, straining to see the snowy images and hear the crackling audio.

They had only a short time before the cruiser's orbit took it out of range, so Nicholas went quickly through what his team had found. A tiny time clock set into the screen counted down the seconds left in the transmission window. Nicholas seemed less enthusiastic than some of his colleagues, whose faces popped up in the picture occasionally to make comments. Behind him, when the image cleared enough to make them out, Benny could see the walls of the ruined settlement Nicholas was describing. He seemed to be going over the same information again and again, as if holding something back.

'So it's just some more ruins, right?' Benny asked after a few minutes, feeling that perhaps she was missing the point. 'Better preserved, but more of the same.'

Nicholas turned away from the camera, as if consulting someone else, or listening to their opinion. 'No,' he said when he turned back. 'No, it's not that simple.' The picture broke up completely for a few seconds. '– as straightforward as that,' Nicholas was saying when it returned. 'I'm not sure how much more I should transmit over an open channel.'

Kamadrich leant closer to the screen, and to the tiny camera built into its housing. 'If you're in any doubt, send us an encrypted report on the secure channel. This may be very sensitive.'

Nicholas nodded, his movement made jerky and artificial by the transmission. 'That may be best.'

There was a burst of noise from the screen, though whether it was interference or the protestations of Nicholas's team, Benny could not tell. Then the time clock clicked away the last second, and the screen snowed over for good.

'So what was all that about?' Benny asked Kamadrich after everyone else had drifted away.

Kamadrich shrugged. But her usually calm face betrayed a hint of anxiety. 'Well, we'll soon find out,' she said.

The secure transmission was received a few minutes later. Kamadrich punched the day's one-time code into the console, and rapidly read the text as it scrolled up the screen. She was so close to the screen that Benny was unable to see any of it.

'So?'

Kamadrich turned from the console. For a split second she seemed pensive. Then she shook her head, exasperated. 'What a waste of time,' she said. The frustration was clear in her voice. 'It's just more ruins.' She punched the delete key. 'Tell them to make a quick survey and press on,' she told the communications technician.

Benny watched Kamadrich leave the cabin. She wished she had seen the message – she could not help but feel there was rather more to it than Kamadrich was letting on. If only she had been fit enough to lead the team. Was Nicholas out of his depth? Or was he just making an archaeological mountain out of a molehill?

Of all of them, Bjork was the most angry. When Nicholas read out the message from Kamadrich, he snatched the printout from him in disbelief. They were standing in a room that was still practically intact. It had black openings for windows, and a grassy floor, but compared with the ruins they had found up till now it was in amazingly good condition. Unlike the other buildings in the settlement, this one seemed to have escaped the worst effects of the volcanic eruption that had destroyed the community and killed its inhabitants. The jungle had grown back and reclaimed the surrounding land, but the buildings had somehow been kept clear of creepers, vines and other vegetation. They were frozen in time, caught in the volcanic ash.

'You're joking. A quick survey and move on?' Bjork snorted in disgust.

Nicholas gestured at the paper. 'That's what it says.'

'But didn't you explain? Didn't you tell them what we found in your message?'

Nicholas turned away. 'Of course I did. Maybe they've found something similar. Maybe they want to follow up later. I don't know what's going on any more than you,' he lied. He turned to Callum, who was keeping watch. 'What are they up to?'

Callum was standing by an opening in the stone wall. 'They're still hanging around on the edge of the jungle,' he said. 'Rumbling, the way they do now. Here. They haven't come into the clearing, though there are more of them now. I think they're getting bolder.'

'I wonder what we've done to upset them.' Nicholas crossed to Callum at the window and looked out into the gloom. 'The steggies are usually so placid.'

Bjork joined them. 'They haven't actually attacked us or

anything,' he pointed out. 'Though they do seem agitated.'

'I've never seen so many together at once.' Callum turned to Nicholas. 'Do you think it's to do with this place, with the lava?' he asked.

'Possibly,' Nicholas conceded. But before he could say more, Bjork grabbed his shoulder.

'They're on the move.'

Outside, the steggodons were slowly, furtively, leaving the shelter of the jungle and grouping on the edge of the clearing.

'You'd better warn the others,' Nicholas told Callum. Some were asleep, others were finishing the initial surveying in other buildings within the settlement. Callum nodded and ran from the room.

The steggodons gathered in the clearing. They shuffled together, entwining snouts and kicking at the ground. The place was sacred to them, and now these intruders had come, had tried to make it their own. The steggies did not, could not, articulate their feelings so precisely, but they felt a shared unease. Fear. Agitation.

It was dark, and they knew instinctively that this was the best time to drive the intruders out. That this was the best time to reclaim their land. The feeling swelled and grew, and a steady rumble transmitted through the air, shared by the rubbing of leathery skin, amplified by the crowd mentality, the herd spirit.

Benny could not sleep. The transmission was bothering her, and she was annoyed that Kamadrich had not shown her Nicholas's encrypted message before she erased it. Eventually, she decided that there was no point in lying in bed getting cross, and so she got up.

She was not quite sure what she should or could do to help Nicholas, or even if he needed help. Probably he was getting overenthusiastic about something mundane. She decided to play back the recording of the video transmission. She might be able to read something into Nicholas's words, or make out enough of the background to come to some conclusions.

The comms cabin was deserted apart from the duty technician, who woke with a start when Benny came in. He was handing Benny a coffee and explaining (again) how he had not really been asleep as such when the message came in.

It was an audio signal on a radio frequency – old technology but reliable. A burst of static and then a voice, loud and clear. Benny was too distracted by the shouting and screaming in the background to take in what was being said. The voice was not Nicholas's – it sounded more like Bjork.

'Help. Help us. They're attacking, hundreds of them. You have to get us out of here. Now. Can anyone hear me? Is anyone there?'

The technician and Benny stared at each other as the sound faded. Then the technician grabbed for a control pad, desperately trying to retune to the signal. Benny was shouting into the microphone, knowing that she could not be heard but not knowing what she was saying.

Kamadrich was suddenly in the room with them. 'Did the cruiser pick up the transmission?' she asked calmly.

The technician checked a readout and nodded. Where there had been a cacophony of sound, there was now silence as Kamadrich checked over the readings.

'Then there's nothing more we can do,' she said at last. 'They'll send a shuttle.'

NUSEK'S GAMBIT

Commander Skutloid held the china teacup delicately between the clamped fingers of his ceremonial armour plating. His reptilian tongue licked the surface of the tea, scooping it into his thin mouth between husky rasps. 'Excellent, as ever,' he commented as he set down the cup. 'And how can I help you? I know from experience that you rarely offer tea as a merely social diversion.'

Braxiatel laughed. 'Well, now you mention it, I do have a small problem you can help me with.'

'Good,' rasped Skutloid, smacking scaly fist into armoured palm. 'I always enjoy helping you out. What is it this time, eh? A stray cruiser that needs to disappear? A few mercenaries for undisclosed duties on an unnamed planet? You know, I think it's you that makes my retirement to this forsaken place bearable.'

'I'm afraid it's nothing so exciting this time. A simple question, no more.'

Skutloid slumped back in the chair, obviously disappointed. 'Oh. Well at least the tea is good. Fire away, as we say in my profession.'

Braxiatel took a sip of tea, then put his cup aside. 'Tell me,' he said, 'what exactly was the Gamalian Gambit?'

Skutloid did not reply for a moment. 'Is that a serious question?' he asked at last.

'Oh yes. Yes indeed.'

'You would like to know what the Gamalian Gambit was?

The stratagem that enabled Hugo Gamaliel to win at Bocaro from a position of certain defeat and against overwhelming odds. The initiative that set him up as an unstoppable force in this sector, that gave him a victory so astounding that he scarcely had to fight another battle. And you would like to know what it was?'

Braxiatel smiled, used to Skutloid's sarcastic tirades. 'I apologize for my ignorance, but the history books are unclear and it is not a period with which I am myself immediately familiar. And you, as head of the Strategic Institute here at St Oscar's –'

'As head of the Strategic Institute here at St Oscar's,' Skutloid interrupted, 'I should like to know as well.' He leant forward, the light gleaming on the dark eyes shielded behind the blast screens set into his green face. 'Let me tell you, if I knew what the Gamalian Gambit truly was, do you think I would be skulking about in this hell-hole? No, I'd be leading my troopers to glory as ruler of half this quadrant.'

Braxiatel considered this. 'So, you don't know?'

Skutloid laughed again. 'Of course I don't know. Nobody knows. That's why it was so brilliant. We used to play through the scenarios at battle school. Always the same, Gamaliel well and truly annihilated. Nobody has a clue how he did it.'

'How interesting,' Braxiatel murmured. 'What about the institute's simulators? Surely they are up to the task.'

'I doubt it. It's supposed to be insoluble. Gamaliel's last stratagem, one of my tutors called it.' He held out his cup for more tea. 'He must have been a lousy tactician to get himself into such a hopeless position in the first place. Though you could argue that the Knights of Jeneve were rather rash to commit their entire force to a single confrontation, however safe a bet it might have seemed.'

Braxiatel poured from the silver teapot. 'Mind if I have a go?' he asked.

'What, run the Battle of Bocaro through the institute's simulators?'

'Why not? The untrained mind may come up with something new. Be a bit of fun, anyway.'

Skutloid snorted. 'Please yourself. Just say I sent you – they'll give you some machine time.'

'Thank you.'

The commander sipped at his tea again. 'I don't suppose,' he asked after a while, 'you have any of those chocolates? You know, the square ones with the soft mint in the middle?'

The canteen was quiet. Deathly quiet. The tables had been pushed to the walls, and a sheet hung up on them to serve as a screen. The RGB projector was sitting on a table in the middle of the chairs. The members of the expedition left behind at the main base were all gathered into the room. There were about fifteen of them, and Benny was surprised and embarrassed to note that she knew the names of only about half.

Kamadrich stood at the front of the room by the sheet screen. She did not need to wait for the usual noises on such occasions to abate. There was no muted conversation, no scraping of chairs, no shuffling, no latecomers murmuring apologies as they pushed through between rows of seats. Even Gilder was silent and still. Kamadrich coughed nervously. Then she told everyone what by now they already knew.

'We're expecting soon to receive the video images from the shuttle that the cruiser dispatched to investigate,' she finished. 'If they are on schedule, they should pass over the site in a couple of minutes. Then we'll be able to see what's going on.'

She seemed about to say something more, but then she shrugged and sat next to Benny in the front row. As she sat, the lighting dimmed and the projector hummed into life. A pattern of static speckled the screen for a few seconds. Then it was replaced by solid bars of colour.

'They've started transmitting,' Kamadrich whispered to Benny. 'That's the test signal. Their cameras will cut in soon.'

'What do you think they'll find?' Tapshorn asked quietly from the row behind.

Kamadrich shook her head. Benny rubbed at her eyebrow. And an image sprang up on the screen in front of them.

The picture was grainy and faded, the effect of the infrared and the image intensifiers as they struggled to enhance the black reality of Stanturan night. There was so much motion that it took Benny a while to get her bearings. The camera was rushing forward, just above the roof of the jungle. They were seeing the world from the point of view of the small shuttle craft as it dipped towards the ground, and skimmed along above the trees. The picture pitched and rolled, bucked and yawed. It was like playing a speed-racer video game while strapped to a rollercoaster.

Various data streamed across the bottom of the screen. Location references, timestamps, zoom levels, intensity readings. Gibberish to Benny, who was not even sure what the words she could read meant, let alone the acronyms and numbers.

'They're coming up on the ruins now,' Kamadrich murmured. At least the stream of data meant something to her.

It was as if they were suddenly watching a different film. Benny remembered it afterwards in slow motion, though it must have been transmitted in real time. It was her own perception that had raced ahead, slowing the realization, suffering out the story it told. Or, perhaps, she did not remember it at all, and was mentally replacing the sequence with one of the numerous slowed replays that they sat through later, each slightly less numbing than the last until they could think it through logically. Until their brains woke from the shock.

There was nothing. Open space. Bare, exposed earth. There was a short perimeter of stunted and burnt vegetation, and then the jungle gave way to the blackened devastation that replaced the ripped-up burnt-out trees and grass. Once, as her point of view swept across the ground, Benny thought she caught a glimpse of a small pile of stones, the remains perhaps of the major ruin they knew had been there. But with nothing else in the whole area, there was no way to get an idea of the relative size of the structure. It could have been a mountain or a blemish on the lens.

Then they were back among the charred outskirts of the jungle again. The camera slowed and banked as it reached the edge, coming round for a second unnecessary and unwelcome run. It tilted over a burning pile of debris, the flames seeming higher and fiercer for the angle of view. They flared the infrared almost to whiteout before the image-enhancers adjusted for the heat image and levelled off the light spectrum.

Several smaller fires had been sparked off within the jungle, but they were already dying away; the high water content of the bark made the trees fire-retarding. And just for a second in the midst of the inferno, smothered in the oily smoke and caressed by the flames, Benny could see the blackened frame of a groundrider.

There was an air of depression and unease round the camp the next day. Most people had not slept, and most of them looked and behaved to match. Kamadrich was a picture of calm efficiency as ever, despite what Benny decided must be going through her mind. She had seen two-thirds of her expedition wiped out by forces unknown. She did not seem to have friends as such, but several of her colleagues had seemed to be close to her. Yet the next day she was able to give instructions to close off those excavations that were still incomplete and finish logging and cataloguing the remaining discoveries.

It was around noon that there was a shout from one of the trenches. Ironically, Benny found herself running towards the trench where she had been attacked by the rat creatures. Apart from one trip back to try to exorcise her fears, she had made a point of avoiding it, and knew that nobody else had been near it since, either. But now it was being closed up like the others. Several people had gone to remove the equipment and check there was nothing of their own left to be buried when the trench was filled in. That could provide a potential headache and confusion for future archaeologists.

As she reached the trench – just ahead of Kamadrich, she was pleased to note – Benny could hear that the cries from inside were not pain or fear. They were triumphant, euphoric.

One of the archaeologists appeared below them in the trench. He was making his way back from the wall that Benny had opened up, and he was laughing. From where she stood, Benny could see the thinning hair raked across his scalp. She was struggling to remember his name when Kamadrich called out to him.

'Timyan – what is it?' He started when he heard her voice. 'What's going on down there?'

'It's incredible,' he called back. He was craning to see them, head angled back and hand up to blot out the midday sun. Their shadows lay across the trench either side of him, distorted and jagged as the ground dropped away. 'We were replacing the stone, the one Professor Summerfield removed. There's quite a hole where those rodent things pushed through. Lots of damage to shore up.' He paused, tried to blink away the bright light after the gloom of the interior of the excavation. 'Anyway, Grodzki reached inside to clear away some debris, and there it was, just lying there. Inside the wall.'

'What?' Benny called down. 'What was there? What have you found?'

'It's incredible,' Timyan repeated. 'Absolutely incredible. Grodzki's just bringing it.'

As if on cue, Grodzki appeared behind him in the cutting. She was walking slowly, arms held in front of her as she cradled her find, holding it steady and aloft despite its weight. Benny stood rooted to the spot. Theories, suspicions, worries jostled inside her mind trying to find the right slots to slip into in order to make sense, to complete a coherent picture.

Kamadrich gasped out loud – the most emotion Benny had

seen from her aside from the restrained anger and fear at the previous night's video showing. Then she jumped down into the trench.

Grodzki took another step towards Kamadrich, and as she did so she emerged from the shadow of the side of the trench. She was staring at the object she was holding at eye level, her hold beginning to waver under its weight. The sunlight caught it, making it seem to glow. The wings almost glistened despite the mud and grime that caked them. The jewels studded into it reflected starlets of sunshine broken by the dirt and grease.

Carefully, reverently, Kamadrich reached out to Grodzki, and took the Gamalian Dragon from her hands.

Benny spent most of the afternoon in her cabin. The first thing she did, once she had locked the door and pulled the shutters, was to check her rucksack. Sure enough, the Gamalian Dragon – the *real* Gamalian Dragon that she had lifted from Nusek's archives – was still there. She replaced it, wrapped up in a towel, and sat down on her bed. She had a lot to think about.

She tried not to think about Nicholas and what might have happened to him. Loss was, unfortunately, not a new emotion for Benny. And although it got no easier to bear, it was easier to control. For now she was conscious mainly that she had to think through what was happening without help. Braxiatel was too far away to be of use, and Nicholas was . . . gone.

The first thing that Benny decided was that however many 'unique' Gamalian Dragons there might actually be, and wherever they might actually have come from, finding one on Stanturus Three hours before they pulled out was too much of a coincidence. Kamadrich and the others were already making the point that their find was unbelievable. So far they had some circumstantial (and circumspect) evidence that there had indeed been a colony of Gamaliel's people on Stanturus Three. But if there was one single artefact that would prove beyond any doubt that Gamaliel had been to the planet it was the discovery of a long-lost, long-forgotten twin of the famous Gamalian Dragon.

And it was the fact that it was such indisputable proof more than anything that made Benny believe that the whole thing was a fabrication. Even without the knowledge that there was at least one other apparently identical Dragon knocking about, Benny would have been more than dubious. She had been back to the trench just once, had stolen a few moments during a sleepless night to try to come to terms with the memories and the nightmares. It had seemed, thankfully, like a different place in the near-darkness. She had quickly run the beam of her torch across the hole in the wall, then walked briskly back along the trench and returned to her cabin. But despite the speed of it, Benny was sure she would have seen the Dragon glinting in the darkness. She was sure that it had not been there a few nights ago.

In fact, when Benny arranged the facts and suspicions at her disposal, they fell into a surprisingly coherent pattern. Nusek was desperate to establish that Gamaliel had claimed, had visited even, Stanturus Three. There were at least two copies of the unique Gamalian Dragon in existence. Someone on the expedition was trying to kill Benny, and seemed to have succeeded with Nicholas.

Not everything was completely clear. But Benny felt certain that whoever was responsible for the 'accidents' had planted the Dragon so that it would be found when the trench was closed up. It was unlikely that there were two different sets of villains coincidentally on the same expedition, each following a different agenda, so the events and coincidences had to be linked in some way. And whoever the villains were, they must be working for Nusek. That meant that Nusek wanted her and/or Nicholas dead, which in turn meant that he knew something about Benny's Dragon. Or about their visit to Nusek's archives that night in his palace.

Whichever way Benny looked at it, she came back to pretty much the same conclusions. Whichever way she looked at it, it seemed as though Nusek now had a winning hand. Alone,

Benny could not hope to denounce him with any credibility. Even if Nicholas were still around, she doubted that they could argue their case convincingly enough.

In the back of her mind, Benny could see the charred wreckage of the groundrider, flames licking out of its luggage compartment and engulfing the cab. The only sign of life on the whole video, caught on the edge of the carnage.

Life. On the edge.

What if someone had been in the groundrider, had seen what was about to happen? What if they had made it into the jungle outside the devastated area? Or been away from the groundrider on the safe side of the fire?

What if Nicholas were still alive?

Intellectually, she did not believe the supposition for a moment. But on an emotional level she had a quite different attitude. So, less than two hours after Grodzki had found the Stanturan Dragon, Benny was bouncing through the jungle in a groundrider, heading for a patch of burnt-out land three kilometres square obliterated by a focused fission device the night before.

The sun is shining in his eyes, but he can still see them. The lines of troops are marching with measured tread across the landscape. Hundreds of them, stretching into the distance for as far as he can see. The sunlight reflects off their battle armour; their faces are invisible behind the blast shields and anti-rad visors. The polished duralinium glows slightly, an effect of the sun's rather weak radiation emission. But for Nicholas it adds to the overall aura.

He lies, staring up into the sky, seeing the battle lines drawn up and the skyfliers building their attack and defence formations. Staring up into the sky above Stanturus Three and seeing the elaborate preparations on the field of Bocaro. And while the noises of the jungle are stilled, muted by the events of the previous night, while the animals and birds are long gone, searching for shelter and safety, Nicholas hears only the rattle of blaster on armour and the cries of the commanders over the battlenet as they alternately cajole and encourage their troops.

This is not the famous motion holovid of the battle. Nicholas has seen that many times, in all its inaccurate and anachronistic glory. In this battle the armour is practical, not the clanking clumsiness of legend. The Knights of Jeneve mount up, boarding the fireraiders without the contrived help of lifting harnesses and scores of squires.

The lines are drawn. Ready to be crossed and broken. Nicholas smiles into the brightness as the Grand Master of Jeneve signals the outriders, as Gamaliel and his generals struggle to achieve a formation that will deflect the onslaught of the far superior forces – as they prepare to make history, or become victims of it. A shadow crosses between Nicholas and the sun, blocking out his vision of Bocaro. A figure, head and shoulders silhouetted against the sky. The sounds of battle fade into the past, and somewhere, distantly, a bird screeches in terror.

The moment is broken, and Nicholas struggles to shift his bruised and battered body into a sitting position. 'Hello, Benny,' he croaks, his throat dusty and dry.

The edge of the devastation was pronounced and sudden. The scarred and blackened earth stopped abruptly, and the grass took over almost at once. Trees on the edge of the area had limbs stripped from them while their trunks stood virtually untouched. As if to compensate, branches lay on the ground just outside the area, where they had fallen when the trees to which they had been attached had vaporized in the heat.

Benny had found Nicholas from his heat signature. It showed clearly on the groundrider's monitors – he was about the only living thing that had remained within sight of the area. The monitors detected various other animals, including a herd of steggies, but all were moving away from the zone, or at least keeping their considerable distance. Benny's hope was that only Nicholas or another of the archaeologists would be incapable of leaving the area. And she had been right.

Nicholas was lying a hundred yards from the edge of the destruction. He was bruised and burnt, his clothes ripped and torn. But he seemed otherwise to be all right.

'Hello, Benny,' he said as she knelt over him. His voice was faint and laboured. He struggled to sit up, and then his eyes glazed and flickered. He seemed on the very edge of consciousness.

Benny pressed a drink to lips. 'Water,' she said needlessly as he sipped at it. 'What happened, Nicholas? Is there anyone else?'

The sun was in his eyes again as she shifted position, and he turned slightly searching for her shadow. Water trickled down his cheek as he moved. 'The steggies came,' he gasped. 'They dragged me away, attacked the others in the ruins.'

'The steggies did this?' Benny was relieved when Nicholas shook his head slightly.

'No. Afterwards. I managed to escape from them. Tried to get back. Then it happened.' He slumped back, exhausted.

'What?' Benny asked urgently. 'What happened? Who was it, Nicholas?'

But he was unconscious again. Benny knelt beside him, wondering what to do next. Should she try to wake him, or let him sleep? Perhaps she could drag him over to the groundrider and somehow lift him into it. As she looked down at Nicholas, lying on the dry grass, her eye was drawn to a movement behind his head. For a second she thought the grass itself was moving, but then she realized that she was looking at a shadow. A branch above them waving in the breeze, or a bird passing overhead, or –

The hand that came down on her shoulder was large and strong. It almost lifted Benny to her feet even as she was noticing the heavy studding of the protective armour and the stylized dragon emblem that identified Nusek's troops.

There were just three of them in the communications room, and the operator hardly counted. Webbe was not sure quite what the 'developments' that Nusek's message had mentioned would mean, but his guess was that they were not good. In fact, they were mixed.

The positive side of things was the miraculous discovery of another Gamalian Dragon on Stanturus Three. The other turns of events were more difficult to read, though Nusek evidently intended to turn them to his advantage.

'Mastrov is back on the cruiser,' Nusek told Webbe.

'And the archaeologists?'

Nusek nodded. 'Now that we have the Dragon there's no point in keeping them there. The explosion was a good excuse to send in ground troops as well as pulling out the expedition survivors.'

Webbe flicked through the communications log on the screen. 'Any survivors of the blast?' he asked as he skimmed the information.

'Just one. Nicholas Clyde.'

'Convenient. A detonation of that type and just one person survives.'

Nusek smiled. 'Too convenient, really. Mastrov is holding him under close arrest on the cruiser.' Nusek headed for the door. 'The independent hearing will take place as soon as we can arrange it,' he said, obviously expecting Webbe to follow. 'We need to establish the provenance of the new Dragon with all speed.'

'And your claim on Stanturus.'

'Of course.' Nusek waited for Webbe to open the door for him. 'You know that I already have the support of three of the other four?'

'Dependent on the Dragon being proved genuine and your claims to Stanturus Three being upheld by the hearing.'

'Of course.' They were in the corridor now. Nusek was grinning, a wide slash across his face. 'They aren't happy about it, but they know their people will rally to the cause if they don't. The legends, the ties, the memories are too compelling.' He stopped suddenly, turned and grabbed Webbe by the shoulder. 'So close now, Webbe. So close.' Nusek slapped his commander on the back, and continued down the corridor. 'I know you have reservations about the methods we have used, but the goal is almost achieved now. An honourable goal.'

Webbe paused before following. 'It is not in the goal that honour can be found,' he said quietly. 'It is in the means of achieving it.' He exhaled heavily, a faint mist in the cold of the corridor. Then he set off after Nusek.

'We can hardly use Clyde as an expert witness now,' Webbe told Nusek. 'And Kamadrich is obviously unsuitable.' His voice was almost a sneer.

Nusek did not seem to notice Webbe's tone. Or if he did he ignored it. 'Summerfield will give evidence. That should be sufficient.'

'And if she doesn't?'

'Then it will be assumed that she has nothing to say. And that will be interpreted as compliance with the evidence as presented.' Nusek shook his head. 'You seem determinedly pessimistic, Webbe. We have won, don't you see?' His pace slowed, as if he were realizing the truth of his own words for the first time. 'I have won,' he screamed in triumph down the stone corridor.

Model Behaviour

The shuttle was every bit as small, cramped and uncomfortable as Benny had expected. The only saving grace was that the trip was mercifully short. She was transferring from the expedition ship to the cruiser.

They had left Stanturus Three the previous day, and it had taken this long for Benny to persuade the commander of Nusek's troops that she needed to speak to Nicholas about the discoveries they had made. She needed his expert opinion as a historian. Whether he was being held incommunicado in the cruiser's brig or not, she had to ask him some questions about Gamaliel's historical background. Only Nicholas could answer them, and if they went unanswered then there would be many upset people – Romolo Nusek for one. This last argument had apparently swayed the soldier's opinion, and it seemed as though she would be able to talk to Nicholas, at least briefly. Just so long as the commander did not choose to get permission from Nusek himself.

Benny was not sure what was going on. She doubted that Nicholas could help much, though. But it would be useful to talk things through. On the one hand, they were extremely simple, but on the other there were some events and implications that just did not seem to fit. Pieces from the wrong puzzle, lurking in the bottom of the box just when you thought you had completed the picture.

The brig, like most of the rest of the cruiser, was ugly, grey and old. There were patches of corrosion on the bulkheads, and the self-cleaning walls had long ago given up all pretence. Benny and Nicholas sat either side of a force wall, a faint shadow of a line across the metal table the only hint that there was anything between them – unless they tried to touch it, in which case there would be a flare of static, a jolt of pain, and the buzz of an alarm that would bring the guard hurrying in from the anteroom. The table and chairs were bolted to the floor, but it was difficult to tell if the bolts were so corroded that they could never be undone, or if a good blow with a hammer would shear them through.

'So, how are you?' Benny asked, knowing as she said it that this was the question everyone must ask or expect in these circumstances.

Nicholas shrugged. 'I've been better.'

Benny nodded. 'Right, well that's the standard stuff out of the way. We don't have long, and there's lots to talk about.'

'I heard about the Dragon.'

'Yeah. Well, we all know how genuine that is. The hearing should be fun.'

'They won't let me testify, not while I'm official scapegoat.'

Benny resisted the temptation to ask Nicholas to tell her more about what had happened to his expedition. There would be time for that later. There *might* be time for that later. Meanwhile there were more important things. 'I'm going to tell them it's a fake,' she said.

Nicholas's mouth dropped open. His hand was resting palm down on the top of the table, and Benny saw the knuckles tense slightly as he pushed down on it. 'I wouldn't,' he said. 'I really wouldn't.'

'Why not?'

Nicholas laughed, a snort of mock mirth. 'They won't let you, for one thing. Look what they've done to me. It could be that I'm in here to ensure you say the right things.'

'Then they don't know me very well.' Nicholas made to reply, but Benny continued. 'If I say, as the expert witness, that the Dragon is a fake, then that's it. Any hint of foul play and the support of the other warlords will melt away. Nusek will be no better off than he was before all this started.'

Nicholas considered for a moment before replying. 'Look,' he said at last, 'even putting aside what might or might not happen to you and me if you go ahead, I'm not convinced. He'll just wheel in some other experts to say you're wrong, and everything carries on with no change.'

'But if we tell everyone Nusek's plan –'

Nicholas lifted his hands from the table. He clenched them into frustrated fists, then thumped them back down. 'Everyone already knows Nusek's plan. It's obvious. It's so obvious that the steggies probably see through it. He's just going through the motions, making it seem legitimate. If you tell everyone that the Dragon's a fake, they won't be surprised. Of course it's a fake. How could it not be? But he's made the effort. He's gone to the trouble. He's earned the right. Do you think the word of a junior archaeology professor and author of the least academic work on the subject ever to get into a university library will slow him down?' He paused. 'I've been thinking about how I got here. You know, the "why me?" stuff. And the fact is, Nusek chose his two tame experts very well. Both convincing and accomplished enough to back up his claims. But neither respected nor established enough to discredit him. You back him up and it's more weight to his argument. Denounce him, and who are you anyway? Does your academic background, your standing in the archaeological or historical community give you the right or the credibility to stand up to Nusek? I tell you, mine certainly doesn't.'

Benny stared at him. She was sure there must be an argument she could use, some point that Nicholas was missing. She hoped there was. 'What if I can prove the Dragon's a fake?' she asked at last. 'Would that do it?'

Nicholas considered. 'Maybe. Yes, maybe. He'd have to start again, anyway, and that delay coupled with the loss of face might persuade the other warlords that they need to consider a different approach. They're none too enamoured of Nusek after all.' He nodded slowly. 'What have you in mind?'

Benny did not have anything in mind. But she was thinking quickly. 'What if I produce the third Dragon at the hearing.'

Nicholas shook his head. 'No, that might actually bolster his claim. It's less credible that there are just the two than that Gamaliel had hundreds of the things all over his empire. If anything it will reflect badly on you.'

'Well,' Benny said, thinking through what they already knew, 'the two Dragons we've looked at so far – the original and the copy I had – are absolutely identical. Too identical to both be the products of the sort of workmanship and tools the Knights of Jeneve and their craftsmen would have had.'

'Yes, that's possible.' Nicholas was leaning forward, so close Benny could reach out and touch him without effort. Except for the force wall. 'If you can prove that all three are so minutely identical that two of them must have been copied from the original using modern technology.'

Benny grinned, pleased with herself. They had a plan.

'It might work,' Nicholas said again. 'But there's no guarantee.'

'I'll check the new Dragon, make some notes, prepare some reports.'

There was a clank from behind her, followed by the protesting shriek of the door's hinges. The guard was standing in the doorway. 'Another minute,' he said.

'OK, we're nearly done.' Benny waited until the door had slammed shut again. 'Anything I can get you?' she asked.

'Out of here?'

'Unlikely. For now anyway. I've a friend who may be able to persuade them to let you go. And after the hearing there won't be much point in keeping you.'

'It's how they plan to get rid of me that I'm worried about.'

Benny stood up. 'There is something *you* can do for *me*,' she said.

Nicholas looked surprised. 'Oh?'

'You may have more time to think things through. So give

some thought to this.' Benny quickly described the problems she had run into getting copies of documents.

'So?' Nicholas asked when she had finished.

'So, I don't think the Knights of Jeneve were wiped out at Bocaro.'

'What?'

'I think the order survived and that they're still around. I think they're deliberately covering their tracks.'

The door squealed open again.

Nicholas was staring at the table and shaking his head. 'No, no you're wrong, Benny.'

'Am I?' The guard was gesturing for her to leave. 'Think about it.'

'No,' he said again. 'Don't waste time on that, Benny. Believe me, you have to be wrong.'

If Nicholas said anything else, the closing door cut it off. There was something in his voice that had not been there earlier. He had been worried, anxious, as they spoke. But what Benny could hear in his voice as the door closed she took for incredulity. It was on the shuttle, returning to the expedition ship, that it occurred to Benny that it might be fear.

The first problem, perhaps predictably, was that they would not let Benny have the Dragon. At least, she could examine it – in fact as the expedition's archaeological expert she was expected and encouraged to do so. But she knew there was no way that the commander or Kamadrich would let the Dragon out of the strongroom. If the commander had his way, it would have been on the cruiser under heavy guard. As it was, Kamadrich had managed to have the Dragon kept in the strongroom on the expedition ship, with a single trooper on the door and Kamadrich and the commander in possession of the only keys.

So, Benny set up her equipment in the strongroom. It was rather cramped, and the guard insisted on standing inside the room to watch.

'I'm not going to escape out of a window with it, you know,' Benny told him. He didn't smile, and he didn't move. So she gave him a bundle of cables to hold and worked round him.

Once Benny thought it through, it really was not much of an inconvenience. All she needed was a three-dimensional model of the Dragon, like the model she had already made of the other two Dragons, and then she could compare the models. With three sets of data, she could begin to decide how best to present her case. The trick was to start off as if she was endorsing Nusek's claims, and get so far before anyone realized otherwise that they could not stop her.

An hour later, armed with an optical disc, Benny returned to her cabin. 'Just tidy up when you're done,' she told the guard without a trace of a smile as she left. As she locked her cabin door she could imagine him still standing, cables in hand, wondering where best to start to sort through the Heath Robinson arrangement of baffles, lasers and power amplifiers.

Feeding the disc into her console, Benny was in buoyant mood. She had the evidence. All she needed to do now was to present it. And she reckoned if anyone could talk their way out of Nusek's machinations then Bernice Summerfield was that someone. She whistled a popular tune from the late twentieth century as she set up the projection fields and watched three Gamalian Dragons shimmer into existence round her room. A few adjustments, and the images floated towards one side of the room, merging, coalescing, becoming one.

Benny sat back and looked at her handiwork. A single composite Dragon turning slowly in the space above her bed. She clapped her hands together, and walked round it. Then she dived through the image on to her bed, turning on to her back so she could see the Dragon again. The wing tips were perfectly aligned, the tongue a single fork of fire licking out of the blur of the mouth, the tail curling and rippling behind the creature.

Blur.

Ripple.

Benny leapt from the bed and stared at the hologram from inches away. The mouth was blurred. Just very slightly. And the tail was rippling, the scales shimmering as the models interacted and set up an interference pattern where they did not perfectly match.

She swore, considered, and swore again. Then Benny scrambled for the console. She punched up a series of readings, measurements, proportions. Three columns of figures scrolled slowly past her finger as she traced the line between them. The first two matched exactly, but she knew that. They were the readings for the Dragon she had found on Dellah and the one she had switched it with in Nusek's archive.

But the figures in the third column were slightly different. Very slightly, sometimes by a few microns, sometimes as much as a millimetre. But the amount did not matter – they were not identical. That was enough.

She slumped back on to the bed, and stared at the Dragon revolving above her. Her mind was racing, working through the possibilities. But there was only one that fitted.

The two Dragons Benny had modelled first had matched exactly. But the third, the Dragon found on Stanturus, did not. And that could only mean one thing. Benny and Nicholas had been wrong. The Dragon, the original Gamalian Dragon, had not been removed from the archives, copied, then put back. Two copies had been made, and *one of the copies* had been returned to the archives. The reason that two dragons matched exactly was simple. They had both been made by the same laser sculpting system working from the same three-dimensional model. And the model was not perfect, either because of time or inaccuracies inherent in the system, or the margin of error within the laser system.

What it boiled down to was that Benny had one of the copies, and the other was in Nusek's archives. The Dragon sitting in the middle of a contortion of equipment in the strongroom was the original Gamalian Dragon, removed from the archives and 'found' on Stanturus Three. And since the dragon found of Stanturus Three really was the genuine, original Gamalian Dragon, Benny's plan to prove it was a fake was doomed to failure from the start.

So she lay on her bed, and stared at the holographic image slowly rotating above her head. Its eyes sparkled as they caught a light source that was no longer there, making it seem as if the Dragon were smiling, mocking. 'I want to go home,' she said to it eventually.

They were close enough for a real-time video link. Nusek and Webbe were in Nusek's study. Mastrov's face floated above the desk. The holographic audio imaging was slightly distorted so that the voice came disconcertingly from slightly above and behind the face.

'So, Summerfield wishes to return home, back to the university.' Webbe respected Mastrov, but that respect did not extend to liking and the disdain was barely hidden in his voice. 'You are passing relatively close to Dellah, and she has already agreed to attend the hearing next week. So what's the problem?'

'Perhaps nothing.' There was no emotion in Mastrov's reply. 'But her manner has been changed. Since she examined the Dragon she has been quiet, reserved. Hardly ventured out of her cabin, eaten little but drunk much.'

'What do you suggest?' Nusek asked.

'There is a possibility she will not cooperate. I suggest we eliminate that possibility.'

'We need an independent witness,' Webbe said quietly.

Nusek raised his hand. 'We still have Clyde. There is no evidence to directly link him to the explosion. And the fact that he was there, that he survived, may even strengthen his evidence.'

Mastrov nodded. 'A brave man, almost killed in his determination to bring us the historical truth of these momentous findings.'

Nusek smiled. 'Indeed.'

'And Summerfield?'

Nusek sat back, hands resting on the desk, fingertips touching. 'I think perhaps you should also go to Dellah, Mastrov. We cannot have a suspicious death on the ship. But an accident at the university, an independent witness who everyone knows was there on Stanturus Three when the Dragon was found and who was about to endorse the findings there . . .' He opened his hands by way of completing the thought. 'Sad news for the chairman of the hearing to bring before us all when it opens. Sad indeed.'

Webbe coughed, breaking in on the moment. 'Do we yet have a chairman for the hearing?'

'Indeed. I received the signal of acceptance this morning. Someone with considerable skill and experience in these matters, it seems. Someone above reproach who will be respected and listened to by all parties. His very presence will endow the proceedings with an aura of respectability and a sense of occasion.' Nusek smiled, looking from Webbe to Mastrov's floating face. 'The perfect candidate, by all accounts.'

Benny was surprised they had agreed to let her go home. She was less surprised that they had put her on the slowest, most outdated shuttle on the cruiser. A carrier pigeon with a broken wing could probably get there quicker. She was cross that she had not been permitted to see Nicholas again, and angry at herself that she was running away. She tried to rationalize it as going home to think things through, to talk to Braxiatel about what to do next. But in truth she was running away, and if she attended the hearing the following week on a station in neutral space, she had no idea what she would say. Probably she would agree with anything Kamadrich said, and hope that Nusek would simply let Nicholas go afterwards. He had no reason to hang on to him after all.

Benny sat in a window seat in the small cabin. The shuttle could seat twenty, but there were just herself and the flight crew – a pilot and navigator.

'Not long now, Professor,' the navigator's voice was echoed and distorted by the speakers. 'Just waiting for our other passenger to board.'

At that moment, the main door swung open with a hiss, and a figure stepped into the shuttle. He was carrying a small bag, and looked around as if embarrassed. Benny shrank down in her seat and stared out of the porthole at the wall of the docking bay, hoping futilely that he would not see her. The seat moved slightly as he sat down next to her.

'Jolly good idea, going back to Dellah for a few days before this hearing thing,' Gilder said. 'It's been a pretty hectic few weeks, and I expect there's lots of work piling up back at the university.' He shuffled in his seat in an effort to get comfortable. His bag was hugged to his chest, chin resting on it so it seemed as if his whole head had been removed and placed on top. 'I expect you'll have lots of marking and mail to catch up on.'

Benny said nothing. This was going to be an even longer journey than she had anticipated.

Knight Visitor

Benny watched the last of her credit tick away on the readout in the public-access booth at the spaceport. It was raining outside – it was *always* raining outside – as she stared unseeing through the large window and across the levelled landscape of Dellah. The sun was inching its way down over the brown tops of the university buildings, reflecting off the glass of the Theatrology complex and drenching the tall needle of the control tower. The rain, meanwhile, was drenching the spaceport workers as they readied a shuttle just outside.

Braxiatel was not answering, so she accepted the mail system's husky suggestion that she leave him a message. She kept it short to make sure he got it: 'Hi, it's Benny. I'm back. Call me.' If her credit ran out she was not sure what would happen to it. It might get erased, which would be bad enough. Worse still, they might want Braxiatel to pay for it, which would not reflect well on Benny at a time when she was counting on his help and advice more than ever.

It occurred to Benny on her way back to her rooms that Braxiatel might be away. This did little to cheer her up. She had been forced to accept a ride with Gilder back to the Archaeology Department, since she could not afford any other means of travel and it was too far to walk. Having listened to his oily explanations of how much he was helping to organize the university on the long shuttle journey, she reckoned she could cope with an hour skimming through the rain between islands. If he thought he was doing her a favour, and that she was diligently going to check her mail and messages at the department, that was his problem. One thing she definitely did not want was Gilder's financial advice, however good it might actually be. So she could not admit her lack of funds, and played along with his workaholic fantasy. They rode in the lift together to the third floor where Benny's office and seminar room was located, and she made a great show of heading towards it. Gilder continued in the lift.

It was quite late in the evening by now, and the place was deserted. Having got this far, Benny did indeed check her messages, not least to allow the rain time to abate. She had only two messages of any interest aside from the usual department notices and reminders. One was a final demand for payment, and the other a circular to everyone on a list of people interested in the feeding habits of Mitsushan Quantoctresses which Benny had been put on by mistake. She hoped.

By the time Benny had finished, the rain had got worse. She made her way back to the main entrance, finding some little comfort in the memory that her bicycle was still parked outside and some little solace in the fact that it did not appear to have been stolen or vandalized. She checked quickly that nobody had coated the seat with contact adhesive (once was enough), wiped it dry with a grubby hanky, hitched her heavy rucksack higher up her back, and set off.

The light was worrying for its financial implications rather than anything else. Benny, after all, had nothing to steal. And she was quite prepared to believe that she had left the light on. It would be typical of her porter, Joseph, to have assumed she did it deliberately and not switched it off. It would not be drawing much power, but at the moment every shilling counted and she was not sure how the direct-debit system for the power usage worked. It might be debiting as she used it rather than at periodic intervals. The last thing Benny needed right now, she decided as she threw open the door to her rooms and strode in, was to have her power cut off.

A somewhat hasty assessment, she decided a moment later. The initial relief at seeing her familiar rooms, lined with books floor to ceiling and covered in pizza boxes, dirty mugs and various discarded articles of clothing wall to wall, was dispelled by the sight out of the corner of her eye of the dark figure stepping from behind the door. No, Benny decided as she made a tired, half-hearted and unsuccessful attempt to avoid the heavy blow that was crashing down on her head, *this* was the last thing she needed.

She was already losing consciousness as she rolled on to her back and stared up at her attacker. The figure was dressed completely in black, with a blast helmet concealing its face. It was holding a hand blaster, and pointing it at Benny's head. There was a click that might have been the door closing or opening, or it might have been first pressure on the trigger. Then everything went blurred and faded into darkness.

'It's good to have you back.'

Benny rubbed her temples and blinked a lot. It felt as though Symon Dextro's Tom-Tom Ensemble had decamped from their usual venue at Cordelia's and taken to practising inside her head. 'Do you mean back on Dellah, or back in the land of the living?' she asked between drum rolls.

Braxiatel laughed and handed her the wet cloth he had been using to bathe her forehead. 'Both, I suppose. Though I second your suggestion that Dellah and the land of the living may be two entirely different places.'

Benny spent some time trying to wipe her headache away before giving up and dropping the cloth. She was lying on her bed, and she guessed Braxiatel had carried her through from the living room.

Braxiatel was sitting on a chair beside the bed. The accumulated detritus that had previously all but hidden the chair was carefully arranged on the floor, exactly as it had been on the chair, presumably so that Benny could put it back just as she liked it. Braxiatel was tinkering with two white hemispheres, poking inside one with a tiny screwdriver. He looked up, and saw Benny watching him.

'Your porter,' he explained. 'I'll soon have him fixed for you.'

'Thanks.'

'Seems simple enough. Bit too simple perhaps.' He smiled suddenly and brilliantly. 'Would you like me to tweak the personality circuits a bit? They don't seem to be at the optimal setting for you.'

'Like Agent Mike was, you mean?' Benny considered. 'No,' she decided. 'I dislike Joseph just as he is.'

'Fair enough. A little personality clash does lend a certain frisson to an otherwise bald and undemanding relationship. Sorry about the window, by the way. Not my forte. You probably need a glazier for that. And your cat ran off when he saw me.'

Benny sat up, and immediately wished she hadn't. 'Look, you'd better tell me what's going on.'

'Well, I got your message. So I came over. When I got here, the outside door was open. And you were lying on the floor in there with a blaster at your head. The owner of said blaster took one look at me and took off. Through the window.' He placed the two halves of the sphere together and twisted them. 'There, that should do it.' The sphere lifted hesitantly into the air, groaned, and wobbled off towards the door. 'He'll be all right after a good lie down. Or whatever.'

'I know how he feels.' Benny swung her legs off the bed. 'I need coffee. Who was it, by the way? I mean who hit me?'

Braxiatel followed her through to the kitchen. 'Don't know, didn't get round to introductions. Very rude. Someone who knows how to take out a porter, though – single blaster shot with no collateral damage.'

'You mean they didn't hit anything else.'

'I mean they're a very good shot.'

Benny rummaged in the back of a cupboard, and eventually came out with a bag of coffee beans. 'Knew they were in there somewhere,' she said. 'Will Joseph remember who shot him?'

135

'Perhaps. But I doubt if he saw anything more useful than we did. How do you ever find anything in here?'

Benny smiled. 'Practice,' she said. 'Or panic.'

Braxiatel declined the coffee, making himself a cup of tea instead. They sat at the table in the lounge, and Benny went through everything that had happened on her trip. Much of it Braxiatel already knew from her infrequent messages. But he made her go through it all again in as much detail as she could remember. Talking seemed to help her head recover, so Benny was happy to oblige. Also, it was good to have such an attentive listener, and one who did not comment or condemn. He just listened, occasionally nodded, occasionally asked for a clarification. By the time Benny neared the end of her account, it was dawn.

She finished with her conclusion that the Knights of Jeneve were still very much in existence. She expected this to get some sort of reaction, especially after Nicholas's. She was disappointed. Braxiatel nodded again without speaking.

'Oh, come on,' said Benny. 'I think as deductions go that demands some comment.'

'Indeed.' Braxiatel stood up and walked to the window. There was a breeze coming through the broken glass, ruffling his hair as he stood with his hands behind his back looking out at the next building. 'I reached much the same conclusion myself a little while ago. It does indeed explain a lot of the peripheral activities we have both observed.' He turned back towards Benny. 'Let me make some breakfast, and then I'll tell you what I have discovered and surmised.'

'OK.'

'And while I do that –' he reached inside his jacket pocket and drew out a plain white envelope '– this is for you.'

Benny took the envelope. Her name was printed on the front. 'From you?' she asked, surprised.

'In a way, I suppose. It's your formal invitation and summons to attend the Inquiry into the Findings and Discoveries on Stanturus Three. Delivered by hand, for no very good reason other than I knew I would be seeing you.'

'But –' Benny was confused '– how did you get it?'

'Mmm?' Braxiatel was almost at the kitchen door. 'Oh, sorry didn't I tell you? I'm the independent chairman and chief arbiter for the hearing.'

'You must have pulled some strings for this,' Benny said, waving the invitation when Braxiatel returned. He was carrying a tray with fresh tea and coffee and some croissants that Benny could not believe he had just found in her kitchen and was unwilling to credit him with having baked himself. Probably Joseph was in an obliging mood.

'Maybe a few. Short ones,' he conceded.

'Short and curly, knowing you.'

He adopted a hurt expression. 'Please. All I did was have my name mentioned in the right places. I do, after all, have some considerable experience in chairing all sorts of things. Some much more delicate than this, I can tell you. And since I'm also a renowned expert in –' He broke off as if searching for the right word or phrase. 'In things,' he eventually went on, 'I was an obvious choice.' He beamed at Benny and poured her coffee. 'The leading players, as it were, also trust me as an independent arbiter.'

'You mean the warlords? Trust you?'

'Well,' he said as he raised his teacup to her, 'maybe they're a little wary of me too.'

This was certainly plausible. If they knew anything about him, Benny decided, the warlords were probably scared witless of Braxiatel. Those who had wits. And those who didn't would have something that sounded very similar.

Braxiatel finished his tea and started on a croissant. As he ate he told Benny about his own findings and suspicions, tying them in to her own story and theories in a way that impressed her almost as much as the way he managed to eat a croissant without leaving flakes of it all over the plate and table.

'Newark Rappare was coming to see me when he was killed,' Braxiatel explained. 'I don't know, but I think he wanted to trade the second Dragon for an escape route and money. He must have known my reputation as a collector and reasoned that I would be interested in his offer.'

'So he secretly made a second copy.'

'Exactly. It was his insurance. He knew, or suspected, that whatever the copy was for he knew too much. Either that or he wanted to move on. He had quite a reputation of his own for copying artefacts and antiques. His studio is very impressive, you know.'

'Really?' Benny was not terribly interested.

'There was a bit of a mess on the floor when I looked round. Probably the mould, the plasticrete surround that the lasers gouged the Dragon copy from. I'd guess he destroyed the other one himself, or hid it away.'

They discussed Rappare's skills as a forger for a while. His real artistry had been in his knowledge and understanding of the materials to use and how to make them appear aged to the right degree.

'So what about the Knights, then?' Benny asked. 'You said you had concluded the order still exists as well.'

'Indeed. I made some inquiries about the Dragon, and put together that data for you as well. But even doing that I sensed I was being sidelined at times.'

'I know the feeling.'

'So I pushed a bit further on things, called in some favours, aroused some interest.'

'And?'

'And yesterday morning I had a message from someone who claims to be the Grand Master of the Order of Jeneve. He felt we should exchange information.'

'Really?' Benny was leaning across the table, croissant flakes sticking to her jumper and coffee mug clutched between her palms.

'They've been meaning to get in touch for a while now, apparently. Like me, they are collectors of knowledge, though he would divulge little more than that. I explained what was happening here, about Nusek and the various Dragons. Of course he knew about the discovery on Stanturus Three, as does everyone else. I think that more than anything triggered his call.'

'So what happens next?'

Braxiatel pulled out a pocket watch. 'There is a representative of the Order of Jeneve here on Dellah. At the university, in fact. He has been briefed by his superiors and is empowered to divulge to us the true nature of the Gamalian Dragon.'

'The true nature?'

Braxiatel shrugged. 'Their words, not mine. Ask him yourself.'

'What? Where? When?'

'About the Dragon. Here. In about ten minutes.'

Benny stared at him. 'You're serious, aren't you?' Braxiatel stared back. 'Yes, of course you are.' Benny drained the remains of her coffee. 'I need a shower.'

Braxiatel busied himself looking through Benny's bookshelves. Benny sat on the sofa, hands clutched together in her lap, feeling as if she were waiting for a time bomb to go off.

'He's late.'

Braxiatel answered without turning. 'Perhaps he took offence at my leaving him a message to come here. It is raining, after all, and he'll have just traipsed all the way over to Theatrology.'

Before Benny could answer, the door clicked open. A figure stood silhouetted on the threshold, the rain running off his broad-brimmed hat. A cape swirled round him in the draught from the broken window blowing out through the open door. He was carrying a briefcase. As the man stepped into the room, he pulled off his hat, shaking the water off outside the door behind him. Then he turned, and Benny saw his face for the first time.

'You!' she exclaimed.

'Professor Summerfield. How nice to see you again.' His voice was rich and cultured, his eyes alive with interest. He stepped forward, discarding his cape, which Benny could now see was a water-retardant academic gown. 'And you must be –'

'Irving Braxiatel.'

'Splendid. Excellent.' The man held out his hand. 'Dr Archduke. I specialize in Obscure Theatrical Forms, albeit under the auspices of the Literary Department rather than your own excellent establishment.'

'Indeed.' Braxiatel sat down and motioned for Archduke and Benny to do likewise. 'That must have been something of a disappointment for you, given that I imagine the only reason for your so-called specialization was to meet me.'

Archduke's manner changed in an instant. The façade of bonhomie and academic bluster was peeled away like a mask. 'It seems you are indeed as informed and intelligent as I was told. I apologize for having taken so long to make your acquaintance, but certain other matters have warranted my attention since I arrived here. May I ask, as a matter of interest, why you rejected my application to join your department? Did you even then suspect my true motives?'

'No. My own motive was a little more mundane. I read some of your papers.'

'So did I,' Benny put in, anxious not to get excluded from the conversation. 'The pantomime paper was quite an experience.'

Braxiatel snorted. 'A case in point, if I may say so. Anyone who can write about the development of pantomime without making comparisons with the anarchic societies of today which mirror some of its internal philosophy, or even mentioning the Comedia Del'Arte in which it has its Earthly roots, would be misplaced in a Theatrology Department.' He paused for an instant, then added, 'Oh yes they would.'

Archduke shuffled uncomfortably. 'Er, yes, well. Um.'

'Tell us,' Benny suggested, 'about the Knights of Jeneve.'

Archduke rallied to this subject. 'I can tell you a little, yes. I am only a relatively lowly member of the esteemed order, and I know little more than I am empowered to tell. And what I can tell you relates directly to the so-called Gamalian

Dragon. But first, I need to explain a little of the background to the Order of Jeneve.'

Benny listened carefully, oblivious to the wind blowing through her broken window or the rain outside. She wished that Nicholas were with her to hear the story, but she put her disappointment and anger to the back of her mind, and listened to Archduke.

'The Knights of Jeneve is a learned military brotherhood set up over three hundred years ago in the third quarter of the twenty-third century. As human-controlled space began to recover from its first bout of interstellar wars, then Vazlov Baygent became the President of Earth.

'Baygent is best remembered, as you know, for attempting to ensure that the presidency became an hereditary rather than elected position. He failed, despite being an immensely charismatic and popular leader, but only because he was assassinated in 2276 before he could make his wishes law.

'Baygent was extremely astute as well as ambitious. He predicted that Earth and her colonies and expanding "empire" would be involved in further, more debilitating, wars and conflicts. He foresaw a time when humanity would slip back into a dark age of war and loss of knowledge, and he determined to plan for this time. In secret, he established a set of databases that would eventually be filled with all knowledge – scientific, cultural, literary, artistic. Everything. He entrusted its completion and protection to an existing scientific-military organization which was at once seen as independent yet tied to the political powers. Baygent rechartered and renamed it the Knights of Geneva. This was corrupted over the years until the surviving legends and text spoke variously of the Knights of Geneve, with a G, or Jeneve, with a J.

'All the Knights were fiercely loyal to Baygent and embarked on their new mission with enthusiasm. When Baygent was assassinated, the Knights protected Baygent's young son and made it their personal crusade to find and destroy those responsible for the president's death. They achieved that objective with frightening speed and efficiency.' Archduke paused, as if unsure whether he should continue.

'But I digress,' he said after a while. 'As Baygent had feared, the wars have indeed come again and humanity has been plunged headlong into a new dark age. Throughout this dark time, the Knights of Jeneve have striven to keep humanity's great knowledge intact and hidden.'

He sat back, as if waiting for applause. Benny looked at Braxiatel.

'This explains a lot,' Braxiatel said at length. 'And it is very interesting. I'm not sure I entirely appreciate why the knowledge must be hidden.' He held up his hand to prevent Archduke from interrupting. 'I know there is much you are not telling us, and some of it I think we can deduce for ourselves. But what you have told us so far, while it explains why you wanted to contact me, does not seem directly relevant to the matters in hand.'

'We collect information from wherever we can,' Archduke said. 'Which is indeed why we were interested in making contact with yourself. It is also,' he said, turning to Benny, 'why we tolerate, why we have to tolerate and indeed encourage, pirates like the Grel.'

'And the Gamalian Dragon?' Benny asked.

Archduke nodded. 'May I see it?' he asked. 'Or at least the copy of it that I am told you have in your possession.'

Archduke turned the Dragon over in his hands, caressing the body and wings. Then he turned it to face him, and peered into the Dragon's eyes. He rubbed at one with the end of his forefinger, a delicate motion as if wiping a tear from his own eye. Then he squinted at the result. The Dragon stared back impassively. After a moment, he handed it back to Benny. 'Exquisite. And, as you are aware, a fake.'

'How can you tell?'

Archduke did not answer. He lifted his briefcase on to his lap and opened it. From inside he took a sheaf of papers, and handed them to Benny. 'These are the original construction drawings for the Dragon. Blueprints.'

'Blueprints? But why would anyone have blueprints for a statue, for a work of art?'

'More suppositions,' Braxiatel said as Benny smoothed the papers out on the table. 'I suspect that the Dragon was never intended merely as a piece of statuary. It had a purpose, a very definite purpose.' He turned to Archduke. 'Am I right?' he demanded.

'Alas,' Archduke said as he spread his hands and shook his head, 'I can say no more.' But he was smiling, as if encouraging a child. For Benny's money, patronizing Braxiatel did not seem a particularly good move.

'A purpose,' Braxiatel continued as if Archduke had not replied at all, 'linked to the fact that Gamaliel never won the Battle of Bocaro at all.'

Archduke gasped. The smile was gone from his face.

'What?' asked Benny in amazement. 'But then how did he get the Dragon?'

'I've looked at the data, replayed the scenario on the Strategic Institute's battle simulators several times in the last weeks,' Braxiatel said. 'Everyone assumes that Gamaliel was more clever than them, that he was a better strategist. But I started from the advantageous position of believing that could not be the case. And our friend's reaction to my comment rather confirms my suspicions. Gamaliel did not win at Bocaro – so few troops against so many, an untenable position, a battle he was forced into without adequate preparation or equipment.'

'But what about the Gamalian Gambit, or whatever it's called?'

'A myth, an invention. Disinformation from the very people who claim to hold it in such esteem.' Braxiatel shook his head. 'Gamaliel didn't win. The Knights of Jeneve lost the battle. Deliberately.'

'But why?'

Braxiatel nodded to Archduke. 'Tell her,' he said.

Archduke sighed. 'So that the Knights could continue unhindered while everyone thought they had been destroyed.

So that Gamaliel would start his crusade.' He paused, looked to Braxiatel, but got no reaction. 'And so that Gamaliel would have the Dragon.'

'Why?' Benny asked again. It was fast becoming her favourite word.

Archduke stood up. 'I have outstayed my welcome,' he said. 'I should go.'

Benny saw him to the door, and helped him into his cape. He shook her hand before he left, holding it for a moment longer than necessary.

'As I told you when we first met, knowledge above all,' he said as if this were an explanation for everything. 'Knowledge above all.' Then he stepped out into the rain and was gone.

DEATH IN THE NIGHT

There was, as Mappin Gilder had anticipated, an awful lot to catch up on. He had not spent much time on it the previous evening despite his good intentions. The next round of department budgetary negotiations were due to start in a week or so, and there was some paperwork associated with a couple of students who were scheduled to arrive late for this term.

It was getting late. He had spent all of the morning at work, and it was a half-day for the department, so the building was practically empty. He rubbed his eyes, checked the time again and decided that enough was enough.

Numbers were Gilder's first love. He liked the beautiful way they fitted together, the way that you could create patterns out of numerals, could see mathematical progressions in a sequence of sums. Helen's beauty in a balance sheet. It had taken him a while to find anything at all to interest or involve him in the recent expedition. The way the scanning equipment worked, the mathematics behind it, had been his only compensation for an otherwise devastatingly boring time. He was glad to be back at work. Real work.

But he also felt some guilt still at what had happened. He had made the scanner his own toy, his mission. And he had made a mistake. There had been some sort of accident, true, but he still felt the guilt. He should have realized the signature patterns did not match the situation, that he was measuring something else. But he had not, and Summerfield had been injured as a result.

There was no way that Gilder could apologize. For one thing he did not know how. He had no experience. But he had seen her at work, had seen that she found the same fascination in archaeology as he found in numbers. And he had at least begun to appreciate how she felt about her work. As he locked his office door, Gilder found himself wondering if Bernice was in her office. Perhaps she too would be catching up on her budgets and balances, or marking whatever it was that she marked. Perhaps he should check. Perhaps invite her out for a coffee, discuss the acquisitions budget and the expenses from the expedition. Perhaps . . .

Without having made any conscious decision, Gilder found that the lift stopped at the floor where Benny's office was located. She had been so polite on the shuttle trip, after all. And she had gladly accepted a lift with him back to the university, eschewing the moving pavements and underground speed pavements, flyers and the carrier tunnels (so economical). Yes, he would ask her if she had any comment on the latest round of corporate results and the recovery of the galactic stock exchange.

There was movement along the corridor. A door opening in the gloom of the dim light as the building conserved power for the half-day (a cost-saving suggestion of Gilder's own). Was it? Yes, it was Professor Summerfield's office. The door was open, the light clicked off, the female form silhouetted in the doorway as she stepped into the corridor. The figure turned towards Gilder. And froze.

Gilder was surprised. 'Oh, I thought you were Prof– er, Bernice.' He looked past her to the office door, now closed. 'Is she with you?'

'No.' Her voice was as silky as ever. 'No, she's not.'

Gilder nodded, for all the world as if he had expected this. Then he frowned. 'Then what were you doing in her office?' Another thought occurred to him. 'And why are you here? I thought you were going back to Tharn for the debriefing before next week's hearings.'

She stepped forward. 'A slight change of plan. I needed to

see Professor Summerfield. Some things to check.' She was almost standing on his toes now. They were eye to eye. 'A problem to eliminate.'

Gilder fancied he could hear the clicking of gears as he stared into her eyes. He peered closer. There seemed to be something moving within her eyes: tiny text – and numbers – streaming in reverse across the iris, right to left.

'Several problems,' she breathed, and he was aware that despite their proximity and the fact that he could hear the sound of her breath, he could not feel or smell it.

A smile switched on across her face, framed by the blonde hair, not quite reaching her digital eyes. Her hand ran down his cheek, and Gilder stood rooted to the spot. He tried to clear his throat, out of embarrassment. Then in pain as the hand gripped it. The smile was fixed in position as she squeezed.

Her face went red first, then her hair. Then the world. And Gilder felt himself slipping to the floor, half supported by her hand still fixed to his throat.

One thing that Benny had definitely missed was a decent pint of beer. So it was not a difficult choice to leave Braxiatel to pore over the diagrams and blueprints that Archduke had provided and make for the bar for a little rest and recuperation. She was not surprised to find several of her students in the bar.

Polybus Arex and Anne-Marie Rose were arguing at a table while Marjorie Marjorie tried in vain to mediate. Benny joined them, accepted Polybus's offer of a drink, and avoided their questions about her expedition as best she could by pleading that it was *sub judice* until after the hearing.

Benny saw her across the bar. She stood out for several reasons. First, she was not drunk. Second, she was standing absolutely still, turning only her head as if scanning the bar for someone or something in particular. Third, Truby Kamadrich was the sort of person who stood out wherever she was. Benny waved almost before her surprise registered. Kamadrich waved back and headed across the crowded room.

Benny excused herself from the others and met Kamadrich halfway. They grabbed a table as it became empty, and Benny wiped some of the spilt beer from its stained surface with the back of her hand.

'Hey, what are you doing here? Can I buy you a drink?'

Kamadrich declined the drink. 'I wanted to see you. Before the hearing,' she said. 'I think you have things you want to say.'

Benny regarded Kamadrich through a beery haze. 'Yeah. Yeah, I do.' She took another swig of her pint. 'How's Nicholas?'

'He's fine.' Kamadrich locked her gaze on Benny. Her eyes were very wide, very alert. They seemed almost to be moving inside. 'They're trying to kill me, Benny,' she said quietly, looking away. 'I wasn't sure at first. But then, on the cruiser . . .' She shuddered as her voice tailed off. Then she seemed to pull herself together. Her hands were clasped together on the damp table in front of her as she leant forward. 'I want you to get a fair hearing, Benny. If there is something, anything, not above board here then we need to root it out. We need to expose Nusek for what he is, denounce him if there's any hint of foul play.'

Benny nodded. 'Foul play. Right. I'll say.' She leant forward too, her own elbows in the beer on the table top. She told Kamadrich about the attack, about how someone had actually tried to kill her, here on Dellah. In her own rooms. Kamadrich nodded attentively, as if reliving her own experiences through Benny's words.

She considered telling Kamadrich about the Knights of Jeneve and about what Braxiatel had discovered. But the bar was crowded, and they were having to shout to each other anyway. So instead Benny agreed immediately when Kamadrich suggested they go back to Benny's rooms and talk things through properly.

The night air had a distinctly sobering effect. It was drizzling, the rain spotting into the puddles left from the earlier downpour. By the time they reached Benny's rooms, she reckoned she was fully recovered from the effects of the beer and ready for a large burger. Except she was also sober enough to know she couldn't afford one. So she decided to settle for coffee instead.

'So tell me all about it,' Kamadrich said as they arrived. She did not comment on the state of the apartment, or on the broken window.

'Mmm,' Benny said, wondering where to start.

Kamadrich seemed to mistake this for inebriation. 'Why don't you put on some music?' she suggested quietly. 'Some of that jazz you're fond of, perhaps?'

Benny nodded, but said nothing. If Kamadrich thought she was drunk that might be all to the good. She needed to think through some things. There was something here that was not quite right. Something . . .

'Shall I make some coffee?' Kamadrich asked when Benny still said nothing.

Benny grinned. 'Yes, do. Coffee. Great. Black, please.'

Kamadrich looked at her for several seconds, then nodded and headed for the kitchen.

Benny was feeling considerably more with it when Kamadrich returned. The smell of the coffee revived her still more, which was good because Benny knew as soon as Kamadrich brought it that she would not be drinking any.

'So,' said Kamadrich, voice silky-sweet and coffee untouched on the table beside her, 'tell me all about it.'

'It was the accidents, I suppose,' Benny said. 'That's when I knew there was someone on the expedition who was sabotaging things. Trying to kill us, perhaps. Nicholas was less convinced, thought I was paranoid.'

Kamadrich nodded seriously, attentive.

'Then there was the business with the scanner and the rat things. That's when I was sure it was Gilder. But I didn't know if he was doing it out of spite, so the department could get the insurance money, or because he was somehow involved with Nusek already. He's the new boy here, and I don't know what he did or who he did it for before he arrived.' Benny picked up her coffee mug, looked down into the steam. Smiled at her foggy reflection on the surface of the liquid. 'Just shows how wrong you can be, doesn't it.'

'Oh?'

'The jazz – well that might be a good guess. Or excellent eyesight.'

'My eyesight is better than excellent.'

'I bet. But the coffee was the clincher. Nobody knows where to find the coffee in this place. It's the most important thing, and so it's the best hidden. So you must have been here before and had a good search through everything. Very professional, very careful. But nobody just finds the coffee. Even –' Benny stopped. 'No. No, I won't tell you anything you don't already know. After all, that's what all this is about, isn't it?'

'Is it?'

'I wondered why you seemed so young.'

'Jealousy?'

Benny laughed. 'No. Well, in a way I suppose. So accomplished yet apparently so young. But now I know.'

'I'm not as young as I seem.'

'Or as accomplished.' Benny was still staring into the coffee, looking for answers in its dark depths. 'Truby Kamadrich is probably so old she doesn't get out much these days.'

'She doesn't get out at all now.' Kamadrich was standing beside Benny.

Still Benny did not move. She did not seem to hear Kamadrich or register her presence. 'I guess a good archaeologist would have known that. Not that anyone else here picked up on it. Too busy seeing shillings in their eyes.'

'But we didn't want a good archaeologist.'

'No. No you didn't.' Benny looked up at Kamadrich at last. Her face was twisted into a sneer and she could feel the hate rising in her gut. 'And you know what? More than anything else in this whole miserable bloody business, that's what really pisses me off.'

And with that, Benny stood up. As Kamadrich's hands reached out, Benny flung the steaming coffee at her.

The dark liquid hit Kamadrich full in the face. Benny did not wait to see the effect: she was already diving for the broken window, rolling as she hit the ground, up and running, arms working, feet pounding, brain racing, blood pumping.

It took only seconds for her to isolate the pain and desensitize the area. The woman who was not Truby Kamadrich blinked the coffee from her eyes and swung round. Summerfield was gone, through the window. Her heat traces were indistinct, the hot coffee making the whole picture a livid orange. Temperature and humidity readings were edging off the top of the scale, but they would soon settle down. There was no permanent damage.

She leapt through the window after Benny, landing on her feet and setting off down the shallow incline along the edge of Goodyear College. It was dark, but the image-enhancers and heat-signature readout were working again. A probability program determined Benny's most likely course, and the sensors strained to pick up an image in that direction. All the while, she kept running.

The university was big, sprawled across islands, divided up and linked by walkways and bridges. But Kamadrich would not tire until she had found Benny. The same determination and energy that powered the cybernetic cryvoks in Nusek's palace had been enhanced tremendously before being put to work inside Mastrov's frame. A junction of the path, a split-second decision, no break of step. Somewhere in the distance a footfall in a puddle. The slap of boot on paving slab. The sounds of the quarry relayed through acoustic sensors which adjusted for atmospherics and weather conditions, peaked the wave form and filtered out static, fed the improved sound into Mastrov's brain and betrayed Benny's position to within a metre.

The Goll guards on duty at the black gates to the Advanced Research Department paid no attention to Mastrov's running figure, just as they had ignored Benny's hasty stumbling gait less than a minute earlier. By the time she reached Pierce College, Kamadrich could hear Benny's laboured breathing, could get a heat signature on her body – as distinctive as a DNA trace – as she staggered onward, could sense her breath on the moist breeze.

Kamadrich was walking now. Stalking. Enjoying the one-sided chase. Benny was expelling energy at an unsustainable rate. Collapse would follow shortly unless she rested. She saw no reason to expend her own power unnecessarily. And besides, it added to the fun.

A change of perspective. She paused. Benny was still moving, her speed constant, but energy loss, determined by body heat and estimated perspiration level, had flat-lined. She was in a vehicle of some sort. She broke into an easy run, long regular strides eating the ground between them.

A moving walkway, the connection between Pierce College and Prospero Plaza away over the water on the next island. She was close enough to see Benny turn, zoomed vision registering the widening of the eyes, measuring pupil dilation in the fading light as Benny saw her in the distance. Then Benny was off, running again along the pavement, pushing an Ootsoi out of the way, staggering into a Goll, leaping over a surprised Pakhar.

Kamadrich followed, forging a passage along the moving bridge with ease. The Goll turned to face her, its broad heavy body in her way, hand held up to stop the slim human woman. She kept going, didn't pause, briefly registered the impact, calculated the body weight and probable damage and bruising. The shouts and the splash were discarded as superfluous data.

Ahead, Benny had reached the backs of the buildings that faced on to Prospero Plaza. A collection of tubes and pipes hung from the side of one of the domed red-mud structures. Various pieces of Menlove Stokes's unfinished sculpture dangled free, blowing in the slight wind, jangling together as they moved. The cat's cradle of garish clashing colours reached up the whole side of the building, across the roof and down the other side. It resembled nothing so much as a clown's wig at the end of an eventful circus on a bad hair-day.

The assassin reached the base of the structure before Benny was halfway up. She paused to assess the best route to climb up after the woman, pulled at a tube and read off the tensile strength and weight tolerances. Then she started up the side of the building, hand over hand, easily and precisely, gaining on Benny with every movement.

They reached the top at almost the same moment. Benny turned, caught in the moment of grabbing a thin pipe that fell the length of the building, stretched across the Plaza below and attached to the glass splendour of the Theatrology Building opposite. But she had no time to climb down now. No time to devise a new plan. No time to seek an alternative escape route. No time.

Kamadrich walked across the roof towards her. The heat signature was flashing across her retina, the target sensors going wild as the kill range reduced to point-blank. Benny pulled a handkerchief from her pocket, every movement registered, recorded, analysed and rated for threat. Nil rating.

Time to intercept: 5 seconds. The 5 faded to a 4 to a 3. Kill-kill-kill flashed in scarlet across the bottom of her vision as she reached out to Benny, her face seen red through the countdown. Through the 2, the 1.

Zero.

BREAKING GLASS

Kamadrich, or whoever – whatever – she really was, crossed the roof of the building towards her. Benny felt in her pockets, vaguely hoping to find some weapon she knew was not there. But it was something to do while her mind desperately sought a course of action. It was only a matter of a few moments before the woman knocked Benny senseless, or shot her, or strangled her, or hurled her off the top of the building.

Benny pulled a handkerchief out of her pocket. She stared at it, and was about to drop it and start running round the top of the building screaming and shouting for help when an outrageous thought occurred to her. She pulled the hanky from the corners, testing its strength. It was made of Jeruxian linen, and if it could withstand the strength of a Jeruxian sneeze then Benny reckoned it was easily up to the task she had in mind.

Kamadrich reached out for Benny, who took a step backward. She felt her heels hit the low edging around the top of the building before it sloped away into the night. She swayed backward, slightly off balance, reaching forward to redistribute her weight, knocking Kamadrich's hand aside as she did so. She grabbed at the orange pipe that extended above her head, hanging down and across the walkway far below until it connected with the Theatrology building opposite.

Kamadrich smiled, a sudden twist of the mouth as if in

response to an instruction flashed from her brain to her face. She reached forward again.

Benny twisted round, looping the handkerchief over the pipe above her head. 'Bye,' she called, 'got to fly.' Her voice was louder than she had intended, strengthened by her fear. Then she grabbed the free end of the hanky with her spare hand, and leapt into space.

More by luck than planning, Benny was facing forward, so she could see the glass building rushing towards her. She put her head down, hoping to shield her face in the space between her outstretched arms. She wondered briefly what Kamadrich was doing on the rooftop above and behind her, then worried about what would happen when she hit the side of the Theatrology building. On balance, she decided, she would probably bounce off, fall the remaining thirty feet to the ground and break her neck on arrival.

The cold damp air was rushing past her, making Benny's ears sing. She risked a glance ahead, saw an expanse of glass rushing up to meet her, and instinctively let go of the hanky bringing her arms round to protect her face as she fell.

The hanky fluttered to the ground. Above it, Benny continued on her course like a projectile. She was curled into a ball, rolled forward into a crash dive, striking the large window dead centre. The noise was deafening as the window exploded into fragments. Benny hit the floor with a jolt, slivers of glass showering down on her. She lay motionless for a moment, listening to the screech of the intruder alarms. Then she heaved herself to her feet, dusting glass from her jumper and shaking it from her hair.

Outside, framed by the jagged glass remaining in place, Benny could see Kamadrich standing at the top of the building opposite looking down at her. Without waiting to see what the woman would do, Benny turned and ran. The floor crunched under her feet, and the sirens shrieked around her. She ran without knowing where she was going or what she would do when she got there. If she got there.

Benny was in a corridor, offices and seminar rooms either

side. She skidded round a corner, regained her balance and sprinted. The night lighting was no more than a red glow, the noise was deafening. Another corner, another turn, was she going round in circles? Where were the lifts? Benny looked round as she ran, searching for somewhere useful, somewhere to turn to escape from the infinite corridor. If she had not turned she would have seen the figure step out in front of her. As it was, the first clue she had that anyone was there was when she ran straight into him.

She struggled for a moment, but the strong arms held her tight, lifted her up slightly, and dumped her back on her feet.

'Is it you making all the noise?' Braxiatel asked.

'Er, yes,' Benny gasped, trying to catch her breath. She pointed back down the corridor. 'But I'm not sure I'm on my own yet.'

Braxiatel peered down the corridor. 'I don't see anyone. But best not to take any chances.' He turned. 'Come with me.'

The hole in the side of the massive building was relatively small, a black starburst in the otherwise moonlight-bright structure. The assassin watched for movement. She had seen Benny land inside and struggle to her feet. The building was almost deserted, only one other heat trace, so it was easy to track the target as she ran round the main corridor. The images met, and headed off in a new direction.

Still she waited. There was no point in following unless and until she had an idea where Benny was heading. Following down the pipe might not be the optimal route for interception. The heat signatures flared, flickered as they reached the far side of the building. Then suddenly they were gone. Kamadrich rechecked the readings, replayed the previous few seconds, ran a diagnostics program. But the traces were gone from the sensors.

She waited for an hour in case the signals were shielded by some structural anomaly of the building. But still there was nothing. Then she climbed down the tubular sculpture and headed for the spaceport. She had a shuttle waiting. If Bernice Summerfield was going to cause any trouble, it would have to be at the Stanturan Inquiry. And Kamadrich would be there, waiting for her.

Braxiatel had led Benny quickly through the Theatrology building to his study. On the way she had summarized her encounter with Kamadrich. 'I never expected the glass to break,' she finished breathlessly. She had to shout to make herself heard about the alarm siren.

'You were lucky,' Braxiatel told her unlocking his door. 'I only let Stokes put that pipe across because I thought it might come in handy. But to get out rather than in.'

'Is that why the glass broke?'

Braxiatel closed the door behind them, shutting out some of the noise of the siren. 'You were moving slowly enough to get through the osmotic shield. Anything as fast as a bullet or missile, say, would bounce off and activate the defences. It was designed to let someone out rather than in, of course.' He tapped a sequence into the numeric keypad by the door.

'And then you can climb up the pipe.'

'No. That would take for ever. It disconnects at this end, and swings you down to the ground. Much quicker, and considerably less strenuous.'

'I wish I'd known.'

Braxiatel crossed to his desk. 'You're safer in here. From what you say she's using heat imaging and some sort of advanced sensory input to track you. In here we're shielded.'

Benny joined him at the desk. It was covered with papers. Some she recognized from the sheaf that Archduke had given them. Others were covered with scrawled notes and calculations. 'Shielded from what?' she asked, picking up one of the pages of notes.

'Just about everything,' Braxiatel told her as he took back the paper and replaced it on the desk. 'Excuse me a moment.' He lifted a communicator from a nearby shelf.

She moved round the large desk so she was seeing the

papers the right way up. Most of the area was taken up with the main blueprint Archduke had provided. It was unfolded, and weighted down with various objects. A small brass plaque which read 'Custodian of the Library of St John the Beheaded' held one corner in check. Another corner played host to a small glass tankard which was engraved with what looked like a medieval skyline. She lifted it up, holding the paper still with a finger as she held the glass to the light. Italian, probably sixteenth or seventeenth century. From Murano at a guess. She turned it and read the flowing script on the back: 'The Armageddon Convention – Your Contribution Really Made a Difference'.

Braxiatel was beside her again. 'Everyone got one of those, regardless of contribution. Well, nearly everyone. I told them a bird flew into the building,' he continued as Benny replaced the tankard. 'They're not convinced but at least they'll turn that terrible noise off.' Even as he spoke the siren died away, faltering and fading to nothing. 'Mind you, they seem more occupied with some Goll complaining about being pushed off a bridge. I could hear her exercising her vocabulary in the background.'

'What will Kamadrich do?' she asked in the silence.

Braxiatel shrugged. 'She has no reason to connect the two of us, I hope?' Benny shook her head. 'Good. Then she'll probably wait around for a while, then go home. She won't expect you to resurface, and since that was her intention anyway she may well consider her mission accomplished.' He returned his attention to the papers on the desk. 'As you can see, I've been making some progress here.'

'So I see. I thought you'd be a bit tidier, I must say. It's quite a relief to see the work in progress.'

Braxiatel clicked his tongue. 'A tidy desk is the sign of a tiny mind,' he said. 'The mind must be free to make its own intuitive leaps, to make connections and conclusions that would otherwise be tidied away. How else can you make progress, think the unthinkable, conclude the illogical, achieve your intellectual peak experiences?'

Benny sniffed. 'And have you discovered anything useful?'

'I think so, yes.' Braxiatel cleared some of his notes from the main blueprint. The diagram showed various cross-sections of the Dragon statue. Some areas had measurements and construction materials noted. Others were simply blacked in. It was to several of these black areas that Braxiatel pointed. 'These bits are interesting.'

'Oh? But they don't show anything.'

'Exactly. There's no point in including them on the plans at all if they don't show anything. They've been deliberately obscured.'

'You mean to prevent us seeing what's there?'

Braxiatel nodded. 'That's precisely what I mean, yes. We are permitted to see, to deduce only so much and no more. Whatever mechanisms and circuits are in these areas, we are not supposed to be aware of them. A crude but quick way of keeping us literally in the dark.'

'Unless they want us to know there are things we don't know.'

'A dangerous game, but possible,' Braxiatel conceded.

Benny looked over the other parts of the blueprint. There was an exploded area showing what looked like circuit diagrams at one point. 'Wait a moment,' she said. 'Did you say mechanisms and circuits?'

'Indeed. There is more to the Dragon than meets the eye.' He gestured to a cross-hatched area running round the inside of the Dragon. 'Lead shielding, presumably to protect the innards and keep them secret. Scan the statue and it would appear to be solid. The extra weight helps the illusion.'

'So what is it? What's it for?'

'It's a camera,' Braxiatel said simply. He traced through the circuitry. 'Video input here, through the eye. Image buffer, quite large but these things were a couple of centuries ago. Probably holds, oh, about two years of real-time video and audio. Nowadays you could probably package the whole system within the lens itself.' He pointed to another schematic. 'Here's the transmitter. Quite ingenious: it uses the camera lens – the only break in the shielding – to transmit packets of video data and perhaps to receive remote instructions.'

'And where is the lens?'

'Oh, it's the Dragon's left eye.'

She nodded. 'So that's why Archduke looked into the Dragon's eye. He was checking to see if it was the one with a lens.'

Braxiatel laughed. 'He was showing off. There's no way he could see a lens that size with his naked eye.'

'Well, like I said: what is it and what's it for?'

Braxiatel straightened up from the table. 'I think it's a bug,' he said. 'I think the Knights of Jeneve allowed Gamaliel to capture the Dragon. They knew he would adopt it as his emblem and standard, so they had a direct audiovisual link to Gamaliel's war room.'

Benny crossed the room and sat down on the sofa in the far corner. She rubbed her eyes with the heels of her hands. It was turning out to be a long night. 'Is it still working?' The thought had suddenly occurred to her. 'Is the Dragon still transmitting to the Knights? Because, if it is . . .'

But Braxiatel was shaking his head. 'No, the transmitter's components would degrade quite quickly. The booster in particular might only survive for as little as a hundred years. They've used some organic-based compounds and crystals to enhance the signal which have a very limited life.'

'Pity. Otherwise, the Knights could provide us with the evidence we need. Nice video images of the Dragon being modelled and copied plus who knows what other incriminating goodies.'

Braxiatel thought about this. He frowned, smiled, then clicked his fingers. 'Wait a minute.' He leant over the plans again, immediately deep in study.

After a few moments, Benny joined him. 'What is it?'

'The transmitter's no use to us. It can probably transmit a local signal still, but without the booster that's no good. It would only have a range of about a kilometre. But the video circuit itself is rather more robust.' His finger jabbed at the plans. 'The camera should still be operational, and there's a good chance that the local cache memory will still be working.'

'So what does that mean?'

Braxiatel was rubbing his hands together and smiling. 'It means that, with a bit of luck and a following wind, if we can recover the original Dragon, we can access the local storage and get the audio and video data for the past year of so. The incriminating evidence you were after.'

'Sounds good. But how do we get the Dragon?'

'Please,' Braxiatel admonished, 'one thing at a time.' He pulled a small key from his pocket and unlocked the bottom drawer of his desk. From inside he withdrew a pair of fluted glasses and a chilled bottle. 'Champagne? Or is it too early in the day for you?'

'It's never too early in the day for champagne,' she told him.

'There are still a few puzzles.' Braxiatel sipped at his champagne. They were in a small sitting room off the study.

'You're telling me.'

'I mean, academically rather than immediately relevant to our current problems and opportunities.'

Benny drained her glass. 'Such as?' she asked as Braxiatel refilled it.

'Such as the Dragon myths themselves. We know from our recent researches that they predate the Battle of Bocaro by quite a while.'

'There are references,' Benny agreed. 'So I assume the Knights did indeed have a dragon emblem of some sort. They built the Gamalian Dragon to fulfill the myth, in a sense. The best lies are shrouded in truth.'

Braxiatel raised his glass to her. 'That's a good thought. Very axiomatic.'

'Thank you. I picked it up somewhere.'

'You're right, of course,' Braxiatel went on. 'Gamaliel had

to believe he was capturing something significant. The stuff that myths and legends were made of. So they created a statue that fulfilled all the requirements. A Dragon more in keeping with the stories, perhaps, than the actual original.'

'Dragons are interesting,' Benny said. 'I was telling Nicholas and Reddik. There's a sort of duality in them. A dichotomy between the Eastern and Western mythology of old Earth where they originate.'

Braxiatel agreed. 'A bit like your steggies on Stanturus. You said they seemed to change character in the presence of certain people, or when they felt threatened. To become unpleasant and aggressive.'

'I suppose so. The Western dragon is the scaly, aggressive and unpleasant one. Eastern dragons are more cuddly and easier to befriend.'

'It makes a lot of sense, actually.' Braxiatel topped up his glass. 'The Dragon that Gamaliel got is representative of warlike aggression. A fire-breathing monster, all sound and fury. But Chinese dragons are not like that at all, for example. Everything is to do with information, or rather with knowledge, according to what Archduke told us. There's a lot he didn't tell us, mind you. But the dragon of Eastern culture and myth is smaller, and has no wings. It is a generally benign creature which represents learning and knowledge.'

'So, two types of dragon, and two sides to the Knights of Jeneve.'

Braxiatel nodded. 'Seems that way. Which begs the question: whatever happened to the *original* original Dragon? It would not necessarily look anything like the image we all have of the Gamalian Dragon.'

Benny paused, glass halfway to her mouth. Then she put it down, worried that she might drop it. She was aware that her mouth was still open.

'What is it?'

She picked the glass up again, the moment gone. An idea on the edge of her mind had slipped quietly away before she could usher it in. 'Oh, nothing. We probably ought to talk to

Nicholas about all this when and if we next see him.'

'Nicholas. Yes.' Braxiatel stood up. 'Yes, it's probably time to start considering our plan. Certainly we need to rescue poor Nicholas Clyde from his incarceration. The inquiry is the obvious place. They won't be expecting you to attend now, so they will have to produce Clyde. Probably with a promise of a pardon and freedom if he cooperates.'

'So we rescue him there?'

'We?' Braxiatel frowned. 'I am entrusted with the position of impartial chairman, don't let's forget. And whatever happens, I must appear to be impartial throughout the proceedings.'

Benny glared at him. 'Impartial? After everything?'

He held up a finger. 'I did say *appear* to be.' He smiled. 'And whether I actually remain impartial or not, whatever that may mean, I do have a few suggestions for how we might proceed.'

Talisman Station was relatively small, a tiny dot spinning slowly on its axis in the middle of the empty blackness of interplanetary space. Neutral territory. It had been a guidance beacon, big enough for a crew of twenty and a lot of sophisticated navigational and guidance equipment. Then in the war it had been stripped of every component, however useless, and the crew had been taken off to attend to more important duties, and in some cases to die for them.

Now the station belonged, technically, to one of the warlords who held dominion in the sector. It was a technicality that nobody was likely to challenge. The lord in question was less than enamoured of this useless space hulk, but was more than happy to let Romolo Nusek refurbish it and repair the systems for his independent inquiry at no cost. After all, he had admitted to a friend when he thought Nusek wasn't monitoring his call, if he was going to have to follow Nusek on some half-arsed crusade across the quadrant he might as well get something out of it for himself. Nusek had smiled at the sound of the words and promised himself that the man would indeed get something out of it.

At the risk of seeming overoptimistic, Nusek had begun the repairs even before he dispatched his expedition to Stanturus Three. So it was that, less than a week after the archaeological team returned, Nusek was installed in his own office on board Talisman. Adjacent offices were set aside for his head of security, Webbe, and for his special adviser, Mastrov. Knowing how well the two failed to get on, Nusek has made sure that his office was between theirs. They were both excellent at their jobs, and professionally they worked together well. But their philosophies were completely at odds. Webbe had a refined and definite idea of what constituted honourable behaviour. Mastrov had no understanding at all of the concept.

With two days to go before the inquiry started, all three were on Talisman. The first Press Association staff had arrived and their technicians were setting up the broadcast suite under Mastrov's supervision. The two expert arbiters, who together with the inquiry chairman would form the judiciary team, were unpacking. One was a senior academician from Deyton Beta called Alain Lassita. The other was the noted columnist for *Historiography Today*, Martha Gannymede.

The chairman himself, Irving Braxiatel no less, was due the next day. Nusek had been surprised and pleased to persuade Braxiatel to take part. His very presence should ensure that there was no question of impropriety, no suggestion of jury-rigging or fabrication. And given that it was such a coup to get him, Nusek did not see how, even after Mastrov's recommendation to the contrary, he could reasonably deny Braxiatel's single request.

Braxiatel had asked for the original Gamalian Dragon to be brought from Tharn so that it could be presented as evidence and compared with the newly discovered Stanturan Dragon.

Ironically, the smallest ship was given the largest and best-equipped docking bay. It was the smallest ship for a simple reason: it was Braxiatel's own. And while the other arbiters had each brought a small entourage of pilots, co-pilots, navigators, secondary navigators, secretaries, advisers, and even (in Martha Gannymede's case) hairdressers, Braxiatel preferred to travel alone. He piloted the ship himself, and since his memory was excellent and he never took advice from fools or had trouble with his hair he had no need of the other experts his colleagues had chosen to bring along for the ride.

The station crew, all troops seconded from Nusek's own personal guard for the occasion, formed an honour guard to greet the noted chairman. He smiled politely, asked after the families that none of the soldiers had seen or been permitted to communicate with since they were signed up, commented on how brightly their buckles and badges shined, and complimented them on their efficiency.

'You will sweep the ship for unauthorized weapons, transmitters, drugs, that sort of thing, won't you?' Braxiatel asked the guard commander, who assured Braxiatel that those were indeed his orders. Or something similar.

'Jolly good.' Braxiatel leant forward conspiratorially. 'Must make sure everything is seen to be above board, mustn't we?' Then he winked, commented again on the excellent turnout, and accepted the offer of a guided tour of the facilities offered by Talisman Station.

The guards, comforted by Braxiatel's words, gave the ship only a cursory scan. Which was how they missed the false floor in the hold and the figure concealed beneath it.

Braxiatel preferred to travel alone. But on this occasion at least he had not done so. When the guards were gone, and Benny had heard the main hatch clang shut behind them, she lifted up the false section of flooring and heaved herself into the hold. Then she linked the ship's systems to the main station systems and downloaded a map of Talisman. It didn't take her long to spot the secure area where Nicholas must be.

The docking bay was not guarded. Most of the other visitors had provided their own security in the form of the flight crew, who had nothing better to do than remain on their ship performing vital maintenance, drinking and playing cards. Braxiatel had declined the guard commander's kind invitation for a security detail on his docking bay. And his vague comments about having his own deadly anti-intruder devices keyed to his personality index and retinal patterns were as effective in keeping Nusek's men away from his ship as they were false.

So Benny was able to make her way through the station with relative ease. There were few people about, and anyone she did see returned her smile and went about their business. Nobody knew anybody, except for the real celebrities like Nusek and the arbiters. Just so long as she didn't run into anyone who did know her, Benny would be fine.

The one place that Benny did expect trouble was the secure area where Nicholas was – she hoped – being held. She was not disappointed. There was a control suite in the foyer, cells off a corridor behind it. A guard sat, bored, at the control desk. Her feet were up on the desk and she was picking at her nails. Her blast helmet lay on another chair, her blaster was holstered at her side.

On the whole, Benny decided, this was as good as she could reasonably have hoped. And she had come prepared. Braxiatel had given her a needle blaster. It was too small to pack much of a punch, but it should render the woman unconscious, at least for a while. And its size meant it fitted into Benny's clenched fist so that just the tip of the needle protruded.

'Hi,' Benny said as she stepped into the foyer.

The guard quickly drew her feet off the desk and tried to look efficient and in control.

'I'm with the press people,' Benny continued, pretending not to have noticed. 'Here to talk to Nicholas Clyde. He's through there I take it?' She pointed up the corridor behind the desk.

'Er, yes,' the guard admitted, confused. 'But I haven't been –' She got no further because the impact from Benny's needle blaster knocked her senseless from her chair.

'Thanks.' Benny said, picking her way over chair and body to the desk. There was a bank of monitors set into its surface. Most of them showed empty cells. But one showed Nicholas. He was lying on his back on a low bunk, using his holdall for a pillow. He was holding his keypad, his trophy from his first expedition, Benny remembered. Now his talisman on Talisman. She found the door release for the cell and smiled at Nicholas's look of surprise as the door swung open.

'Surprise,' Benny called.

They knew the guard would not stay unconscious for long. Meanwhile, they needed to use what time they did have to try to get back to Braxiatel's ship. They got about halfway. Then the clatter of running feet warned them that the search had started. Benny pulled Nicholas down behind a drinks dispenser just in time to avoid a squad of guards running towards the secure area.

'I think we've been rumbled,' Nicholas said.

'I think we have. We need somewhere to hole up for a while.'

Nicholas's eyebrows went up about an inch.

'It's an arcane Earth expression meaning to hide,' Benny explained.

They found an empty equipment room, just one of many now that most of the equipment was gone. 'So what do we do now?' Nicholas asked as they sat opposite each other on the floor, backs resting against the empty component racks.

'You know, this is the first real opportunity we've had to spend some time and have a proper talk. How about,' Benny said, 'you tell me what happened on Stanturus Three?'

THE HISTORIAN'S TALE

'The temperature was almost unbearable. It was bad enough working at the initial site, but out in the open with the heat from the groundrider engines as well, it was stifling.

'We took frequent breaks, got through a lot of water. But we were in high spirits. We were going out to make or uncover history, we were sure of it. We made good time to the secondary site. But there was little there. We spent a few days surveying, cataloguing. Then we moved on, further north, to another small cluster of ruins. And when we arrived it was even more impressive and promising than we had dared to hope.

'The satellite images suggested some earthworks, maybe some ruins, but most of it buried underground. They were wrong. Most of the structure was still intact and above ground. It was overgrown, covered in creepers, but certainly not buried. We had to leave the groundriders when the earth became too uneven. And we had to hack our way through the last fifty metres of undergrowth. But towering above us the whole time we could see the buildings.

'It was as if they had been carved out of living rock. There didn't seem to be any appreciable gap between the slabs of stone. A more sophisticated building technique than we saw at the initial site. The doorways were huge, too. There was some evidence of hinges rusted into the stone. But the doors themselves had long disappeared.

'But when we got inside, it was all a façade. The insides of the buildings were gone, completely destroyed. The ground was broken up and uneven as if a great river had swept through taking everything with it. And in a way it had.

'Bjork insisted we survey the whole area before we report back. So we sent nothing but routine signals for three days while we mapped out what still existed. There was one room that was practically intact, windows blown out and floor overgrown, but intact. The rest were washed away.

'Then Callum and Krama found the basement. It's strange, but until then we really didn't know what had happened there. We had all the evidence – the smoothed but sloping rock floors, albeit overgrown; walls and whole buildings swept down; even piles of ash and clinker. But it was only when we freed the entrance to the basement area, if it was indeed a basement and not the level where the ground floors had once been, that we knew.

'The lava had washed over the entrance, not through and out the other end. Everything down there was calcified, encased in a fine dust. The lava might not have got to them, but the volcanic ash had rained down and filtered through. Perhaps the eruption itself buried the whole area, sealed it from the lava's path.

'We cleared a way in. It wasn't difficult. It was as if someone had already been there, had already unearthed the remains, then sealed it again like a shrine. Which of course they had.

'The steggies were there the whole time, did I mention that? Probably not. They were everywhere – you forget to notice them after a while. So quiet and placid. Usually.

'But here they were more agitated. Like they were when Kamadrich was around, as if they could sense some hidden tension or danger. There seemed to be more and more of them all the time. Gathering on the edge of the clearing we had made. And they were getting noisy, a sort of rumble of disapproval as if they didn't care for what we were doing to their jungle. We ignored it. Took it for granted. Wondered what Tapshorn would make of it when we told him. Assumed we would see him again, have a drink and talk it over. Laugh at his theories and tell him they were just dumb animals.

'Dumb animals. Jesus.

'That was what we found, do you see? The bodies, preserved in that basement, calcified where they fell. Hunched over the solidified equipment or just going about their business. A snapshot of a civilization caught at a moment in time. A moment in time before its descent into the jungle.

'They were steggodons. Gamaliel never went to Stanturus Three – that's what's so ironic about this whole thing, this whole setup. The ancient civilization that influenced the development of this whole quadrant – steggies.

'Dumb animals.

'Except they didn't seem so dumb now. Not frozen into the acts of intelligent, sophisticated living. And not gathered outside in the night, making that awful noise, clustering, herding, at the edge of the clearing just beyond the light.

'But we didn't worry. We were euphoric. At first. We finished the initial survey and sent an encrypted signal. We waited for the reply. Callum, Bjork and I stayed up half the night waiting for a reply. The others were sleeping, or finishing off their survey work if they were too excited to rest. And still we waited for the reply.

'And what a reply Kamadrich sent: "Do a quick survey, and then move on." We should have realized, I suppose. Should have known she was in Nusek's pocket from the start – that this was the last thing she expected or wanted to find. But to go to such lengths to hide it, to conceal the truth.

'They came for us that night, while we were still numbed by Kamadrich's instructions. I was with Bjork and Callum when the steggies started moving towards the buildings. Towards us. We thought at first they were just getting braver, coming closer. Perhaps looking to see what we were up to.

'They rushed us. We were tired and confused, but we managed to beat them off. Somehow. I remember Bjork smashing at them with a spade. Brooke had the main lights set up for some video imaging. He planned to work through the night. He turned the lights round so they shone right at the steggies as they charged at us, again and again. You know, they didn't like that. They preferred the dark, preferred to have the advantage of seeing us while we could not see them. It was the lights that drove them off.

'They were all over us when the lights came on. Callum was wrestling with one in the room I was in. It had its snout round his neck, was throttling the life out of him. Bjork was laying into two others with his spade. I had only my bare hands, and three of them came for me. I struggled, punched, fought. They pressed down, bore me to the floor. Then the lights came on.

'They just ran. Except that the steggies that were holding me took me with them. I shouted – screamed, probably – for help. But there was so much confusion that I don't think anyone heard me. And we were running, racing across the clearing and back into the jungle. They carried me for ever. It seemed like for ever. We passed the groundriders a good three kilometres away. It was getting light by then, and they had slowed.

'I don't know what they intended to do with me. Was I a hostage, a prisoner or some sort of sacrifice to appease whatever gods they might have left? I don't know. And thankfully I never found out.

'We had just passed the groundriders when I heard the thrusters. The steggies heard it, too. They stopped, listened, seemed unsure. They were getting agitated, the way they do. Then the gunship swept over us. It was low, so low you'd think you could reach up and touch it. Low enough for the steggies to drop me and run. I just stood, shielding my eyes from the morning sun, and staring.

'It was a standard ship, from the cruiser I guess. Nusek's emblem was stencilled on the side in black. My first thought was that they had come to help, had got a message somehow. But it was there too quick. I started back towards the settlement. I could see the ship complete its sighting run, though I didn't know that was what it was. It banked into the distance, turned, and came back at me. Out of the sun.

'Even when the gunports flipped open, I didn't realize what was going on, how far they'd go to keep us quiet, to suppress what we found. When the bay opened underneath the ship like a giant mouth and spat out a rolling grey cylinder, I still didn't realize. What was it? Supplies? Equipment? I even started to walk back towards the camp. Towards the ship. Towards the cylinder. Towards impact.

'It detonated about thirty feet above the main building. A second eruption over the settlement. But this one was far more effective at blotting out the civilization of Stanturus Three. An unnatural airburst.

'The blast wave knocked me off my feet. It came a moment after the sheet of flame exploded outward from the cylinder. The whole thing cracked open as if it could no longer contain the forces inside. The whole world whited out, disappeared, died in that instant. I felt the heat of it. I could smell the disintegrating jungle.

'Then I dreamt. Until you woke me.'

They sat in silence for a while. Then Benny told Nicholas about everything that had happened to her. He seemed numbed by the memories, but he listened to her story, making infrequent comments.

'The steggies ritually dismember their dead,' Benny told him after she had finished her story. 'I've seen them do it, very unpleasant. Maybe they do the same for other animals, too. Anyway, it explains why we never found any bodies in the ruins.'

'They couldn't do that to the bodies we found. They were as good as stone.'

'Perhaps that was why they were so concerned about your being there,' Benny suggested. 'Maybe the place had some special religious significance as a result.'

'Maybe. Not that it matters now.' He was holding the keypad again, turning it over in his hands, stroking his fingertips over the keys. 'So many dead,' he whispered. 'So many.' He looked up at Benny, his eyes red. 'Was it worth it?'

Benny put her hand over his. 'Of course not,' she said. Nicholas looked away. 'They could never afford for anyone to know what really happened. Nusek would forfeit for ever his claims to Stanturus, and his dreams of glory. But right now he has the winning hand and the inquiry is about to begin.'

'What can we do?' Nicholas asked.

'If only we had some proof. It's just our word at the moment.'

Nicholas stood up. 'At least we're free, though.' He helped Benny to her feet. 'Thanks for that.'

'My pleasure.' She straightened up, stretching in an effort to alleviate the discomfort from sitting so long on the hard floor jammed between the rows of shelves. 'Right, it should be clear by now. Let's try to get back to Braxiatel's ship.' She heaved her rucksack on to her back.

Benny reached out for the door control. But the door slid open before she touched it. A group of guards stood outside. One of them stepped forward. It was Webbe.

'It seems you were right, Mastrov. Here they are, all ready and waiting for us.' He held out his hand to Benny. 'You know what I want.'

She handed him the needle blaster without comment. A trooper scanned them for other weapons. Behind him, a woman stepped into the room. She was tall and slim with long blonde hair and eyes that danced in the halogen lighting.

It did not surprise Benny that Mastrov was the woman she had known as Kamadrich. She nodded to Benny and Nicholas. 'How nice to see you both again,' she said, her voice like cut silk.

'I wish I could say the same,' Benny replied as one of the guards gestured with a blaster for them to follow.

'Oh, but I was looking forward to it, Professor Summerfield.' Mastrov's smile was fixed. 'Which is why I kept your heat signature in my memory. It can now be erased, I fancy.'

An Independent Inquiry

As far as the general populace were concerned, the whole thing was a lot of fuss about nothing. But it was certainly of interest to the more influential and powerful denizens of the quadrant. These included those who took an interest in power politics, and those who determined the make-up of the democratic bodies, those who decided whether or not to accept the new laws beginning to filter through from Earth and other potential powers for the future, and those who determined the vidcast schedules.

So, like it or not, a huge audience for the region tuned in to the whole Stanturan Inquiry, as it was now known thanks to the star billing it received in the arcanely named *Aural Schedule*, the vidcast schedules infospool with by far the widest distribution.

Taking an especial interest in the event were the four other warlords from the Gang of Five. They were pretty much resigned to following Nusek, whom they each privately considered to be less objectionable than at least two of the other candidates. But nonetheless, they put aside enough of their differences to gather together in a conference centre on Klapidon Major that boasted the largest holowall and most powerful AI predictive software for parsecs around in order to watch the events virtually live. They studied every exchange with care, looking for the slightest slip from Nusek's team and made bets on the exact running time of the proceedings. They also drank copious quantities of beer, while elsewhere in the sector their various forces engaged in skirmishes and small battles whose outcomes were used to determine what toppings to have on the pizza.

The broadcast opened with a close shot of the Stanturan Dragon (actually it was the Gamalian Dragon, but like everyone else the director could not tell the two apart). The camera pulled back to show the Dragon, side by side with its twin in a blastproof display case on the desk in front of the inquiry chairman, as if they were watching the whole affair with him and waiting to give their own judgement. The proceedings had then started with the promise of controversy when Nusek apologized even before the formal opening for the absence of his chief archaeologist. He declined to name her, but explained that she had in effect ticked the box on her contract marked 'No Publicity' and that in any case she was on leave and unavailable as she was 'having children'.

The warlords in particular watched this performance with interest. They had a good idea what the unnamed archaeologist's real name might be, and looked forward to Braxiatel's reply. It was a disappointment when it came, which set the tone for the first day of the proceedings. Braxiatel seemed to suffer a short coughing fit, after which he told Nusek straight-faced that this was entirely understandable and not at all a problem given the ratificatory nature of these proceedings. Several of the warlords' advisers and aides were sent scurrying for dictionary discs at this point, but otherwise it was hardly worthy of note.

The real reasons behind the absence of Nusek's chief archaeologist were not hard for Benny and Nicholas to fathom as they watched the broadcast in their cell. Anyone who had known the real Kamadrich, or who recognized Mastrov, would have had something to say.

The process the inquiry followed seemed to be straightforward. They watched basically the same proceedings played out for each of the witnesses who appeared the first day. Tapshorn and a couple of the other archaeologists gave evidence about the expedition's exemplary organization, but were not asked about what happened to all the other archaeologists who had gone off with Nicholas. Tapshorn additionally told more than anyone wanted to know about the habits and physiology of the steggodons. Timyan and Grodzki both gave accounts of how they had found the Stanturan Dragon, the only slight discrepancy being that they had both, apparently, seen it first.

In each case, Nusek or occasionally Webbe questioned the witness. Braxiatel then cross-questioned them if he chose. Usually he did not bother. It seemed that the other two arbiters were not permitted to put questions themselves, though they could ask Braxiatel to put them on their behalf. If he wanted. In theory, at the end of the inquiry, all three arbiters would decide between them whether the expedition's finds were genuine and if they were whether this constituted proof that Gamaliel had been to Stanturus Three, giving Nusek a valid claim on the territory. In practice, Benny imagined that the other arbiters would go along with whatever Braxiatel said. The problem was for Braxiatel to manipulate the inquiry so that the findings he wanted to deliver did not seem at odds with the evidence given.

Assuming that Braxiatel wanted to find that the whole thing was faked and set up from the start, and Benny was keenly aware that making any assumption about Braxiatel was hazardous in the extreme, the first day was not going well. All the evidence pointed to a normal expedition that had, in the course of events, made a remarkable discovery. And this was hardly surprising, because all the witnesses who gave evidence that day truly believed this to be the case.

For the whole of the first day, Braxiatel was as helpful and considerate to Nusek as he could be. He made a great show of taking copious notes, having checked first that none of the cameras were angled to show that he was really using the time to redesign St Oscar's databases. He asked few questions, and those he did were for clarification, at the suggestion of Lassita or Gannymede to make them feel wanted and necessary, or to allow Nusek to score a point. In idle moments he replayed famous chess games in his head and toyed – briefly – with the idea of opening the impenetrable case in front of him and switching round the two Dragons when nobody was looking. But, having worked out how to break into the case, do the switch, then close it again and still have change from three seconds, he discarded the idea.

His good behaviour had the desired effects. For one, it lulled Nusek into believing that things would go all his way without incident. For another, it meant that Nusek had no objection whatsoever to Braxiatel taking time during a recess to chat with the vidcast technicians in the broadcast suite. Braxiatel noted with a smile that a tall blonde woman stepped into the shadows at the back of the room as he entered and resisted the temptation to introduce himself to her. Then he casually suggested how the technicians might retune their video booster to take advantage of local solar activity and reduce the necessary power consumption.

The first day ran so smoothly and according to expectations that the second day some of the more populist networks managed to persuade their sponsors and 'friends' that they should return to their normal schedules and simply include the less boring bits in regular news bulletins.

But within an hour of the inquiry reopening on the second day, these schedules were once again discarded in favour of 'special news bulletins from Talisman Station' which brought on-the-spot coverage. This was in fact identical to the regular programming on the other channels apart from the pink 'newsflash' logo included at the top corner of the screen. Flashing.

Braxiatel looked over the day's schedule that Webbe had handed him the night before. Then he looked up and surveyed the inquiry room. His inquiry room. He smiled at Nusek.

'I see,' Braxiatel said, 'that you plan to wheel on a couple more archaeologists from the expedition, one of them being the catering manager. Presumably this is to attest to the nutritional value of the diet provided and its complete lack of hallucinogens.'

Nusek smiled weakly, and looked at Webbe. Webbe shrugged.

'And then,' Braxiatel continued, 'we are due to hear from some experts on Gamalian history and the sculpture of the time who will swear, I suspect, that the Stanturan Dragon is genuine and very much in keeping with what one might expect to dig up on any one of a hundred worlds where Gamaliel stamped his mark. The strong implication thus being made that Stanturus Three was one of these worlds. Yes?'

Nusek flinched. 'Er, yes. That is,' he corrected himself, 'I do not know of course until they give evidence quite what they will say, but that may well be the case.'

'Hmm.' Braxiatel studied the list again, ignoring Nusek's whispered conversation with Webbe at the desk in front. 'That sounds every bit as enthralling as yesterday's events.' He looked up. 'May I suggest a change of pace?' He pulled a folded sheet of paper from his inside jacket pocket and opened it out on the table in front of him.

'Of course,' Nusek said.

'Good. Then I suggest we dive straight in and call the two expert witnesses listed here on your original schedule.'

Nusek's eyes widened.

'I call Dr Nicholas Clyde and Professor Bernice Soberfield.' He held the paper at arm's length and squinted. 'I do apologize, *Summerfield*. Both of St Oscar's University on Dellah.' He folded the paper up and returned it to his pocket. Then he looked quizzically at Nusek, who was opening and closing his mouth like a goldfish. 'Problem?' Braxiatel asked politely.

It was Webbe who answered. 'I think there is a slight misunderstanding, sir.'

Braxiatel was surprised. 'Oh?'

'That schedule was drawn up some days ago, and the two experts you mention are unfortunately unavailable to give evidence at this time.'

'Really?'

Webbe and Nusek both nodded.

Braxiatel pulled the paper from his pocket again and reread it, as if to check the details. 'Having children, perhaps? I'm sure they would welcome the publicity just now.'

'I don't think so, sir.'

'Don't you?' Braxiatel was leaning forward, his demeanour suddenly stern. 'Why don't we ask them? They are I believe in the euphemistically named secure area of this station. Or in the cells, for the rest of us.'

Mastrov watched the events played out on the monitors in the broadcast suite. She considered cutting the transmission, but it was better to let things proceed for the moment. Cutting the transmission might make it appear that things were worse for Nusek than was actually the case. She was sure that whatever Benny and Nicholas might say they could not back it up with any proof. And without proof, things were sure to go Nusek's way in the end.

The same thought was in Benny's mind. She had enjoyed watching the last few minutes, but she was uncertain how Braxiatel planned to work things to his advantage even with their help. If he had a plan.

The cell door opened, and Webbe stepped in. On the screen, Nusek was asking for an urgent recess for procedural reasons. Braxiatel made a play of speaking quietly with the other arbiters before turning down the request.

'Come on.' Webbe's tone was as bored as ever, almost resigned.

'Are we going to the inquiry?' Benny asked as they left the cell. 'Or are we going to have a little accident on the way?'

Webbe seemed genuinely shocked and angry. 'What do you take me for?' he asked.

Benny turned to answer and spotted something lying on the bed in the cell behind her. 'Wait,' she cried, 'I need my rucksack.'

Webbe caught her arm. 'I don't think so. You're going to give evidence, not to have a picnic.'

'No, no I do. There's evidence in the rucksack.' Benny bit her lip. She hoped that had been the right thing to say. It was the truth after all, and she had a feeling, a hope, that Webbe appreciated the truth when he could get it.

Braxiatel called Nicholas first. He let Nusek ask his usual questions about the preparations for the expedition, establishing that everything about how Nicholas had been recruited and joined the expedition had been above board. After a few minutes it seemed like Nusek was back into the swing of things, and that everything was again going his way.

Nusek finished his questions by asking if Nicholas had been present when the Stanturan Dragon was discovered.

'No,' Nicholas replied. 'No, I was not.'

'Thank you. You may go now,' Nusek said quickly with a furtive glance at Braxiatel.

Braxiatel was scribbling on the pad in front of him. He let Nicholas get almost to the door before he looked up. 'I did have a couple of short questions, Dr Clyde, thank you.'

Nicholas returned to the chair in the centre of the room where the witnesses sat.

'First,' Braxiatel said, 'let me assure you that the publicity you receive here will in no way damage your academic standing. I believe you may have expressed some concerns.'

'No,' Nicholas said simply.

'Indeed?' Braxiatel seemed surprised. He looked over to Nusek, then made another note on his pad.

Benny watched from a bench by the door. If nothing else, she decided, Braxiatel was having fun.

'Now,' Braxiatel was asking, 'is there anything else that happened on Stanturus Three that you think we should know about, that you think may have a bearing on our deliberations here? Think carefully. Any little thing may be of relevance.'

So Nicholas told them. He recounted something of the various accidents. He described how Benny was to lead the offshoot expedition and how the rodent creatures attacked her in the trench.

'Is this relevant?' Nusek demanded, leaping to his feet. 'I must say it seems to have precious little bearing on the matter in hand.'

'Must you?'

Nusek breathed heavily. His cheeks were red with anger. 'We discounted Dr Clyde as a witness as we learnt that his academic standing is not what it might be,' Nusek said. 'He is only recently qualified. His views do not seem relevant to the debate.'

Braxiatel nodded slowly. 'Recently qualified or not, he is here and he does profess to have views.' He tapped the display case in front of him with his pencil. 'This Dragon –' he paused to check he had the right Dragon '– is only recently discovered. Is it not relevant to the debate?'

'That is entirely different.'

'I don't think so. Dr Clyde's expertise may have lain undiscovered for as long as this antique, if antique it be. That does not diminish its value, however.' Braxiatel turned back to Nicholas, the matter evidently closed. 'So tell us about your expedition, Dr Clyde. I love a good yarn.'

Nicholas continued his story without interruption until he told of discovering the steggodons. At this point there was some considerable commotion. Chairs shuffled, reporters whispered into comm units, observers and guests exchanged comments and both arbiters turned to Braxiatel for guidance on how to react.

'This just is not true,' Nusek said above the background noise. 'There is no registered data to back this up. The report he cites is just a routine message – survey proceeding as planned. We can produce the comm logs.'

'Thank you, Romolo Nusek, I'm sure you can.' Braxiatel banged his palm on the desk for quiet. 'Let's allow him to finish, shall we?'

Nicholas finished. He described the steggies' assault on the archaeologists' camp, and how he was carried off. Then he described the arrival of the gunship and the explosion. Nusek was on his feet before Nicholas was through.

'This is monstrous, an absurd allegation,' he shouted. 'And completely uncorroborated.'

'Indeed?'

'Of course.' Nusek was breathing heavily. He turned to Webbe, who was looking pale. The commander shook his head, his whisper heard by all in the sudden silence. 'There was no strike authorization, and the cruiser returned with a full arsenal.'

'But there was an explosion?' Braxiatel asked, eyebrow raised.

'Yes,' Nusek all but shouted. 'Yes of course there was. The footage from the gunship we sent to investigate proves that.'

'We have started an inquiry into what happened,' Webbe said. 'So far with no satisfactory result.'

Braxiatel considered for a moment. 'Perhaps you will send me the video footage you refer to. I shall examine it later.'

Nusek and Webbe exchanged a few hushed words. 'I'll mail it to you now,' Webbe agreed when they had finished.

'Good,' Braxiatel said. 'In the meantime there still remains, even if we put aside this tragic mystery, the question of whether the civilization of Stanturus Three was indeed indigenous. Sadly there is no proof either way remaining, whoever was responsible.'

Nusek laughed. 'Professor Tapshorn described the current indigenous life in some detail yesterday. A low mammalian life form, I recall.'

'Oh?' Braxiatel leafed through some papers. 'I believe he actually described them as sophisticated herbivores with a highly developed herd mentality and cooperative skills.'

Webbe motioned to Nusek, and they exchanged hushed whispers. 'I am reminded,' Nusek said when they had finished their muted conversation, 'that several samples of the life form were taken for observation when the expedition was withdrawn. They are currently on the cruiser which by happy chance is moored close to this station.'

'Fortuitous indeed,' Braxiatel agreed.

Benny was thinking fast. Producing a steggie would certainly strengthen Nusek's argument, but no more than not producing one. But there again, given the way the steggies reacted to aggression, it might also unsettle Nusek himself. She doubted he had ever seen a steggie close up. So she nodded vehemently as Braxiatel glanced her way.

'I think perhaps we should take a look at one of these animals,' Braxiatel announced as if the whole thing had been his idea. 'How long will it take to get the cruiser here?'

'Ten point four minutes,' Nusek replied. If he realized how the fact that he just happened to have a cruiser nearby and to know to the second how long it would take it to travel from its current position to the independent inquiry would be interpreted by those watching at home, it was not until after he had spoken.

Webbe, by contrast, shielded his eyes with his hand.

'We will recess for fifteen minutes then.' Braxiatel was already on his feet. 'Summerfield, do you have a moment?' he asked brusquely as he swept through the door.

'Er, yes,' she said quickly as she followed him out. 'Sir.'

They exchanged a few quick words in the corridor.

'How's it going do you think?' Braxiatel asked.

'Got them rattled. They certainly didn't expect that stuff from Nicholas.'

'That's what worries me,' Braxiatel said. 'Nusek seemed genuinely surprised and I'm sure Webbe knew nothing about it.'

'A good act?'

'Possibly. Or maybe Mastrov didn't give them all the details of what she's been up to.'

'The steggie might unsettle them some more, get them making mistakes.'

'Good,' Braxiatel said, 'because it's all up to you now, you know.'

Benny didn't. She gulped, nodded, and followed Braxiatel back into the inquiry room.

The steggie was led in by a guard. It seemed bemused by the whole thing, and certainly it did not give the impression of being the recent descendant of a highly civilized race. It stood bewildered in the centre of the room, hunched over and swaying from side to side so that its snout swung in front of it. It turned slowly round, seemed irritated to find Nicholas standing cautiously nearby and slunk away from him.

It was as if the animal had been bitten. It seemed suddenly to sense without looking that Nusek was at the table behind it. The steggie spun round, eyes staring wide and scared into a billion homes as it was confronted with Nusek's thin smile. Then it gave out a high-pitched shriek, and laid into him with its snout. It took Webbe and three troopers to drag the creature away. Many media experts thought (wrongly) that the resultant test of strength would become the most repeated clip in vidcast history, finally displacing an old monochrome video recording from an ancient children's programme in which an animal defecated on the studio floor and then dragged its keeper through the mess and into a camera to the obvious hilarity of the three presenters.

'You call that civilized behaviour?' Nusek shouted as the animal was taken away. Of the millions watching at home, even those who frequently went through a very similar sort of procedure with their spouse or children, could see his point.

After another short recess to calm things down a little, Braxiatel called for Benny to give evidence. Again Nusek asked his standard questions. He seemed in buoyant mood, obviously happy he had dispelled the threat from Nicholas and confident that he would do the same with Benny.

'And you are the author of the popular archaeological

textbook *Down Among the Dead Men*?' Nusek asked finally. His tone suggested that he did not think people would regard this as adding credibility to Benny's subsequent evidence.

'Yes,' Benny said loudly. 'Have you read it?'

'Has anyone?' Nusek asked with a malicious grin. 'No further questions, sir.'

'I must say,' Braxiatel noted as Nusek returned smugly to his seat, 'that I enjoyed *Down Among the Dead Men* immensely. A highly competent piece of work if I may say so. An accessible democratization of the science.'

Benny was pleased to see that the grin was gone when Nusek sat down. She made a mental note to look up *democratization* when she got a chance.

'Now then, Professor Summerfield,' Braxiatel continued, 'is there anything else you feel we should be aware of?'

Benny nodded thoughtfully. 'Yeah. A couple of things, I guess.' She looked round at her expectant audience, trying not to guess how many people would be watching the vidcast by now. 'First off,' she said, 'the Stanturan Dragon up there is a fake. It was made by Newark Rappare, who was subsequently murdered because of his involvement.'

'More lies,' Nusek shouted above the sudden hubbub. 'Baseless slander.' He pointed at Benny, arm straight out across the table. 'You had better be able to prove these unfounded accusations, young lady.'

'I repeat,' Benny said as she stood up and went towards the door, 'it's a fake. It was made by Newark Rappare on Dellah.' She stooped down and retrieved her rucksack from under the chair where she had been sitting for Nicholas's evidence. For a moment as she turned and crossed back to the centre of the room, her eyes met Webbe's as he sat beside Nusek. His lip curled slightly, but what emotion was behind the movement Benny could not guess.

'He actually made two copies, you see. He kept one for insurance,' Benny said reaching inside the rucksack. 'I have the other one here.' And she pulled the third Dragon from inside the rucksack, hastily removing the undergarment which had somehow got draped over the wings and returning that to the rucksack. Then she raised the Dragon for all to see. 'A worthless fake,' she said.

But her words were lost in the noise. Nusek was on his feet, shouting incomprehensibly. Almost everyone else was shouting too.

After almost a minute, Braxiatel stood and raised his hand for quiet. It took a few moments, but he got it. 'You have some comment?' he asked Nusek quietly.

'Yes I have.' Nusek's voice was shaking slightly. He was still on his feet, his cheeks burning brilliant red. 'This proves nothing. Just because a misguided young woman can create a copy of the Gamalian Dragon – anyone can do that.'

'Anyone?' Braxiatel asked, apparently surprised. 'I was led to understand that the original was closely guarded at your palace on Tharn and rarely if ever examined in sufficient detail to make what appears to be an excellent copy. Wasn't that one of the reasons you cited in your original deposition for the Stanturan Dragon being genuine?' He hunted through his papers again. 'I have it here if you need to refresh your memory.'

Webbe was scribbling furiously on a sheet of paper. He handed it to Nusek, who scanned it and handed it back.

'You are right, of course, sir.' His voice was calm and quiet again. Dangerously so. 'I understand that Professor Summerfield did, however, make a three-dimensional model of the Stanturan Dragon during her time with the expedition. That would certainly provide sufficient detail to create a copy.'

'That's true,' Benny conceded. She walked to the arbiters' desk and set down her Dragon in front of the display case containing the other two. 'But I can prove what I say.'

Benny's eyes met Braxiatel's for an instant. Less than three seconds later, somehow, Benny stepped aside to reveal that the impenetrable display case was open. She lifted the two Dragons from inside, ignoring the gasps from her audience, and placed them beside her third Dragon. 'This is my copy,' she said pointing to it. 'And one of these is also a copy. The other is the genuine Gamalian Dragon. And the genuine Dragon is the only one that is lined with lead shielding to protect the video circuitry and microphone concealed inside.'

She waited for the noise to die down again. 'We can't scan or X-ray the Dragons, because of the lead. But they are a bit brittle and fragile now due to their age, either real or forged. I've kept mine wrapped up – in socks mainly,' she added helpfully.

'Just what are you intending?' Nusek asked, his voice barely more than a husky whisper.

'Well, we have a choice, don't we,' Benny told him. 'Either you tell everyone what you've really been up to – about your deal with Rappare and why you killed him, about how you replaced the original Dragon with a fake and had Mastrov plant the original ready to be found on Stanturus Three, or . . .'

Everyone leant forward in what Benny thought was a superb demonstration of autosuggestion and collective behaviour.

'Or?' Nusek gasped.

'Or I smash the Dragons one by one and let their innards prove me right. Either way, you lose.'

In the broadcast suite everyone was leaning forward. They were either staring at the monitors or watching events in the inquiry room through the one-way glass wall that gave them a ringside seat. Everyone except Mastrov.

'I think that's quite enough excitement for everyone for one day,' she said quietly to the chief technician. 'Cut the power to the cameras. Now.'

He turned to tell her what to do with her excess excitement. Then he saw the blaster she was holding, and nodded dumbly. He pressed a button and the monitor labelled 'Broadcast Signal' blanked out.

'Hey.' The director turned to the chief technician. 'What do you think –' Then he saw Mastrov's gun. 'Er, OK. Cut it there,' he said nervously. 'That's a wrap.'

The steggodon was confused. It was unused to this world of grey where there was no vegetation and the ground was the same colour as the sky. It was distrustful of the two short-snouts who were leading it through the grey world.

The animal was also getting very hungry. It was grinding its teeth together, but there was no food between its large, textured teeth. Its teeth would wear out and get replaced up to eight times during a steggodon's natural life, getting bigger as the creature grew. The teeth would be replaced from the back of the mouth – the new teeth pushing the old ones out forward. Each tooth got more worn as it approached the front of the mouth, and the steggie could feel the rough edges of its frontmost tooth with its tongue. Soon it would be ground away completely, making room for the next one. The animal was desperately hungry. It needed to eat most of the time, but since being bundled into a crate on Stanturus, it had been offered nothing more substantial than a bundle of dry leaves. So it ground its teeth noisily together, trying to let the short-snouts know that it was hungry.

But they seemed to take no notice, encouraging and cajoling it down the hot, grey metal of the drab world.

The steggodon's digestive system was not its only inefficiency. Its sweat glands, too, were insufficient for losing enough heat, and so it used water to help cool down. The loose skin trapped moisture and it cooled the animal down as it evaporated from between the folds. But it had no water. Not even cool mud which it might plaster itself in.

The creature was agitated anyway. It could sense the tension and potential aggression of the short-snouts as they prodded it forward. It was hungry, tired, hot and irritated, and the encounter with the noisy short-snout under the even hotter gaze of many small suns had brought it almost to breaking point. Almost.

Then one of the short-snouts, the one pushing from behind,

hit it again with the short stick that sizzled and hurt when it touched the steggie's hide. And that did it. Rather than simply increase the speed of its doleful shuffle for a short while, the steggodon pulled itself upright from its slouch, turned, and whacked the short-snout full across the face with its powerful snout.

Caught slightly off-balance, the short-snout crashed to the floor, banging its head against the wall as he fell. The steggie trumpeted loudly in triumph, encouraged by this small victory and sensing that it might escape. It barged into the second short-snout, knocking him backward so that he tripped over his colleague. Then it laid into them both with its snout, hitting them again and again until they were both quite still.

The steggie looked down at the short-snouts. Slowly, carefully, it wrapped its snout round the arm of one of them and began to pull. They might have imprisoned and tormented it, but the steggodon instinctively felt that even these creatures deserved the dignity of a proper death ritual. It strengthened its grip on the arm, pulling harder.

The short-snout's eyes snapped open and its face twisted in pain as the steggie felt something give in the shoulder joint. The short-snout looked up, saw the steggodon, and screamed in pain.

The sound echoed round the corridor, startling and frightening the steggie. It let go of the short-snout's arm, watched for a moment as the fingers scrabbled weakly at the ground, and then hurried away.

The inquiry room was in hushed silence. Still. Benny stood at the front of the room, Dragon statue held out in one hand, ready to fall. Time stood still for a few brief moments. In that time nobody spoke or moved. The only change was the increase in tension in the muscles of Benny's forearm. The red transmission lights on the cameras snapped off, though if they noticed nobody commented. And as if on cue people shuffled, murmured, gasped.

Nusek stared at the nearest camera, his brow creased for a

moment in thought. Then he laughed. A loud, high, nasal laugh. 'You're bluffing.' His voice was full of conviction. But Benny could see his eyes, and they were far from certain.

She did not let go of the Dragon. She hurled it at the floor.

The sound was explosive, rattling off the metal walls and stunning the audience. The Gamalian Dragon cracked, splintered, shattered into a thousand fragments bursting across the floor. A nerve ticked high up in Nusek's cheek, just under his eye. Otherwise his expression did not change.

'Still think I'm bluffing?' Benny asked, breathless and hot.

Nusek glanced at the nearest camera, then sat back and folded his arms. 'Yes,' he said.

Benny kicked at the debris at her feet. The inside of the Dragon had been formed from a composite material which had shattered into a white powder. 'A fake,' she said.

'Of course. It was the Dragon you brought.' Nusek's lip curled into a half-smile. 'All you have done is to confirm my own theory. That was the copy you say this man Rappare gave you.'

'It was the Dragon I brought,' Benny conceded. 'But I didn't say Rappare gave it me. In fact, I removed it from the imperial archives on Tharn.'

Nusek's smile faded. 'So you might say. I say the other two Dragons are genuine. But it doesn't matter.'

'Doesn't matter?' Benny asked, her voice almost a whisper. 'Doesn't matter?'

Nusek leant forward over the table. 'We have only your word for the composition of the Dragons. We all know that the Dragon you just destroyed was a fake. But we have only your unproven hypothesis for the composition of the genuine Dragon. Who is to say they wouldn't all smash into powder?'

'The genuine Gamalian Dragon has a video circuit and microphone built into it.'

Nusek leapt to his feet. 'So you say,' he cried, thumping his fist down on the table. 'But you offer no explanation for this wild theory, no source for this assumption.'

Benny felt herself colouring, struggled to keep her anger

and nerves out of her voice. 'Hugo Gamaliel was allowed to capture the Dragon at the Battle of Bocaro. The Knights of Jeneve had built it to be a surveillance device, a bug, to observe Gamaliel's war room.'

Whatever reaction this information would have elicited from the audience was pre-empted by Nusek's scream. 'Lies. More lies.' He turned to Braxiatel, red spots burning on his cheeks. 'How much more of this absurdity must we endure? I know – we all know – that Hugo Gamaliel would never have allowed himself to be duped in such a way.' He turned back to Benny. 'You are asking us to believe that the greatest soldier of our past, the most brilliant strategist ever, was outwitted by a troop of mock-medieval chivalrics. That is completely and utterly absurd, and you know it.'

He stepped out from behind the table. Benny thought for a moment that Nusek was going to come over and hit her. But he stood his distance. 'I challenge you to prove what you claim,' he said pointing straight at her. 'Smash the other Dragons. They are worth nothing compared with the honour of our greatest figurehead, an honour I intend to uphold and enhance.' He took a step towards her. 'Smash the Dragons,' he repeated, 'if you are up to it. I challenge you.'

Benny stood and stared at him. She looked at Braxiatel and the other arbiters, then she looked to the audience. Nobody moved a hair. Everyone was watching, and waiting. For her.

'You can't do it,' Nusek breathed, just loudly enough for Benny to hear.

Benny sucked in air, felt the blood run from her face. She grabbed the nearer of the Dragons, not knowing or caring which it was, not sure how she could even tell.

'You can't do it,' Nusek said again, 'because of who and what you are. It isn't that you're lying – maybe you even believe what you say. It's who you are. We researched you, looked into your murky background, found lots of intriguing things – and *failed* to find a lot, too, I admit. But I know you.'

Benny stood, Dragon in hand. Once again poised, frozen,

caught in the act. All she could see was Nusek's face, all she could hear was his voice.

'I *have* read your book. That probably surprises you, but it was the most basic research we could do. Two things come through as clear as daylight, or so my psychoanalytical team tell me. You want to know what they are?'

Benny knew what they were. She would never admit them, never wished or expected to hear them articulated to her. She felt rather than saw Braxiatel's mouth open slightly and then close again in sympathy. She knew she had to listen. Yet at the same time, a part of her had no idea at all of what Nusek was about to tell her.

'The first is that you are passionate about your work, about archaeology, about the past. You would spend a month clearing dust from a bone with a single-hair brush if that's what it took to uncover one new fact, to learn one new facet of history, to preserve one atom of the past. We're very similar, you and I. Different goals and dreams, but the same drive and enthusiasm. The same determination.' The nerve ticked again beneath his eye. 'So, what happens when a rock meets a hard place? Something gives. And that brings us to the second observation about your character, *Professor* Summerfield.'

Benny was hearing his voice as if repeated to her in a dream, as if she already knew what he was going to say. Which of course she did.

'When we researched your background, you know, we found it extremely difficult –' Nusek broke off. 'No,' he said after a moment's thought, 'let's be fair: we found it impossible to find much in the way of *real* qualifications that you have, Professor. Oh, there are the usual honorary degrees, professorships and chairs of archaeology. Even a doctorate, though that was mainly down to diligent coursework and repeating the right theories. But nothing based on any actual insight or achievement. In short, with the dubious exception of your coffee-table guide to archaeology, you have achieved nothing original or inspiring.

'Now, we couple that fact with the undercurrents in your

book – the frustration with the bona fide academic community, the hints and not-so-subtle suggestions that reputation is less important than the work itself. And what's the result?' He leant forward, hands on hips. 'I'll tell you what. A massive chip on Professor Summerfield's shoulder, that's what.'

Nusek turned away. A deliberate gesture, calculated to hurt her still more.

Benny blinked the tears from her eyes. 'Turn round, damn you,' she shouted. 'I want you to see this. I'll do it, so help me.' She raised the Dragon above her head.

'No,' said Nusek, 'no you won't.' Then he turned round. 'You can't do it.' He walked slowly towards her.

Benny tensed, gripped the Dragon tighter, felt its weight. She brought her arm crashing down, smashing the Dragon to the floor. Except she didn't. Couldn't. It was still raised immobile above her head.

'You see? For one thing you could never bring yourself to destroy what might turn out to be a genuine historical artefact.' He was standing close to Benny now. He reached up and took the Dragon from her hand. 'For another –' he might have been talking to the Dragon '– you would sacrifice for ever the chance of that real acceptance into the academic community which you secretly crave so much.' Nusek looked up at Benny, stared into her eyes. 'You could never do it,' he said. 'Though I could.'

She thought for a moment he was going to, almost hoped he was. But then Nusek replaced the Dragon on the desk in front of Braxiatel and stepped away.

'But what would be the point?' he said quietly. 'I now have what I crave so much.'

'There is another reason you don't believe Professor Summerfield would break the statues.' Braxiatel smiled like a favourite uncle patiently explaining a simple matter for the third time. 'And that is because you do not for one moment admit the possibility that your somewhat romanticized image of Gamaliel may be at variance with the truth. Isn't that right?'

Nusek was back in his set, leaning back with hands held behind his head. 'What do you mean?'

Braxiatel shrugged. 'Only that you don't believe the genuine Dragon contains a video circuit at all. You don't think Gamaliel would have fallen for such a ploy. You can't admit the thought that your hero has feet of clay.'

Nusek snorted. 'The whole idea is absurd, if that's what you're saying.'

'Oh? But I thought there was an increasing body of evidence to suggest that Hugo Gamaliel was actually not as clever or philanthropic as he is made out. Isn't that right?' His question was addressed at Nicholas.

Nicholas took a moment to realize he was being asked to comment. But when he did, Benny could see, through the smeared moisture still in her eyes, that he caught on to what Braxiatel was saying.

'Er, yes, yes that's right,' Nicholas said with a cough. 'Gamaliel, it now seems, was something of a corporate bully just out for himself. He covered up his frauds with an inept crusade which just happened to catch the public imagination at the time.'

'Rubbish,' Nusek snorted.

'It's true,' Benny joined in. 'He cheated his way to victory. There was no honour or glory involved at all. A ruthless despot who was just as corrupt and depraved as the government he opposed.'

Nicholas continued. 'A third-rate soldier who dined out on his single victory and financed his campaigns through laundering money from drugs rings, illegal gambling and peddling pornography.'

Nusek was on his feet, shaking his head slowly. He seemed surprised as much as upset by the attack.

'It sounds,' Braxiatel observed quietly, 'as if Gamaliel actually stood for all the centralization and corruption that you yourself are pledged in his name to oppose. Would that be correct?'

* * *

The monitor stood in the corner of the room set into a bank of equipment that nobody seemed to be bothered with. They were all occupied watching the inquiry through the one-way glass. Sound came through a grille set into the wall by the door, linked to the station's communications system. Hardly the 128-bit digital signal the vidcast crew were used to, but good enough to follow the dramatic turn of events in the room below.

Only Mastrov was not completely absorbed by the drama. Her eyes were never still, watching the monitors, checking the output readings, ensuring that the video camera remained blind and dumb.

One of the technicians shifted position. And reflected in the glass, an image appeared. A flickering, black-and-white square. Mastrov turned to see what was being reflected, and saw the monitor.

'What is that?' she snapped, swinging the chief technician round in his seat.

'It's just the image booster monitor. It checks the signal being relayed direct from the master camera to the satellites.' He frowned. 'That's odd, all the cameras are shut off.'

'So what is this?' Mastrov walked over and rapped her knuckles on the small screen. It showed an image of the inquiry room. The angle suggested the camera was sitting right on the desk in front of the arbiters. Benny stood on one side of the frame, Nusek was seated on the other. Nicholas was visible in between them as he commented on Gamaliel's lack of expertise in government. The picture was monochrome, a little grainy, but it was clear what was happening.

The technician joined Mastrov by the equipment. His colleagues were all now watching him as he twisted a switch. The sounds of the inquiry grew louder as a speaker by the monitor crackled into life.

'I don't understand,' the technician said quietly. 'There's a camera in there still transmitting.'

'Transmitting? To where?'

He stared at the small screen. 'Well, to the satellites of

course.' He turned back to Mastrov. But she had gone.

'You're wrong,' Nusek screamed. 'All of you. Gamaliel was the greatest general who ever lived. He wouldn't be taken in by hidden cameras and microphones any more than I would. Your allegations are unfounded and unwarranted.'

'They're not you know.' Benny was actually beginning to enjoy this, watching Nusek get progressively more irate. She wasn't sure how Braxiatel would do it, but she felt certain he would spring some sort of trap soon. Nusek was so worked up he was not thinking before he spoke.

Sure enough, Braxiatel stood up. He left his desk and went over to Nusek, looked down at him across the table. 'Suppose they're not, though,' he said.

'What?'

'Suppose, just suppose, that someone comes along with proof of some of these allegations. What then? What does that do to your goals, your mission, your crusade?'

Nusek was quieter now. He considered Braxiatel's question for a moment. 'It changes nothing,' he said. 'Nothing at all.'

'Honour and glory? A noble cause rather than purely personal ends? Worth nothing?'

Nusek shook his head. 'Nothing. It is the ends that matter, not the means.'

'Sir.' Webbe's voice was calm and quiet. But there was an urgency in it, as if he could see where this was leading.

Nusek glared at Webbe. 'I know your views, Webbe. I know what you believe in, and I know how worthless it is too.'

'No, sir, what I mean –'

But Nusek was not listening to his commander. 'Gamaliel knew that too, don't think he didn't. The end is all, victory is everything.' He stood up so that he was level with Braxiatel, eye to eye. 'He would have done anything to win. Anything at all. And that's the point. It doesn't matter who or what he was, it's what he did. What he did, not how he did it. And that's why I shall win too – that's why you can never defeat me. Because you have scruples and honour. But I know how to win, what it takes. I know that I must and will do whatever is necessary to achieve my goals and ambitions. There is nothing I won't do, and honour and nobility be damned. Nothing.'

Braxiatel turned to Benny. A nod, no more. Then he spoke to Nusek again. 'Nothing? You'd kill, as Gamaliel did?'

'Yes.'

'You'd cheat and lie, as Gamaliel did?'

'Yes.'

Braxiatel shrugged and stepped aside. It was like a chess move – a path laid open for Benny, a direct sight of the piece to be captured. Her attention was focused on the target. Behind her the door crashed open, but she barely heard it. Check.

'You'd fake archaeological evidence? Set up a bogus inquiry to establish your claims as genuine even when there's not a jot of truth in them?'

Mastrov's shout was close to Benny's ear as she ran across the room.

But all Benny heard was Nusek's reply, almost screamed back at her. 'Of course I would, you fool. Do you really think I'd have gone to all this trouble if I wasn't determined to win?'

Checkmate.

They ran. Braxiatel hurriedly excused himself from the other arbiters while the audience struggled to absorb the enormity of what they had heard. The fact that Nusek seemed unperturbed by his self-incrimination gave them a few moments to escape. But Mastrov was explaining to him about the broadcast image even as Benny grabbed the nearer of the two Dragons and stuffed it into her rucksack.

Out in the corridor, Braxiatel led Benny and Nicholas swiftly in the direction of the docking bays. Benny was slowed down by her rucksack, Nicholas by the holdall he had grabbed from under his chair as they left. But neither of them was willing to discard their possessions, despite Braxiatel's disapproving looks. As far as Benny was concerned, she and her rucksack had been through a lot together – and besides, her toothbrush was in it somewhere. She imagined Nicholas felt much the same.

'It's only a matter of a few seconds before he calms down enough to realize his dreams are in tatters and his aspirations destroyed,' Braxiatel said as they ran. 'None of the others will follow him now, and he's lost all credibility with the public.'

'We didn't do much for his beloved ancestor's reputation, either,' observed Benny.

'If it were just the people at the inquiry who'd heard, what would he do?' Nicholas asked.

'Kill them all, or bribe them. Set up another inquiry including those who escaped whatever accident he decided had befallen this place.'

The docking bay where Braxiatel's ship was berthed was just a few moments away now. They rounded the last corner. And came face to face with a confused and hungry steggodon.

KNIGHT MOVES

Braxiatel managed to pacify the animal. He seemed to be able to exert a calming influence over the creature. Benny insisted they could not leave the steggodon on Talisman Station with Nusek and his cronies, so Braxiatel led it on to his ship and shut it in a small cabin.

The main difficulty was in keeping it away from Nicholas. Just as they initially had it calmed, the creature caught sight of Nicholas and became agitated again, waving its snout about and trying to hit him. When it was safely shut in the cabin, Nicholas breathed a sigh of relief and they made their way to the main deck.

They were generally agreed that Nusek would not try anything. He might already have lost face in a big way, but there was no chance he would risk further condemnation by murdering the chairman of the inquiry in public. And by the time they had returned to St Oscar's, he would have calmed down enough to realize he had other, more pressing problems to cope with. The clinching factor was that Benny had recovered one of the Dragons, but he still had the other. Original or not, it could still grace the archives on Tharn and lend at least some respectability to Nusek's family history.

It was a little cramped on the main deck for the three of them. Braxiatel took the pilot's seat and quickly made the ship ready for take-off. Benny sat in the co-pilot's position, and Nicholas squatted on the floor behind, bracing himself for the slingshot jolt of the launch. He pulled his lucky keypad from his jacket pocket, and nervously turned it over in his hands.

It was not until they were clear of the station with no signs yet of pursuit that Nicholas seemed to relax, and Benny too felt a weight lifted from her. Braxiatel set the autopilot and swung his chair round so that they all sat in a small semicircle looking at each other and trying to keep their legs from getting too tangled up together.

'Well,' Nicholas said when he realized his two companions were both looking at him, 'I'm glad the inquiry is over.'

Benny glanced at Braxiatel, and found he was already looking at her. Their eyes met for a moment, and she knew in that instant that he was thinking at least some of the same things as she was.

'Don't be too sure,' she told Nicholas.

'Indeed,' Braxiatel agreed. 'I think the inquiry is just beginning.'

'Sorry.' Nicholas looked from one to the other. 'I'm not sure I follow.'

'It always bothered me,' Benny said standing up and stretching in the confined space, 'that the steggies seem so wary of you.'

Nicholas shrugged. 'Just unlucky, I guess.'

'Yes, I thought that too. After all, they didn't really dote on Kamadrich either. And so I discounted Tapshorn's theory about them sensing a threat or danger of some sort.'

'But,' Braxiatel said quietly, 'Kamadrich was a killer.'

Nicholas's eyes seemed slightly wider, slightly more wary than a few seconds earlier. Benny stared into them. 'So what's your excuse?' she asked him.

The journalists, observers, arbiters and other hangers-on had gone. They had not been long behind Braxiatel in leaving Talisman. Webbe was not surprised, and had told Nusek that soon he would have the station to himself and his own people.

Nusek had wanted to launch an immediate missile strike and destroy Braxiatel's ship as soon as it pulled clear of the station. But for once both Webbe and Mastrov had been agreed that this was not a good plan. Webbe was concerned for the image it might give when the news of his actions inevitably leaked out. Mastrov's reasoning was rather different. She was sure that Braxiatel would expect and anticipate such a move. Better to wait, she said, until Braxiatel was in open space away from enquiring scanners and off his guard. And while Webbe was not convinced that it was worth chasing them down now that the damage had been done, Mastrov shared Nusek's feeling that revenge was of paramount importance.

But while Webbe might not approve of Nusek's sentiments, or of Mastrov's motives, part of his definition of honour was to do with following orders. Another part of his code of honour was pride in a job well done, and he was practical enough and good enough at his job to know that nobody did it better than he. So when those who might pay unwanted attention to such things were gone, the cruiser broke free of Talisman Station. As it launched itself after Braxiatel's ship it was commanded by Webbe himself.

'Are you a threat, Nicholas?' Benny asked. 'Are you dangerous?'

He did not answer. He tapped his keypad against the back of his thumb, then returned it to his pocket.

'You know,' Benny went on, 'that's something else that puzzles me.'

'Oh?' He sounded bored, but his eyes still had an alert wariness about them. 'What?'

'Your lucky keypad. Your antique. Your first find.'

A slight tightening of the lips. 'What about it? It's just a keepsake.'

'Is it? Is it really?' Benny looked at Braxiatel. He was leaning back in his seat watching them. He swung slowly, slightly, from side to side.

201

'You told me,' Benny said, 'that you had never been on an archaeological expedition before we went to Stanturus. Yet you carry with you a relic you claim was your first find on your first dig.' She leant forward, smiled slightly. 'An obvious blunder. I thought at first you were trying to impress me, to convince me you were a Real Historian.' She tried to stress the capital initials. 'But that's just too crass for words. So, am I missing something here?'

Again Nicholas did not answer.

'You see,' Benny said, leaning back, swinging her chair in time to Braxiatel's thoughtful rocking opposite her, 'I also thought it was just a coincidence that your lucky relic was from the same period as the Gamalian Dragon. But now –' she clicked her tongue '– now I'm not so sure.'

Braxiatel's ship was incredibly powerful for her small size. But the cruiser Nusek had sent after her was powered by enormous engines that propelled it through space rather faster if somewhat less efficiently. Webbe was not concerned about how much fuel he burnt, however. They had picked up Braxiatel's transponder exactly where they expected to find it (which was a surprise to Webbe), on a direct route back to Dellah.

The cruiser's guidance systems locked on to the signal. Its mainframe calculated intercept times and probabilities. Webbe sat back in the captain's chair, folded his arms, and watched the two signals slowly closing on the main screen.

'I'm not a big believer in coincidence.' Braxiatel turned back to the flight controls and adjusted a setting. 'Which is why, to give you just one example, I've asked the ship to run some evasive manoeuvres in an attempt to break free from the cruiser that is following us.' He smiled. 'Just one example.'

Benny smiled too. 'Let me give you another,' she said.

'Time to intercept: seven minutes,' a soft, female voice interrupted.

'It's as well to know your situation,' Braxiatel said. 'Now, tell us about this coincidence of yours.'

'Well, it's the strangest thing, really.' Benny's eyes were fixed on Nicholas. His pretence of boredom had evaporated. She had his full attention. 'When we first met, we joked about how your book-learning contrasted with my more practical field experience.'

'I remember,' Nicholas said quietly.

'And do you remember what you said by way of justification? No? I'll remind you. You said "Knowledge above all".'

Nicholas did not move. He said nothing.

And the ship warned them: 'Time to intercept: six minutes, thirty seconds.'

'I didn't think anything of it at the time,' Benny continued. 'But it's an odd phrase. It sounded a little familiar, as if it meant something more than it seemed. As if I had heard it before, and maybe I had. I have certainly heard it since. Twice, that I remember. It was what Reddik said when he left us that morning in the archives on Tharn.'

'Maybe he'd heard it from me.'

'Maybe. But then someone else said it to me.' She nodded to Braxiatel. 'To us both, in fact. Perhaps he's the one I heard it from originally, I honestly can't remember.'

'Archduke,' Braxiatel said quietly.

Benny nodded.

'A formal phrase,' Braxiatel suggested. 'A valediction?'

'I think so. But not one that's referred to in any of the sources you and I have examined during our research.' Benny turned back to Nicholas. 'And how would you happen to know the secret, formal valediction of the Knights of Jeneve?'

'Well, sometimes,' Nicholas said slowly, 'the obvious answers are the correct ones.'

'Time to intercept: six minutes.'

The points of light on the cruiser's scanner were closing on each other faster now. The tiny text which described each symbol – call signs, flight codes, home ports – were overlapping at the edges, blurring each other.

'Boarding party to forward hatch,' Webbe ordered. He watched the screen for another few moments, then made his way forward to join the boarding party.

'Time to intercept: five minutes.'

'What can we do in five minutes?' Benny asked, not really serious.

Braxiatel was already at the controls. 'There is one thing that I think would be of use,' he said.

Benny was at his arm in an instant, trying to make sense of what he was doing. 'Well?' she demanded after a while.

'I'm going to check my mail.'

'What?'

'We're not going to outrun that cruiser,' Braxiatel admitted. 'So we might as well do something useful.' He was scrolling through a list of files on the main viewscreen in front of them. 'Ah,' he said at last, tapping his finger on the screen. 'There it is. Let's run that, shall we?'

Nicholas was standing beside Benny now as she watched the footage again. Even with him standing there with her, she still re-experienced the thrill of fear as the camera sped over the devastated landscape.

'Time to intercept: four minutes, thirty seconds. Window of opportunity for evasive measures now closed.'

'You're telling me,' Benny muttered.

They watched the sequence through for the second time. Braxiatel tweaked some settings on the playback, slowed it a little here, enhanced the colour balance there. A couple of times he froze the image and peered at a couple of readouts. Benny toyed with the idea of putting on her spectacles and peering with him. But she wasn't sure what condition they would be in even if she could find them in her rucksack. And she didn't really need them anyway.

'What are we doing?' Benny hissed at Braxiatel. Not that she was worried about being overheard. But she somehow felt she was more likely to get an answer.

'Something's been puzzling me a little.'

'Terrific,' Nicholas said. 'We're about to be captured by a megalomaniac we've just made look like a stupid crook on a sector-wide vidcast, and something's puzzling you.'

'Allow me to indulge my curiosity,' Braxiatel told him sharply. 'It is in a way for your benefit that I'm bothering to check the facts with this rather antiquated equipment rather than just extrapolating from the known data.'

'Time to intercept: four minutes.'

'What data?' Benny asked.

'Consider, Benny: Nusek was surprised when we suggested he was responsible for this.' Braxiatel gestured at the blackened earth on the screen. 'He didn't just *seem* surprised: he actually *was*. Nusek would never risk the apparent integrity of his archaeological expedition by so obviously murdering members of the team. True, it gave him an excuse to bring in his troops, but from his evidence and demeanour at the inquiry this seems to have been more through paranoia and unease than deliberate forward planning.'

'Mastrov, then?'

Braxiatel shook his head. 'Not without orders, I think. And certainly not without reporting it back afterwards. One thing that I learnt during my research into the Knights of Jeneve,' Braxiatel told them as he checked more of the readings, 'and you will no doubt correct me if I am wrong, Nicholas, was that they were experts in miniaturization technology. The video technology within the Dragon is surprisingly sophisticated and very small for the period. I presume you still practise such skills, eh?' He turned to look at Nicholas. 'Particularly in the arts of warfare, no doubt. All Jeneve technology we have seen so far is both elegant and compact. In particular, judging by some of the schematics of the Dragon circuits and the technical drawings of weaponry captured at Bocaro, the Knights were unsurpassed in the manufacture of microexplosive devices.'

'Time to intercept: three minutes, thirty seconds.'

'What are you saying?' Benny asked slowly. 'What does this footage tell you?'

'It tells me what is plain for anyone with a trained eye to see. Webbe must know it, though I doubt Nusek has bothered to ask him and he's not the sort to volunteer an advantage unless ordered to.' Braxiatel smiled grimly. 'A bit too fair perhaps. But at least he is fair.' He pointed to the screen. The camera was passing over the burning groundrider, swinging low over it and veering off at a sickening angle as the ship turned. 'What these pictures show is an area of devastation caused by a single low-yield nuclear ground blast.'

Benny blinked. She was completely conscious of the act, felt every slight movement in it as eyelids stroked eyeballs, as brain filtered through and decoded Braxiatel's words, then tried again and came to the same conclusions. She went through the motions anyway, testing the logic, looking for a way out. 'But it was an airburst. Nicholas saw the ship come in.' She turned to him. 'You felt the blast wave. You said.'

Their eyes locked, but neither spoke for a while.

'Time to intercept: three minutes.'

The spell was broken, and Nicholas looked away.

'I was curious from the start,' Braxiatel said. He was talking to the screen, to the charred images rolling past them. 'Apart from the coincidence – and you know what I think of coincidence – of one person surviving and that person being you, Nicholas. But then there's the technology. Nusek doesn't have access to the sort of low-yield high-energy material for this. And as I say, it certainly wasn't an airburst.' He turned suddenly to Nicholas. 'A lie should be shrouded in truth,' he said. 'Didn't they teach you that? A couple of unnecessary embellishments and the tissue tears, splits, reveals the truth standing embarrassed behind it. Like finding the court jester weeping by the old king's grave.' He turned back to the screen and shut it off. 'Where be your jibes now?' he murmured so quietly that Benny strained to hear it.

Benny shook her head, though whether disapproving, in a hope of clearing it, or in disbelief she did not know. 'Why?'

she asked Nicholas. 'Why did you do it? What could possibly be worth that cost?'

'Time to intercept: two minutes, thirty seconds.'

'I think, while we still have time, you should tell us the truth,' Braxiatel said. 'What did you really find in the ruins on Stanturus Three?'

Nicholas's voice seemed to be filtered through water, the truth bubbling up to Benny as she floated on the surface. 'What I told you, Benny, was true. Almost all of it. We found the ruins just as I said. Even the volcanic damage and the dust. I managed to persuade Kamadrich – Mastrov – that we'd just found some old ruins. The others were suspicious, but they assumed it was Kamadrich who was playing some game, didn't realize I'd sent a different message in the first place.'

'Time to intercept: two minutes.'

'But Nusek was right. The steggies couldn't possibly have devolved from an intelligent, civilized life form into the creatures we see now. Look at the one in the cabin down the corridor – instinctive, yes. Some reasoning and herd instinct, even. Intelligent? Maybe, for an animal. But no more than that. But the inheritors of a civilization just a few hundred years ago? No way.'

'Then what did you find in the ruins?' Benny's own voice was as removed as Nicholas's. 'If not steggies, what? Were there no bodies at all?'

Nicholas laughed. It was the first real emotion he had shown for a while. And it was anger and nervousness rather than humour. 'Of course there were bodies. That's why the others had to die, why I had to destroy the ruins. Can't you guess even now?' He laughed again, and this time there was a trace of amusement mingled with the other emotions. 'That's the irony of it all, you know. Nusek was right.' He shook his head. 'Would you credit that? He was right all along. He didn't need to fake the Dragon. He didn't need to get us in at all. He just needed to invite a few observers to those ruins.'

'Time to intercept: one minute, thirty seconds.'

'There were bodies all right. Frozen by the heat, by the volcanic ash raining down on them. They must have died in agony. At least my team died quickly when they had to. And for a reason. But this was horrible – the expressions, the fear, the pain, scarred across their faces for us all to see. And the uniforms, charred and torn, but still intact. The insignia still identifiable – on the uniforms, the equipment. The Gamalian Dragon emblem. Oh yes, they were Gamalian troopers. He had an outpost on Stanturus Three, just as Nusek wanted everyone to believe.'

'Time to intercept: one minute.'

Benny was suddenly aware of Nicholas's hand on her shoulder. Had he just put it there? Or was he just holding her harder now?

'That's why, don't you see? That's why I had to do it. We can't afford for that to become known. We can't let Nusek expand in this sector. The support this little victory would engender for Nusek would be extremely dangerous, don't you see that?'

'Dangerous to the Knights?' Braxiatel asked quietly.

'Of course to the Knights.' Nicholas was still looking at Benny. 'But to everyone else too. *You* were determined to stop him. You *did* stop him. I had to stop him too. I'm not proud of what I had to do, that people had to die. But it's just a question of degree. You must see that.'

'Interception imminent,' the ship warned. 'Brace for impact.' The room switched to red emergency lighting. A klaxon sounded close to Benny's ear. But she noticed none of this.

'No,' she said, and she could see that Nicholas heard her above the klaxon. 'No, I don't see that at all.'

She turned away just as the deck fell from beneath her. Her feet jolted back into the floor as the stabilizers compensated for docking impact. From down the corridor came the sound of the clamps on the main door being blown from the outside, followed by the violent hiss of pressure-compensation.

A hand caught Benny's arm as she almost collapsed. She turned, and Webbe smiled as he lifted her back on to her feet.

'Romolo Nusek would be grateful if you would join him at his palace,' Webbe said. 'I'm afraid he won't take no for an answer.'

Teetering on the Brink

The journey back to Tharn was not physically uncomfortable. Braxiatel's ship was taken into the cruiser's docking bays, and its occupants given quarters within the cruiser itself. Benny, Nicholas and Braxiatel each had a room of their own, and they shared a living area and bathroom. The steggodon was left where it was on Braxiatel's ship, not least because none of Webbe's troopers was keen to go near it.

Benny's immediate concern was to escape. However, this soon gave way to frustration as she realized that neither of her companions seemed at all interested in trying to get away. Braxiatel, when she broached the subject with him for the fourth time, patiently pointed out that they had nowhere to escape to. Even if they got back to his ship, it would be of little help – the cruiser could outrun them again just as it had before. Benny's vague suggestions of sabotaging engines and creating diversions met with a raised eyebrow and a sad smile.

Nicholas was more infuriating. He and Braxiatel seemed determined to engage in academic and philosophical discussions for which Benny was in no mood. When she interrupted (again) to suggest they ought to do some forward planning, Nicholas reminded her, 'Knowledge above all.' Actually, he got only as far as 'Knowledge above –' before he saw her fist. He caught her hand expertly, mouthed an apology and continued his argument. She almost punched him again.

Eventually, Benny got bored with the lack of response and decided that perhaps she was missing something. The journey would be about twelve hours altogether, and there were only around seven of those left. So she slumped into one of the easy chairs in the lounge area and listened to Braxiatel talk about the merits and disadvantages of the Gamalian Dragon's lead shielding. There were three chairs arranged in a triangle round a low glass-topped coffee table.

'Surely,' Braxiatel was saying to Nicholas, 'the shielding would merely hamper the video and audio signals. That would be more of a problem than the possibility of X-rays or scanning. The chances are that Gamaliel took the Dragon at face value and never dreamt of examining it in any detail.'

'So why bother?' Benny asked, partly to show she was paying attention and now a part of the discussion.

'Exactly. Why not use some osmotic material that would let the signals out but retard scanning wave forms?'

'Like a one-way mirror?'

'Yes, something like that.' Braxiatel turned to Nicholas. 'Certainly the technology was available, so why use lead? There must be another reason.' He leant forward slightly, and Benny sensed that he already guessed the answer to the puzzle. 'Am I right?'

Nicholas seemed uncertain. 'I can't say,' he muttered with obvious embarrassment.

'But do you know?' Braxiatel leant back in the chair and addressed his next observations to Benny. 'You see, lead did have a very specific use in those days. One it has had for a long while, in fact. It was used as shielding, true, but not to keep emissions out, but to keep them in.'

Benny could see what he was getting at. 'Radiation shielding?'

Braxiatel nodded. 'You know that, of course, Nicholas. With your knowledge of the era, you must know that.' Braxiatel stood up suddenly and walked to the corner of the room. 'They should have a drinks cabinet just here,' he said indicating the exact spot. 'So what is it?' He had not turned,

211

was talking to the space where the drinks cabinet was not. 'A smart device of some sort obviously. Fission grenade?' He turned on his heel and stared at Nicholas. 'The size is about right.' He walked slowly across the room again as he spoke, away from Benny and behind Nicholas so that he had to turn to watch, so that he had to show that he was listening. 'But if so, then why didn't the Knights explode their bomb? Its purpose must have been to wipe out Gamaliel's forces at some later stage.' He stopped immediately behind Nicholas's chair. In a stride he was at Nicholas's side, looking down at him with his intent, piercing stare. 'Well,' he snapped, 'why didn't they do it?'

Nicholas did not answer. He stood up, and left the room. Benny and Braxiatel exchanged glances. Benny shrugged. But before she could comment, Nicholas was back. He was carrying his holdall, and as he sat down again he pulled from it the stone statuette that they had taken from the tomb of Henri of Bosarno and which the librarian Reddik had given him for safekeeping. He set it down on the low table between himself and Benny.

'This is the answer to your question,' he said quietly. 'The Dragon of Jeneve. The *real* Dragon of Jeneve.'

For a while, nobody spoke. They just stared at the small statue on the table.

Then Benny reached out, stroked her hand across the Dragon's face. 'What happened?' she asked Nicholas. It was hard to think of it as a dragon: it was so very different in style from the Gamalian Dragon. But then it was Benny who had been so keen to explain the differences between the cultural interpretations of the dragon. And here was an object lesson – the fierce, scaly, reptilian fire-breather of Gamaliel, and the lionesque, big-eyed mammalian Dragon of Jeneve.

'We know now what happened, though at the time the Knights were unsure. But given where this was found –' Nicholas tapped the Dragon on the head '– we can be fairly certain now. The Dragon, this dragon, was of great value and significance to the Knights of Jeneve. Indeed, it still is. For reasons of security as well as mystique, nobody ever knew what the Dragon of Jeneve looked like. Nobody except those chosen to protect it.'

'And they were?'

'An elite group of Knights, a sort of inner order known as the Dragon Knights. All we knew until now was that after Bocaro the Dragon Knights were all dead, and the Dragon was gone. Nobody within the order knew what had happened to the dragon, or even how to recognize it.'

'Henri of Bosarno,' Braxiatel said softly.

Nicholas nodded. 'Exactly. The Knights he fell upon and slaughtered as he made his way back to Gamaliel, after the battle was won, were the Dragon Knights. They fought to the death to protect the Dragon. But Bosarno and whoever was with him overcame them and took the Dragon as a trophy.'

'So,' said Benny, 'they couldn't detonate their booby trap for fear of destroying the real Dragon.'

Nicholas nodded. 'That's true. It might have disappeared before or after the battle. It might be lying abandoned and unrecognized on the field of Bocaro. But there was a chance that Gamaliel had the real Dragon too. And we could not afford the risk of destroying it, no matter how slight.'

'Why?' Benny asked simply.

Nicholas shook his head. 'I have told you more than I should already. I cannot answer that.'

Braxiatel sat down at last. He crossed his legs and leant back, staring at the ceiling of the room. 'When we get back to Tharn in a few hours,' he said, 'we are probably going to die. I'd hate to die in ignorance.'

Benny put her hand up as if in school. 'Me too, sir.'

Nicholas's hands clenched and unclenched. 'All right,' he said at last. 'The main reason, not the only reason but the most important reason, why the Dragon of Jeneve is so important is encryption.'

'Encryption?' Benny was lost already.

'Well, decryption, to be exact.'

'A dual key system?' Braxiatel asked. Nicholas nodded,

213

and Benny shook her head in confusion. Braxiatel smiled, and explained. 'The system's been understood for centuries. It's pretty straightforward. There are related pairs of numbers which act as keys. These keys have a special mathematical relationship such that a message encoded using one of the numbers as an encryption key can only be decoded using the other number in the pair. Even the same number won't decode. So you have what's called a private key and a public key. Only you know your private key, but you give your public key to anyone else you want to communicate with. You send them a message encoded with your private key, and they can read it. And they know that it really came from you, because otherwise your public key would not decode it. When they send you a message, they encrypt it with your public key – which they have – and you, only you, can read it using your private key.'

Benny blinked. 'You call that straightforward?'

Braxiatel considered for a moment. 'Yes,' he said. 'But to complicate it a little, you can encrypt your messages to me with both your private key, so I know it's from you, and my public key – so only I can read it. I reply double-encrypted with your public key and my own private key.'

Benny took a deep breath. 'Right,' she said. 'So what's that got to do with Bonzo here?'

'As you know,' Nicholas continued, 'the Knights of Jeneve exist to assimilate and catalogue information. To this end the Knights set up secret cells throughout former Earth space. They established a set of secret archives, staffed by members of their order. They also set up a huge and secret complex to house the main library system they were devoted to creating and maintaining. The information and knowledge gathered was sent in encoded with the Knights' public encryption key. This was then decrypted with the Knights' private key and the data catalogued. They would send out orders and acknowledgements coded in their private key, which only the cells, with access to the public key, could read. Each message was double-encoded with the cell's own public key to ensure it did not get intercepted, but the Knights' private key assured the cell of the authenticity of the message.'

'So what's the problem?'

'The problem was with the Knights' private key. The single data-feed mechanism for encrypting and decrypting was housed inside the emblem of the Knights – a stylized statuette of a dragon.'

'Bonzo!'

Nicholas glared at her. 'For security reasons,' he went on after a pause during which she did not apologize for her irreverence, 'there was only one encrypter. It was guarded by a special elite troop of Knights – the Dragon Knights. The dragon was also the secret emblem of the Knights. But Gamaliel never knew what the emblem looked like. He assumed it was a winged, aggressive, fire-breathing creature of Western Earth mythology. The statue the Knights intended him to capture was made in the form he expected of it. The same form as we also believed, until now, the real Dragon had originally been fashioned in. Since we had nothing but the Gamalian Dragon to refer to, it was an easy mistake. But in fact the statue represents the other side of the nature of the Knights – a benign spiritual being of knowledge derived from Eastern culture. And I must thank you, Benny, for helping us to realize that.'

'Right.' It was Benny's turn to pace the room now. She found that if she walked about a bit, pieces of information seemed more inclined to settle down in her brain and begin to make some sense together. 'But this still seems a pretty poor reason not to use the bomb you'd gone to all the trouble of planting.'

'I agree. If that was the intent. But the device was merely a fail-safe. If Gamaliel had realized he'd been duped, which the Knights would know from their surveillance, the bomb could be detonated and Gamaliel killed. The charge in the explosive was – is – sufficient merely to kill anyone in the immediate area. It could be set off at once when the video link showed Gamaliel was close at hand, or there was a delay switch and a timing mechanism. So the bomb was never exploded for two reasons. First, it was never necessary, and it would have attracted attention back to the Knights just when they'd managed to avoid it. Second, there was a slight danger of damaging the real Dragon of Jeneve if Gamaliel had indeed captured it and it happened to be close by.'

'Well,' said Benny as she slumped back into her chair, 'I'm glad it's no more complicated than that.'

Braxiatel smiled. 'I do have one small question,' he said. 'Where, exactly, does the librarian, Reddik, fit into all this?'

'Reddik, as you have guessed, is an Archivist Major of the Knights of Jeneve.'

Benny swore and closed her eyes.

The librarian's job, Nicholas explained, was to search for any record in Gamaliel's archives that might indicate what had happened to the *real* Dragon. 'Reddik,' he revealed, 'tells me that he is actually the great-great-great-great-grandson of the original librarian charged with this task.'

'Which explains,' Braxiatel said, 'why he keeps the Gamaliel papers and knows their content so well.'

Nicholas agreed. 'The original librarian was a Knight who was captured soon after the battle of Bocaro.'

'Captured?'

'All right, he allowed himself to be captured soon after the loss of the Dragon was discovered. He offered his learning and expertise in archiving to Gamaliel in return for his life.'

Benny was surprised. 'Bit of a risk, wasn't it? What if he'd got his head chopped off?'

Braxiatel picked up the Dragon of Jeneve and ran his palm gently over its surface. 'I suspect,' he said, 'that Gamaliel was actually quite a decent chap really. We have to distinguish between propaganda and reality, both then and now.'

'Reddik and his ancestors searched in vain for the Dragon,' Nicholas said. 'Until Benny's chance comments about Eastern and Western differences in dragon myths caused him to realize that it might be represented on Henri of Bosarno's tomb. He guessed that the Dragon of Jeneve could therefore be hidden inside.'

Nicholas leant forward and took Benny's hands in his. The action surprised her, and for a moment she did not move, returned his smile. Then she remembered what he had done on Stanturus, and she pulled her hands away.

'If it were not for you, Benny, the Dragon would be lost still.'

'It will be again, if Nusek gets his hands on it,' Benny pointed out.

Nicholas nodded grimly. 'That's why,' he said, 'I want you to look after it for us.'

Webbe led the way with Benny, Nicholas and Braxiatel close behind. Several guards followed them as they made their way through the corridors of the palace. Benny assumed at first that they were being taken to the throne room, but as they descended to the lower levels she realized this was not the case. A glance at Nicholas was enough to see that he had come to the same conclusion as herself about where they were actually being taken.

Braxiatel, perhaps because he had no idea of what lay in store, or perhaps because he was more interested in the architecture of the palace, was in an upbeat mood. He tested the guards' patience by suddenly stopping to examine a painting or tapestry; he headed off down a more interesting corridor, to be brought back disappointed at the end of a blaster. He punctuated the sound of their feet on the echoing stone with questions about the castle's construction and history, which Webbe answered in short measure. He commented on the probable nature of the impurities in the water that meant that fire and ice could coexist in such proximity.

But even Irving Braxiatel seemed impressed with their final destination.

Benny and Nicholas had seen the execution chamber only from the observation gallery before. The gallery was high above the ground, running all the way round the huge circular room. But this time they entered at ground level, and the room seemed even bigger from the floor. They had entered through a small side entrance, opposite the main double doors.

The floor sloped more steeply than Benny had thought, almost encouraging her to walk towards the raised circular dais in the centre of the room. There were three steps up to the top of the raised area, and from just inside the doorway they were sufficiently above the level of the dais to see over the edge of the hole cut into the middle of it. The heat from the volcano made the air shimmer and glow above the dais. The air was tinted by the fumes, so that the tortured statues around the edge of the room seemed discoloured and stained. Tainted.

'Fascinating.' Braxiatel was already walking down the incline towards the volcano. He paused as a sheet of flame shot up from the dais, a cloud of yellow smoke following it. Just as quickly it was gone. Braxiatel looked up, following the progress of the rising smoke towards the domed ceiling high above them. 'Force-field projectors,' he called back to Benny and Nicholas, pointing up at the roof. 'Activated by heat, I suspect. If the volcano seems about to erupt, the shields come on to contain the heat until it subsides. I see there's a manual override control by the door.'

They caught up with him, encouraged by the guards. Webbe stopped when he reached Braxiatel, and the guards allowed Benny and Nicholas to stop too.

'You are impressed.' It was not a question. Webbe sounded every bit as bored as he had when he showed Benny, Nicholas and Gilder round weeks earlier.

Braxiatel nodded. 'You're not, though, are you? Why is that, pray?'

Webbe turned away. 'I know what happens here,' he said.

'Well, I think that I can guess.' Braxiatel pointed to the nearest statue, standing in an alcove cut into the wall about ten feet above the ground. It was a representation of a man having his eyes put out by a woman in a long robe. His face was twisted as he tried to turn away, held back by one of the woman's hands. The other held the long-bladed knife. 'I don't care much for the decor, whatever the room is used for.'

Webbe seemed to be about to reply, but at that moment the main doors opened. Two soldiers entered, and immediately moved to either side of the doors. They were followed by Nusek and Mastrov.

'I see that my guests have arrived,' Nusek said as he approached them. His voice was poured over cut glass. 'I think we can dispense with many of the formalities,' he continued as he led the way towards the dais. The guards prodded their prisoners onward, and Benny found herself being pushed down the slope after Nusek and Mastrov by a guard who was holding a blaster to the back of her neck. She hoped he found it awkward to reach over her rucksack.

As she reached the dais, Benny noticed there were low plinths set at intervals round the top. Mastrov was standing by one of them. 'They used to stand traitors' heads on these,' she said. Her eyes were alive with interest and anticipation.

'I think we can find something more appropriate to watch over our proceedings.' Nusek snapped his fingers and pointed to the plinth.

One of the guards who had arrived with Nusek and Mastrov came forward from behind them, and Benny noticed for the first time that he was holding something. He lifted it up, and placed it carefully on the plinth. The Gamalian Dragon.

Nusek adjusted the Dragon's position very slightly, wiped a speck of dust from its wing tip, and stepped back to admire the effect. 'Yes, that will do very well. In fact –' he turned towards Benny '– there is just one thing we lack. And that is something to balance it with.' He strode across the dais to where Benny was standing, guard's blaster still at her neck. 'Don't you think?'

She knew what he was asking, and shucked out of her rucksack. Nusek reached out for it, but instead Benny

219

unzipped the rucksack and pulled out the second Gamalian Dragon. She did not want Nusek rummaging about inside, he might find anything – the Dragon of Jeneve, her diary, or an old sock.

Nusek took the Dragon from her. He held it up to look at it, one side of his mouth twitching into a half smile. He spent a moment looking at the Dragon, then he handed it to Mastrov. She took it to a plinth on the other side of the dais, opposite the first Dragon.

Nusek nodded, obviously happy with the effect. 'Good. Now we can get down to business. Will you be joining us?' he asked Webbe.

'I think not, sir.'

'Ever the soldier. All work and no play, I fear. Unlike Mastrov here.'

Webbe's face was impassive. 'I take no pleasure from these events, sir. And how Mastrov chooses to spend her time is up to her. I cannot believe there is any professional value in the nature or the observation of this business. If you will excuse me, sir, I have other duties.'

Nusek nodded. 'Of course.'

But Webbe was already making his way back towards the door.

'Why do you tolerate him?' Mastrov hissed. Benny could see the contempt in her face, hear the venom in her voice.

Nusek reached out and ran his hand down her cheek. 'The same reason I tolerate you,' he said. 'There is nobody better at what he does.'

Mastrov snorted. 'If you had taken his advice on building support –'

Nusek cut her off: 'I might have succeeded,' he snapped. His hand froze on her cheek and his own cheeks glowed red with anger. 'Your plan failed. *You* failed. Don't forget that.'

Benny thought for a moment that Nusek was going to slap her. But he let his hand drop and turned to his prisoners. 'It isn't really Mastrov's fault, of course. It is yours. And it is a fault we must correct.' He nodded to them, almost pleasant, as if taking his leave after a dinner party. 'Goodbye,' Nusek said and turned on his heel. Mastrov followed him down from the dais.

'I think you mean *au revoir*,' Braxiatel called after them. When they did not respond, he added, 'Sorry, a bit subtle for you perhaps.' He looked round. 'This place is anything but subtle. I don't like it here at all, now I think about it.'

'Time to leave?' Nicholas suggested.

'It would seem prudent, yes. Mustn't outstay our welcome.'

'I'm game,' Benny said. And they turned as if to leave.

There were three guards still with them. The others had followed Nusek and Mastrov from the chamber. But the remaining guards all had their blasters trained on the prisoners.

'There again,' Braxiatel suggested, 'perhaps we could be persuaded to stay. Just for a little while.'

A sound from high above them attracted Benny's attention. She looked up, and saw Mastrov and Nusek emerging on to the observation gallery. The guards had also noticed, though their blasters were not distracted. Braxiatel waved cheerily, and after a moment Benny joined in.

'Oh what the hell,' Nicholas muttered, and he waved too.

They were too far away to see Nusek's reaction, but Benny hoped it was not amusement.

The guards were certainly not amused. One of them nodded at Nicholas. 'You first,' he said with obvious relish. He holstered his blaster and grabbed Nicholas's arm, twisting it up behind his back and pushing him roughly across the dais towards the smoking hole at its centre.

Nicholas was taken by surprise and caught off-balance. He tried to dig his heels in and struggled to force his way back to Benny and Braxiatel. But the guard was a good deal bigger and heavier than he was. His boots scraped on the stone as he was pushed slowly but inevitably towards the lip of the volcano.

Benny and Braxiatel both took a step forward. But the

other two guards jabbed their blasters into them and they were forced to watch.

Nicholas was close to the edge now. He was leaning backward as he tried to resist. Benny saw him turn his head and look back and down over his shoulder. She saw his frightened expression change to resolve as he struggled all the harder, trying to turn so that the guard was on the edge of the hole. But he was held tight in a bear hug now, unable to move his arms. Any second the guard would give a final heave, open his arms, and propel Nicholas backward into the volcano. Any second.

'Wait!'

Everything stopped. Everyone turned towards the voice. Benny assumed at first it was Nusek shouting down from the gallery, though she doubted it was to offer a free pardon.

But the figure that had spoken was in the chamber with them, hurrying down the incline towards the dais. His progress was slow, his old limbs struggling to keep balance on the slope as Reddik made his way towards them.

'What is this? Reddik, what are you doing?' Nusek shouted from above.

But Reddik was at the dais now, climbing the steps, breathless. 'Thank goodness I got here in time,' he said to the nearest guard, the one holding a blaster on Benny.

The noise was deafening. The percussion echoed round the chamber, stinging Benny's ears. She felt the searing heat of the blast, saw the hole appear in Reddik's robes as the energy ate through them. The guard was blown past her by the impact, crashing to the floor behind.

Almost at the same instant Braxiatel kicked the blaster out of the second guard's hands. Then he turned and jumped down from the dais, running up the slope towards the door. The blaster skittered across the floor, the guard diving desperately after it. But Reddik had drawn his blaster from its concealment inside his robes, tracking the guard with it. The guard grabbed his gun, rolled, almost made it to a crouch before Reddik's shot caught him in the shoulder. He spun backwards, colliding with the third guard, who was still holding Nicholas on the edge of the volcano.

Nicholas's guard held his grip as his comrade glanced off them. But the grip was loosened. With surprising speed Nicholas broke free of the embrace. He kicked backward, catching the wounded soldier even as he tried to regain his balance at the edge of the drop. The soldier teetered on the brink, one arm windmilling, the other limp at his side. His scream wailed its way back to them as he toppled over and down. A moment later the scream was cut off by a violent hiss of steam. Flames licked out of the pit, spilling over the edge for a moment and sending Nicholas and the last guard staggering back from them. Then they collapsed back like a breaking wave.

The remaining guard lunged for Nicholas with a cry of anger and determination. Nicholas clenched his hands together into a single fist and swung at him. The guard took the blow under the jaw, his own full weight behind the impact. His head snapped upward and he went over backward, slamming to the ground without time for a cry. His head lolled to one side, eyes wide in unseeing surprise.

It had taken only a few seconds from the time Reddik fired his first shot. But already there was noise from the gallery. Nusek and Mastrov were shouting instructions. Guards were rushing to positions on the balcony and training blasters on the chamber below.

'Terrific,' Benny said. 'Now what's the plan?'

'We die with honour,' Reddik said, 'as soldiers should.'

Nicholas was with him, the two of them standing back to back, guns raised, as if about to begin walking at the start of a duel. Benny was not impressed. Dying with honour was, in her book, a very poor second to not dying at all. She looked round for Braxiatel.

He was at the main door. But he did not seem concerned with escape. He was crouched at a control panel set into the wall beside the door. As Benny watched, there was a small explosion of spark and flame from the panel. Then

Braxiatel straightened up, rubbed his hands together with apparent satisfaction, and walked quickly back down the slope towards them.

'You've done something clever, haven't you?' Benny accused him as he approached.

He nodded. 'I jammed the lock on the doors for one thing.'

Benny pointed up at the gallery. 'We do have other problems,' she said. 'They don't actually have to get in to get us.'

'Oh, that,' Braxiatel said dismissively.

'Fire at will.' Nusek's angry voice carried to them clearly.

'Your name Will?' Benny asked. It wasn't much of an epitaph, but she thought it would do under the circumstances.

Braxiatel was watching the gallery with interest, his hand shading his eyes as if he were looking into the sun. Nicholas aimed his blaster up at the guards, but Braxiatel gently pulled his arm back down before he could fire. 'Not a good idea, actually,' he said.

The guards all fired at once. It was spectacular. The noise was deafening, and the blasts screamed across the air above them, rolling and slicing through the chamber like fireworks. It was over almost at once. Those guards still standing had their mouths open is disbelief. Some threw down their weapons as if they were hot. Others just stood and stared at their dead comrades. Nusek seemed actually to be jumping up and down in anger and frustration.

'So what exactly did you do?' Benny asked as the echoes died away.

'I turned on the force field. With a few minor adjustments so that it angled the energy from the blasts back at the gallery. Some will have been absorbed, but that will dissipate through whatever the force field usually dissipates the heat through. I'm afraid they'll work it out in a minute, though.'

'Can they turn it off?'

'No, but they can come down here and try again.'

Benny smiled. 'I thought you jammed the doors.'

'I did. But there are other doors. Come on.' He was striding quickly across the dais, heading for the door where they had been brought in. Reddik and Nicholas were close behind Benny as she followed. She plucked a Dragon – her Dragon – from its plinth as she passed, tried to bundle it into her rucksack as she walked. She gave up, and carried it instead.

'I wonder where they do dissipate the heat,' Braxiatel said as they walked up the slope. 'I hope they don't just project it back –'

Behind them the volcano erupted.

'They do,' Braxiatel said above the noise. 'The fools.'

A tower of flame shot out of the dais, dripping over it and spilling into the room. Clouds of smoke billowed out and in a moment Benny was choking on the fumes. She could see through the thick air as Nicholas stumbled and fell, losing his blaster and sliding back down towards the dais. Braxiatel continued unperturbed towards the door. Then the door opened, and several guards ran into the chamber. One collapsed immediately, seized by a fit of coughing. Another ran straight towards Benny and Braxiatel.

The guard was still pulling his blaster from its holster when he reached them. Braxiatel shrugged in response to Benny's enquiring raise of an eyebrow. She swung the Dragon at the guard, and its head connected with his temple. The guard groaned and flopped to the floor, hand still on blaster butt. There was a quiet tinkling sound as something small hit the ground beside him. Benny stooped down, checking to see that she had not damaged the Dragon. But the noise had been made by a small piece of rounded glass. She picked it up, and could see tiny filaments set inside.

'Do you know what I think this is?' Benny asked Braxiatel as she stood up. But he was looking away from her.

Benny looked across the room, following Braxiatel's gaze. And saw Nusek and Mastrov entering the room by another door.

* * *

As soon as he entered the room, Nusek's priorities were changed. 'The Dragon!' he shouted, running towards the dais. The flames had died down again now, though they were still flickering above the dais. Pools of oily liquid burnt smokily across the dais and the nearby main floor. One of the plinths cracked in the heat, the base crumbling and the stonework collapsing in a cracked heap.

Nusek had his arm over his face to ward off the heat. He stumbled up the steps, avoiding the burning liquid. The plinth in front of him was in the middle of an oily fire. In the midst of the flames the Gamalian Dragon stood like the phoenix. Flames curled round its wings and glowed off its scales. He was vaguely aware of a figure running towards him, but his attention was entirely on the Dragon. His Dragon. He had to recover it. His emblem, his inheritance from Gamaliel.

Nicholas recovered from the fall, shaking his head as he stood up. In front of him was Nusek. Nusek, standing in front of a pool of fire, on the dais. In a second Nicholas made a decision. He ran back down the slope, hurled himself at Nusek, intending to knock or carry him into the burning abyss. Then something hit him, hurled Nicholas sideways across the dais. He slammed into a plinth, rolled through fire, struggled to his feet and turned to see what had collided with him.

Mastrov.

She was walking towards him through the fire. The draught from the heat blew her blonde hair back from her face. Her eyes burnt, part reflection part hatred, as she closed on him.

Nicholas made to run past her, to break for the nearest doorway. But Mastrov was too fast for him. She grabbed him by the shoulder, pulled him back. The strength of her grip convinced him at once that he could not win the fight. He tried to pull free, dragging her towards the centre of the dais. With his spare hand he fumbled in his pocket.

* * *

Braxiatel had swiftly dealt with two guards. Another lay coughing violently by the door. From the sound of it, the rest were at the main doors trying to break in. But Benny reckoned it would not be long before more soldiers found an open door.

Benny and Braxiatel were too far away to help Nicholas as he struggled with Mastrov. Benny was running back towards them as they wrestled closer and closer to the edge of the pit. Nicholas was shouting, holding something up to show her. Suddenly he threw it. Benny caught it, just as Mastrov took advantage of Nicholas's distraction and hurled him away from her, over the edge.

'No!' Benny shouted. But it was too late. As he fell, Nicholas managed to reach back and grab Mastrov's leg. For a moment he held on, and Benny thought he might manage to pull himself back from the fiery abyss. But then Mastrov lost her balance and crashed to the ground. Nicholas shouted to Benny, he was telling her something – something important, but she couldn't hear him above the sound of the fire and the volcano. Then he disappeared from view, pulling Mastrov's thrashing body after him.

Benny looked down to see what Nicholas had thrown her. Through smoke and tears she saw that it was his keypad. 'He wanted me to have it.' Braxiatel was standing beside her. 'It meant so much to him.'

'I think now would be a good time to make use of it. We may escape in the confusion, and I think we owe it to our friend.'

'A good time? For what?'

Braxiatel frowned. He reached down and lifted Benny's hand up, the hand holding the keypad. 'Why do you think he was so careful to keep this with him? Why do you think he lied about what it really was? Why do you think it dates from exactly the same period as the Dragon?'

Benny looked at him blankly

'What Nicholas wanted you to have,' Braxiatel said quietly, 'is the detonator for the Gamalian Dragon.'

On the dais in front of them, Romolo Nusek reached through the dying flames. His hand closed round the Gamalian Dragon – his inheritance, his destiny.

Beyond Nusek, the main doors finally crashed open, and a group of soldiers ran into the room, blasters unholstered.

Somewhere below the dais, within the burning shaft of the volcano's mouth, Mastrov clutched and clawed her way towards the top. The sensory circuits were suppressing the pain and pumping drugs through her system. Servos strained and whirred, one eye ran in a molten mess across a polished cheek. Her left arm had stopped working, and the temperature readings splashed across the retina of her remaining eye were flashing danger signals.

Inch by inch she struggled back towards the surface.

'What do I do?' Benny asked.

'Tap in the code phrase – the key that will detonate the device.'

'But I don't know what it is,' she sobbed. 'God help me, I don't know.'

Nusek screamed and snatched his hand away from the Dragon. The metal had been heated by the fire until it was almost at melting point. The flesh of his hand fused to the statue, and as he moved the Dragon was pulled off its plinth. Then the weight of the statue tore it from his hand, lifting and removing layers of burnt skin, and it fell to the floor. It bounced, rolled, skidded towards the edge of the volcano.

'No!' Nusek screamed. He hardly noticed the pain as he dived after the Dragon, clutched, fumbled, almost caught it. Watched it roll over the edge. He ignored the heat and leant over. The Dragon was resting on a small ledge just a few feet down the shaft. He reached down, arm stretched to its limit, fingers grazing the hot surface of a wing.

'I just don't know it.'

Across the smoky room, the guards levelled their blasters.

'I don't think,' Braxiatel said, 'that guesswork is any substitute for knowledge at a time like this. Do you?' His last question was directed at Reddik, now standing with them.

'Of course,' Benny whispered, wiping her cheek with the back of her hand. And she tapped in 'Knowledge above all'. The words glowed at her from the readout. She smiled at Braxiatel and Reddik, and pressed the commit key.

Nothing happened.

THE DRAGON AND HIS WRATH

The steggodon was growing frustrated with the tiny grey world in which it was confined. One of the short-snouts – the kind female – had given it food and water when it was first shut inside the grey box. But it had seen nobody for a long while now, and had heard no signs of life from beyond the smooth, cold, grey wall. It was as confused, hungry and angry as ever. It knew there was a way out, because it remembered where it had come in, and where the short-snout had opened a hole in the wall to bring it food. For a while now it had been battering at the wall, butting at the crack with its head and smashing at it with its forelimbs. But while the wall was getting dented, it remained closed.

It took a chance blow just above one of the rough supports along the line for the wall to split open and give way. A part of the wall pivoted on the remaining support, swinging open at the top left. The other support snapped under the strain, and a piece of the wall crashed to the floor. The steggie stared for a moment at the opening it had made. Then it ran from the box, looking for a way out of the grey world and back to the greenery of the forest it knew must lie beyond.

Benny stared in horrified disbelief at the keypad. She shook it, and was about to fling it away when it emitted a warbling sound. The sound stopped almost at once, and the readout flared back into life.

```
Time-delay Destruct Sequence Initialized
```

The tiny screen cleared, and was replaced by a number

```
1000
```

As Benny watched, it flipped to

```
999
```

A countdown.

Braxiatel, looking over her shoulder, clicked his tongue disapprovingly. 'I was hoping for a small diversion,' he said. 'And I was hoping for it sort of now.'

The guards were approaching them warily. Their guns were raised, and they stepped slowly forward, fanning out, cutting off any chance of escape except through the door immediately behind. On the dais, Nusek was lying full length, leaning down into the pit. Suddenly he pulled himself back and rolled away from the edge.

A moment later, a huge fireball erupted from the shaft. It mushroomed out above Nusek, the force of the heat knocking several of the guards off their feet. The others staggered away as oily black smoke drifted across the room. In a moment it was impossible to see the guards. Or, Benny realized, to be seen by them.

'Come on,' Braxiatel urged grabbing Benny's hand. 'As distractions go, that isn't at all bad.' He dragged both her and Reddik back towards the door. From out of the smoke came the confused sounds of shouted questions and orders.

The smoke was clearing. A little. The heat had reduced. A little. The soldiers were grouped round the dais, uncertain what to do, awaiting orders. In front of them, watching Nusek as he lay across the dais, stood Mastrov. Or what was left of her.

Nusek was reaching into the volcano again, the flames from below flickering across his face as he stretched and strained. The tips of his fingers gained a slight purchase on the Dragon's wing tip. He rolled it slightly, lost his tenuous grip, watched the Dragon roll back.

He leant slightly further. Any more and he knew he would pitch forward into the fires below. Just a few more inches. The muscles in his shoulder ached from stretching. He lunged at the Dragon, brushed against it, rolled it, caught it.

Then it slipped from his grip, wobbled, tottered on the edge of the shelf on which it lay. And fell.

The corridor outside was also bathed in a sulphur glow from the lingering fumes and smoke. Braxiatel shut the door behind them, and led the way along the corridor. Reddik and Benny staggered after him, struggling to catch their breath.

They passed soldiers and other palace staff rushing in the other direction – towards the execution chamber. But none of them attempted to hinder their escape, or even to ask who they were and what they were doing. Alarm klaxons echoed along the stone corridors, reverberated down spiral staircases as if trying to find a way out.

Benny clutched the keypad as she ran, checking the readout at frequent intervals. She was surprised each time she looked to see how little time had elapsed since the last.

871

870

869

The soldiers were forming a human chain. Nusek shouted and cajoled, ordering them further into the shaft after the Dragon. He had finally given up trying to reach it himself and seemed for the first time aware that there were others in the room with him.

Mastrov was trying to persuade him to leave the Dragon, and evacuate the area. With her sensitized eyes and infrared vision, she could see the heat patterns deep inside the volcano.

'The whole thing has become unstable,' she told Nusek.

'In a few minutes at most the volcano will erupt. And we don't want to be in here when it does.'

Nusek answered without looking at her. Whether this was because he was so intent on how his guards were proceeding or because he was put off by her blackened and torn body, she neither knew nor cared. Her clothes were charred and ripped. Her left arm was useless, while the right ended in metallic fingers from which the flesh seemed to retreat. Her face was a blackened amalgam of metal, plastic and a memory of skin. Only her hair seemed undisturbed, falling perfectly styled around her ruined features.

'Then be ready to lower the shields as soon as we've got the Dragon.'

'I can't. That idiot Braxiatel has fused the circuits. The force shield won't react to any control instructions.'

'Well at least it's activated. It will contain the eruption within this chamber.'

Mastrov grabbed Nusek's shoulder, turned him to face her. 'It will not,' she said quietly. 'The eruption will meet the angled shields, fold back in on itself looking for another route. Then it will burst through the walls at ground level. From the moment the eruption meets the shields, it will take less than ten minutes for the whole palace to be consumed.'

It was impossible to tell from Nusek's expression whether he understood her, or even if he had heard. He turned back to the shaft, to the line of soldiers, arms gripping arms as they braced on the edge of the shaft, lowering their comrades down into the blistering heat. 'Then get them,' Nusek said at last. 'We will recover the Dragon. You find and kill the people who did this to us. To *me*.'

'Leave the Dragon,' Mastrov snarled. 'It isn't important.'

Nusek turned to her again. His cheeks fiery red with anger. 'Find them and kill them,' he screamed at her. 'Kill them, you hear me?'

Mastrov held his gaze for a beat. Then she turned and started up the incline towards the main doors. She limped

233

slightly as she went, the rhythm of metal on stone slightly irregular as she walked.

'That way to the ship, surely,' Benny called as Braxiatel turned down a corridor to the left. The smell of sulphur was everywhere and getting stronger.

615

614

'No, this way to the library,' he shouted back. 'Reddik, show us the way, would you?'

'The library? You're mad. We have to get out of here.'

609

608

But Braxiatel was shaking his head. 'We have to save as much of the information from the Library as we can.'

'You're joking,' Benny screamed at him. 'At most we can carry a couple of books each.'

'It's better than nothing. Leave it here and it will be lost for ever when the volcano erupts. Without the shields, there's nothing to contain it. And when that countdown reaches zero, if the Dragon's still stuck down the shaft . . .'

596

595

'All the more reason to make sure we get back to your ship.'

Reddik tapped her shoulder. 'I do have a digital copy of the archive. There's an optical sphere in the cavern.'

'Yes, but even so.'

Braxiatel was shaking his head in disbelief. 'Then we can save the lot, or copies at least. Why are you waiting, Benny? This is your job – your life – as much as mine.'

579

'Tell me it's my life again in fifteen minutes,' Benny muttered as she ran after them.

More than half the monitors in Security Control were blank. Webbe slammed his fist down on the control console. There was a line down somewhere in the lower levels, probably burnt out looking at the temperature gauges.

Another monitor blanked out, the image disappearing down a pixel in the middle of the screen. He looked along the remaining pictures. They showed a variety of rooms in the palace from various angles. The new camera he had put in the library was still transmitting, as was the throne room and a number of corridors.

His troops were calling in from the lower levels, giving progress reports on the firefighting and repairs to essential systems. But it would not be long before they either had the situation under control or were overwhelmed by it. Webbe punched up a schematic of the palace. His finger traced various possible evacuation routes, not for himself but for his soldiers.

'Thinking of leaving us?' Mastrov's silky voice had gained a slight grating undertone.

'It may come to that before too long.' Webbe turned, and grimaced as he saw the figure behind him.

'Where are they?' She leant forward to look at the monitors and Webbe nearly gagged on the sickly smell of charred flesh. He leant away to try to avoid it.

'I don't know. Half the systems are out, and more are crashing every minute. I'd guess they're heading for their ship. And in that case, you're too late. You'd never catch up with them.' The satisfaction was evident in his voice.

Mastrov said nothing. She was absolutely still, focused on the monitors, watching for any clue, and sign of her prey.

They entered the library at a run. Benny went immediately to the bookcase which concealed the route down to the cavern and kicked it as she had done before. It clicked open, swinging a few inches away from the doorway behind. Braxiatel helped her to pull it further open, and they stepped through. The smell was even stronger here, pungent, catching at the back of the throat. From somewhere down the corridor came a low rumbling sound.

'I don't think we have much time,' Benny said.

'Come on, then.' Braxiatel pushed past her and set off at a run.

265

264

Mastrov watched long enough to see Reddik follow Benny and Braxiatel through the hidden door. Then she ran from the room, her left leg dragging slightly as she went.

Webbe tapped his chin thoughtfully. So, they had not gone straight back to their ship. He stood up, straightened his jacket, and followed Mastrov.

'I know it's in here somewhere.'

Benny rubbed her forehead. She was not sure she was up to this hectic lifestyle any more.

119

118

Where there had been ice, there were now pools of water. Where there had been pools of lava there was smoke and flame. A yellow pall hung over everything, and in its midst Reddik hunted methodically and laboriously through piles of documents and books.

115

114

'Is this what we're looking for?' Braxiatel held up a plastic box, an eight-inch cube with a hinged top.

'Yes, yes.' Reddik stumbled over to him. 'That's it.' He

opened the lid, checked the sphere was safely inside, and then hugged the box to his chest.

'Come on then, quick.' Benny led the way back through the smoke to the cavern entrance.

95

94

93

There was something there, looming out of the smoky haze in front of them. The shape blurred, moved, grew larger, and resolved itself into a figure. A figure holding a blaster.

Mastrov.

'I thought I might find you here,' she said. 'Though I have to confess, I did not know that *here* existed.'

'Well,' Benny said, 'now you do.'

'And,' Braxiatel told her, 'we're in a bit of a hurry. So, if it's all the same to you we'll just be on our way.'

Mastrov waved the blaster at him. 'Oh, but it isn't all the same to me. We have some unfinished business, I think.' She motioned for them to move back into the cavern, keeping them covered with the gun and her back to the wall. 'So, this is the source of your revelatory information about Gamaliel.'

Nobody answered.

'Nusek was surprised,' she said. 'Genuinely surprised. Did you know that?'

'Then he should have read some of this stuff before he ordered it destroyed,' Benny snapped.

'Before he what?' Mastrov took a step towards Benny. 'Do you think Nusek is at all interested in this lot?' She kicked at a pile of books, watched it topple over into a smoking heap. 'He isn't concerned about history, except when it can help him to fulfil his own aims and ambitions. He wouldn't waste his time hiding or suppressing information. He'd just ignore it.'

'No.' Benny almost laughed. 'No, that's not right. Why else would all this be here?' But there was something that rang true in Mastrov's words. Benny turned to Reddik. 'Why?' she asked him. The keypad was clenched forgotten in her hand.

25

24

'Nusek knows nothing about these documents and papers, not that they are important now,' Reddik answered. 'When he became interested in Gamaliel, it was obvious why. So I provided him with those sources that satisfied his requirements, that showed Gamaliel in a favourable light.'

'And to ensure he never learnt the truth,' Braxiatel said, 'you hid the rest of the documentation, the less favourable information here?'

Reddik nodded. 'If Nusek thought he was genuinely in the right, I reasoned that would blind him to the possibility of failure. If he did not know the truth, was not even aware that there was a truth to know, then he would be setting himself up for a fall.'

'He'd be making it easier for someone who did know the truth to discredit him?' Benny asked. 'Is that what you're saying? Someone like us?'

Reddik nodded. 'Indeed. Exactly like you.'

'A good plan,' Mastrov purred. 'But with one small flaw.'

6

'Oh yes?' Benny gestured to the bubbling pools of lava along the wall behind Mastrov. 'It seems to have gone OK to me.'

4

'But,' Mastrov said, 'you're dead.' She raised the blaster.

2

Servos hissed as she applied first pressure to the trigger.

1

Some of the soldiers lay exhausted on the dais. Two of them, the two who had been at the end of the chain, were led from the chamber, supported by comrades. Their faces were blacked and their hands blistered and scarred.

The guard commander handed the Dragon to Nusek.

'At last.' He held the Gamalian Dragon aloft for all to see. 'My Dragon. My destiny.' It burnt into his hand as he lowered it to face level, leant forward to kiss the burnished metal of the Dragon's head. It's glassy eye stared into his. Deep inside there seemed to be a tiny light, a spark of life growing, blossoming, about to be born.

0 . . . Destruct Confirmed

They rocked on their feet. Reddik lost his balance completely, and Braxiatel helped him back up.

'What the hell was that?' Mastrov turned to look at the wall behind her, in the direction of the noise.

The Gamalian Dragon exploded in a fireball of noise and flame. The guards on the far side of the room were blown off their feet by the blastwave. The walls shook and the floor creaked. High above, the force shields angled the blast back down into the volcano.

From the abyss came a low rumble, rolling, building.

What had been a crash of sound followed by a rumble was now becoming a roar. The wall sparked, shook, dripped and melted. Then suddenly it bulged outward like a balloon. Cracks appeared along its length, and it gave way under the sudden pressure.

Benny and Braxiatel were running, dragging Reddik with them. Through the increasing smoke, Benny saw the lava cascade into the chamber like a waterfall. Saw it splash across the books, start fires and rain down flame. Saw the wave break at Mastrov's feet, hurling her to the floor and washing over her. A metal arm, stripped of clothing and of flesh reached out, gripping, clutching, trying to drag itself clear. Then smoke swirled in front of the image, blotting it from view.

They raced through the corridors of the palace, a ball of flame rolling after them along the lower levels. Lava was already dripping through the walls. Smoke obscured their vision and stung their eyes. They lost their way several times, had to change routes because the heat was too intense at several other times. Once, they almost ran into a pack of cryvoks, escaped from the cages where they were normally confined during the day. Benny held Braxiatel and Reddik back while the animals ran past, whimpering and confused.

But eventually, and to Benny's surprise as much as her relief, they reached the landing pads. Braxiatel's was the only ship, perhaps because all Nusek's ships were on station ready for the start of his aborted crusade, or perhaps because all the others had already fled. Benny was practically laughing for joy, still clutching Nicholas's keypad, as Braxiatel opened the ship's main door.

The hatch lowered gently, slowly, swinging open and down. The inside of the door became a short flight of steps leading up into the ship. And at the top of the steps stood Webbe.

'I take it you've sorted out that bitch Mastrov, then?' he said.

'We did meet, yes.'

Webbe nodded. There was a tiredness, a resignation in the movement. 'Then it's finished,' he said. 'Nusek must be dead by now, and the palace won't last much longer. We can start again. If we survive.' He made his way down the steps. At the bottom he straightened up, and saluted them. 'I wish you well,' he said.

'Come with us. There's no point in you staying here.'

'Oh, Professor Summerfield. There is probably more point now than there ever was before.'

'But why?'

'My men are in there. Dying in there. I have more of a duty

to them than I ever did to Nusek. That's where I belong, with them. Most of them are conscripts – they didn't ask to do this job. I did, though. And now more than ever they need me to do it – to lead them. To save them. They deserve that much at least.'

'What will you do?'

He shrugged. 'The palace is finished. If I have time I shall rally as many of the troops as I can find, and try to get away before the place is finally consumed by the volcano.'

Braxiatel shook his hand. 'We'll signal for rescue ships.'

Webbe laughed, a short, mirthless sound. 'You think there'd be time to get them down?' He shook his head. 'We'll walk out of here. I shall lead them home. And then, well, then we shall see.' Webbe nodded, a short and formal incline of the head accompanied by a click of his heels. Then he strode across the launch pad and back into the palace, his back straight and his head high.

The steggodon was lost, confused and frightened. It had followed what seemed to be the scent of the female short-snout and found its way from the small grey boxes into a world of stone. But now everything was obscured by the stench of the sulphur fumes. It was in a huge cave, an area filled with fire and heat. Parts of the ground were soft, liquid, and the air was burning.

From out of the burning air came a scraping sound. The steggie paused, waited to see what the sound was. Something crawled into view, its shape glinting in the firelight. It was a figure, a short-snout, dragging itself forward with one silver arm. The face turned up towards the steggie. One eye rolled loosely in its socket, and traces of burnt skin hung round what was left of the jaw. The face was framed by a blackened frazzle of what had once been straight blonde hair. The arm reached up towards the steggie. The voice was a dry rasp: 'Help . . . Help me . . . Please.'

The animal stooped down, feeling more than anything else a sense of relief. At last it had a purpose. It did not understand what the short-snout had said, but it was clear that it was dying. And it should die properly, a death fit for one trapped in this hell-world. A death the steggodon hoped it would itself deserve and receive.

It took hold of the arm reaching up for help, grasped it in its snout. And pulled.

The sound of tearing metal and bone ripped through the fumes of the volcano, played a shrieking duet with Mastrov's screams.

They had not bothered to strap in any more than they had run through the preflight checks. Braxiatel's ship lifted clear of the palace, pitched slightly, righted itself. Then it angled back and leapt for the sky.

Far below, the imperial palace of Tharn, the Castle of Ice and Fire, erupted after the ship. The volcano tore through the stonework and blast-resistant masonry like cardboard. A tower collapsed in on itself; another was pushed off sideways and toppled to the ground. The main structure was a ball of flame and smoke.

The shockwave buffeted the ship, pressing its occupants down into their seats as the craft was driven forward.

On the rear-view screen, Benny thought she saw a tiny line of dark figures marching out across the snowy wastes. She imagined one of them looking up at the ship, and waving. But the smoke blacked out the image before she could be sure that she had really seen anything.

When the ship settled into normal flight, Benny pulled open her rucksack. Inside were three things over and above her normal kit. One was Nicholas's keypad, the readout dead and blank. She pulled out the other two and set them on the console in front of her. Two aspects of the same creature. The faked Gamalian Dragon, and the stone Dragon of Jeneve.

Braxiatel set the autopilot and leant back. 'How did you know that wasn't the real one, the bomb?' he asked pointing to the Gamalian Dragon that Rappare had made.

Benny sneaked her fingers into a pocket of her jeans and

pulled out the tiny glass component she had recovered from the floor of the execution chamber after she had clubbed the guard with her Dragon. She held it up on her finger. It was like a contact lens, but with tiny wires and circuits just visible inside. 'This fell off its eye,' she said. 'I think it's a camera. And since I'm an archaeologist, I know it's no antique.'

Braxiatel lifted the tiny circuit carefully from her finger. 'Yes,' he agreed. 'Microminiaturized, and undoubtedly modern, but that's what it is.'

'There was a good chance that the real Dragon's video circuit was no longer working,' Benny said. 'So they put this on the fake. Just to make sure.'

'They?'

'Well...' Benny thought back to their meeting with Archduke in her rooms. 'Archduke looked at the Dragon,' she said. 'He could have placed this circuit on it then. As a backup.' Another thought occurred to her. 'Or you could have done it,' she said.

'We shall never know,' Braxiatel said quietly. 'Whether it was a backup, I mean. There is after all nothing to say that the plans and blueprints with which Archduke was kind enough to furnish us were at all genuine or accurate.'

'You mean, the Gamalian Dragon might not have been a surveillance system at all?'

He smiled. 'I mean that it's as well to take precautions. To plan ahead.' He turned to Reddik, who was sitting on the floor behind them. 'As you did.'

Benny looked down at Reddik. 'And why,' she asked, 'did you say that the documents weren't valuable? After the trouble you went to preserve them.'

'I didn't say they weren't valuable. I said they were unimportant. And so they are, now.' Reddik handed her the box containing the optical sphere. 'They have served their purpose.'

'You mean they're forgeries?'

'Oh no. They are genuine enough. Real documents, books,

243

papers and records from the Gamalian era.' Reddik smiled, his face creasing and the lines of age deepening on his brow. 'But the information they contain is not correct. In short, they lie.'

Braxiatel sighed. 'Of course.'

Benny looked at him. 'Would you like to let me in on this? Of course what?'

'Propaganda, am I right?' Reddik nodded. 'The revelations about Gamaliel's real background and history, the information we used to blacken his name and help discredit Nusek – it's not true, is it?'

'Some of it is,' Reddik conceded. 'But most of what appears in there –' he gestured to the box '– is not. The information was seeded and disseminated by the Knights of Jeneve in order to blacken Gamaliel's name. Gamaliel and his successors managed to suppress or deny most of it. But now the lie is out.' He took Benny's hand and looked up at her. 'It has taken a long while, but now Gamaliel's reputation is irretrievably tarnished.'

'But – why?'

'Because,' Braxiatel told her, 'as well as discrediting Nusek, the Knights needed to show that Gamaliel was not an honourable Robin Hood but a typical, Machiavellian, greedy corporate hatchet man. Discrediting both Nusek and Gamaliel now will prevent a similar situation – potentially with a more adept "champion" – arising in the future.'

Benny was appalled. 'Did you know about this?' she demanded.

Braxiatel picked up the box. 'Whether true or not, the documents themselves are valuable historical artefacts. We did well to save them.' He set down the box, and picked up the Dragon of Jeneve. He stroked his hand across its surface, then handed it to Reddik. 'And this is yours, I believe. Perhaps you will see that it reaches its rightful home?'

'Of course.'

Benny caught Braxiatel by the shoulder. 'You didn't answer my question.'

'Knowledge and suspicion are not the same things, Benny,' he said.

'Knowledge above all,' Reddik said from behind them.

'No,' Benny replied. 'The truth above all. That's what's really important. That's what we scrabble about in the dirt trying to find. That's what we live and die for.'

'You're absolutely right,' Braxiatel agreed. 'The problem is in knowing the truth when you trip over it. Separating the myth from the fact, the legend from the history. The most important truths are shrouded in falsehood.'

'So what do we do now?'

Braxiatel grinned. 'We go home,' he said. 'I think we deserve a bit of peace and quiet.'

Benny nodded. 'And ain't that the truth!' she said.

It was raining. It was nearly always raining. Benny stepped inside the building and shook some of the water from her coat, letting it drip and drop to the tiled floor. The main room was large and well lit, the size emphasized by the fact that most of the exhibits and display stands were below eye level. The clinical whiteness of the freshly painted walls was broken up by the paintings hanging in ordered rows.

Braxiatel was standing in front of the *Mona Lisa*. He seemed to sense that Benny was behind him, and spoke without turning round. 'What do you think?'

She wasn't really sure what to think. The sheer scope and breadth of Rappare's work was staggering. There were pseudo art treasures in this room that seemed gathered together from the furthest corners of the universe and the most distant mists of time. She settled for: 'Impressive.'

'Yes. Indeed. Very.' Braxiatel turned. 'He was an expert at working with materials. Making copies, even of the most delicate or sophisticated artwork, is child's play with modern technology. But getting the form and texture, the feel and the smell so exactly right takes genius.'

They started walking, Braxiatel showing her round the gallery. He pointed out various pieces along the way. Some she recognized, others she had no idea about. At the end of the room was a red velvet curtain. A gold cord hung beside it.

'Is this it?'

He nodded. 'Pride of place. His greatest achievement.' He nodded at the cord. 'Go on.'

'One small tug for a girl,' Benny said as she pulled the cord.

The curtain opened to reveal a recessed display case set into the wall. The lighting was arranged so that there was no reflection from the thick glass.

'I wonder if he knew what he was getting us all into,' Benny said as she stared into the case.

'I doubt it. I'm not sure that we really know yet.'

Benny looked at him. A shadow cut across Braxiatel's face, hiding his eyes. 'What do you mean?' she asked.

'I mean I'm not convinced. A group of pseudo-medieval knights scrabbling about for nuggets of information. A group so dedicated that they preserve their ritual and their ceremony despite having lost the key to interpreting the information they are charged with collecting. Just going about their timeless business as if nothing had changed or ever will change, hiding in shadows from opponents who no longer exist and maybe never did.' He turned to her, the shadow gone and his eyes shining now. 'No, I'm not convinced.'

'There are things we don't know,' she said. 'There are always things we don't know.'

'That's true. That's very true.'

He seemed about to add something, but Benny cut him off. 'Don't say it. I know what you're thinking, and it isn't funny.'

'I was thinking,' Braxiatel told her, 'that there's more to the Knights of Jeneve than they have let on. Some deeper, darker purpose we can only guess at. If we dare.'

'And dare we?'

'I have a few ideas.' He smiled. 'But they can wait.'

'Good.' Benny looked back at the display case. 'I'm in no rush.'

Braxiatel took her by the arm. 'There's still lots of Rappare's stuff worth looking at,' he said quietly.

Benny was still staring at the display case. From behind the glass, Rappare's copy of the Gamalian Dragon gazed back at her. The light reflected off its eyes like fire dancing inside. But behind the fire, deeper inside, lurked the shadow of something darker. She forced herself to look away. 'Yeah, why not?' she said, allowing herself to be led away. Outside the rain splashed against the buildings of the university and washed along its paths.

'Did he do any etchings?' Benny asked.

COMING SOON
IN
THE NEW ADVENTURES

BEYOND THE SUN
by Matthew Jones
ISBN: 0 426 20511 1
Publication date: 17 July 1997

Benny has drawn the short straw – she's forced to take two overlooked freshers on their very first dig. Just when she thinks things can't get any worse, her no-good ex-husband Jason turns up and promptly gets himself kidnapped. As no one else is going to rescue him, Benny resigns herself to the task. But her only clue is a dusty artefact Jason implausibly claimed was part of an ancient and powerful weapon – a weapon rumoured to have powers beyond the sun.

SHIP OF FOOLS
by Dave Stone
ISBN: 0 426 20510 3
Publication date: 21 August 1997

No hard-up archaeologist could resist the perks of working for the fabulously wealthy Krytell. Benny is given an unlimited expense account, an entire new wardrobe and all the jewels and pearls she could ever need. Also, her job, unofficial and shady though it is, requires her presence on the famed space cruise-liner, the *Titanian Queen*. But, as usual, there is a catch: those on board are being systematically bumped off, and the great detective, Emil Dupont, hasn't got a clue what's going on.

DOWN
By Lawrence Miles
ISBN: 0426 20512 X
Publication date: 18 September 1997

If the authorities on Tyler's Folly didn't expect to drag an off-world professor out of the ocean in a forbidden 'quake zone, they certainly weren't ready for her story. According to Benny the planet is hollow, its interior inhabited by warring tribes, rubber-clad Nazis and unconvincing prehistoric monsters. Has something stolen Benny's reason? Or is the planet the sole exception to the more mundane laws of physics? And what is the involvement of the utterly amoral alien known only as !X.